when last seen alive

when last seen Alive

An Aaron Gunner Mystery

Gar Anthony Haywood

G. P. Putnam's Sons New York

G. P. Putnam's Sons
Publishers Since 1838
a member of
Penguin Putnam Inc.
200 Madison Avenue
New York, NY 10016

Library of Congress Cataloging-in-Publication Data
Haywood, Gar Anthony.
    When last seen alive : an Aaron Gunner mystery/
    Gar Anthony Haywood.
        p.   cm.
    ISBN 0-399-14303-3
    1. Gunner, Aaron (Fictitious character)—Fiction.
2. Private investigators—California—Los Angeles—
Fiction.   3. Afro-American men—California—Los
Angeles—Fiction.   4. Los Angeles (Calif.)—Fiction.
I. Title.
PS3558.A885W47   1997   97-37581   CIP
813'.54—dc21

Printed in the United States of America

10   9   8   7   6   5   4   3   2   1

This book is printed on acid-free paper. ∞

Book design by Bonni Leon-Berman

Acknowledgments

For their generous contributions of time and expertise, the author would like to thank:

Detective John Yarbrough
Los Angeles County Sheriffs Department

and

Capt. Brent F. Burton
Los Angeles County Fire Department

Oh, and a long overdue hearty handshake is also hereby offered to my wise and noble agent:

Dominick Abel

For Tessa
With All the Bear's Love
Te quiero mucho, baby!

when last seen alive

It had to scare the living hell out of white folks. One million black men gathered as one in the streets of Washington, D.C.

From the steps of the Lincoln Memorial to the upper reaches of the Capitol Building, old men and little babies, fathers and sons, life-long friends and total strangers swarmed over the Mall, basking in sunshine and peace. Some standing stone-faced, some laughing and embracing, others crying openly, wearing their tears on their faces with the pride of kings, turning in all directions so that their brothers might see how happy they were just to be here, an integral part of this celebration of black manhood known as the Million Man March.

It was a sight Elroy Covington knew he would never forget.

Which was high praise for the event indeed, for Covington was a man whose ambivalence toward his own blackness had always been unassailable. Being an African-American male had never given him any cause for cheer, any more than it had ever moved him to regret. He'd been born black out of chance, not fortune—good, bad, or otherwise—and he had always understood that. So what he was doing here on this momentous occasion, at this colossal demonstration of the very brotherhood and fellowship to which he had never been able to relate, was not easily explained. Other than to say that he'd been curious. Curious to see if his being here would by some miracle move him profoundly, give him some new and wonderful appreciation for the color of his skin he had never known before.

It didn't, of course.

And yet, Covington did not consider the trip from St. Louis a total loss. He at least had something to tell his future grandchildren about, even if he had to tell it with all the emotional attachment of a network news reporter. He had heard the keynote speaker and chief organizer of the event, Louis Farrakhan, address the crowd, sounding brilliant and inspired one moment, delusional and paranoid the next, and he had escaped the wife and the tedium of her company for four whole days. He'd seen the nation's capital, made a few new friends, and was finally able to use the new camera his family had given him for his birthday the previous June. Unfazed by all the hoopla as he was, Covington was glad he had come.

Then Sunday night, his last in the city, he saw a familiar face.

He was having dinner in a restaurant in Dupont Circle. A roomful of people separated them, and several years had passed since their paths had last crossed, but Covington recognized his old friend immediately. There was no mistake. He had come to D.C. fully expecting to see one or two people he knew—this many brothers and sisters in town, how could he not?—but this was something special. This was a ghost sighting, a specter from his past catching up to him in one sudden, inadvertent burst of fate.

Covington should have been afraid, but he wasn't.

Had he turned and run from that restaurant as any reasonably cautious man in his position would have, he could have saved his wife a world of grief, and the police in two different cities a lot of paperand legwork. His friend at the distant table would have failed to see him, and the lie that had been Covington's life for the last five years would have been his to go right on living. But Covington didn't run. He waited to be seen and recognized first, then moved forward instead, smiling like a blissed-out fool, and in so doing guaranteed himself a small but notable place in the historical record of the Million Man March of October 16, 1995.

Of all the black men who attended, Elroy Covington was one of the few who never came home afterward.

The photographs were good.

Twenty-four black-and-white eight-by-tens, shot from a number of ideal perspectives, all exhibiting the same crisp focus and dramatic clarity. Los Angeles City Councilman Gil Everson and a beautiful blonde, caught red-handed wining, dining, and otherwise romancing the hell out of each other. The private investigator who had taken the photographs over the last ten days had no name for the blonde as of yet, but her name was hardly important. What was important was that she was not Everson's wife. Aaron Gunner figured his client would notice that little fact right away.

"This is the wrong woman," Connie Everson said, after cursorily flipping through the photos like a walk-on looking for her one appearance in a screenplay.

"I'm sorry?"

She splashed the eight-by-tens across the cluttered surface of the black man's desk, her disappointment all but overwhelming. "I know all about this woman," she said. "Gil's been seeing her for years."

Gunner could do nothing to disguise his confusion. "I don't—"

"Please, Mr. Gunner. Don't act like you don't know what I'm talking about. The black city councilman without a white woman on the side hasn't been elected yet, they practically find one their first day on the job."

"Then who—"

"I don't *know* who. If I knew who, I wouldn't need *you,* would I?" Everson stood up and began smoothing the wrinkles from the skirt of her canary yellow dress, an obvious prelude to departing the premises. "You're just going to have to keep following him. Sooner or later you'll catch them together, it's just a matter of time."

Gunner watched the councilman's wife prep herself for the long limo ride back home to Ladera Heights and found himself wondering, not for the first time, if the forty-seven-year-old politician to whom she was married had rocks in his head, wooing other women when he could be wooing his wife. Connie Everson was closer to fifty than she was to twenty, but any man who would have held that against her would have had to be blind in both eyes. She was a dark-skinned, full-bodied, raven-eyed fox, Mrs. Everson, and there wasn't a muscle in her body she couldn't move in such a way as to make a grown man cry. Gunner was almost crying now, just watching her play with her skirt.

"You want me to catch him with *one specific woman,*" he said, having completely missed this point eleven days earlier, when Everson had initially hired him.

"Precisely."

"But you don't know who this woman is. You don't have a name, or a description . . ."

"Listen. It's really very simple. The woman I want you to catch him fucking around with will be a whore. A prostitute of some kind."

"A *prostitute?*"

"Yes. A prostitute. Or a porno star. One or the other, or maybe even both, I don't know. She'll be a woman who sells her body to men in one fashion or another, Mr. Gunner. Is that description sufficient for you, or do I need to go on?"

"That depends. Will any prostitute-slash-porno star do, or are we talking about one in particular?"

Everson grunted to dismiss the question, said, "We're talking about one in particular, of course. She'll be black, not white. Younger than myself, though she won't look it. She'll have a pronounced limp. And I suspect she'll be an addict of some sort. A crackhead at the very least, or maybe even a heroin junkie. It wouldn't surprise me a bit if it was heroin."

"I see." Gunner scribbled out a note, looked up at his client again. "You seem to know this woman quite well, after all."

"Know her? Why in God's name would I know her?"

"Well . . ."

"I know my *husband,* Mr. Gunner. That's who I know. I know what he likes, and I know the kind of woman he likes it from. I'm his wife, remember?" She tucked her purse securely under her left arm and said, "Now. I'm leaving. Please don't call me down here again until you've taken the photographs I've paid you to take. Do you understand?"

It would have been polite of her to wait for him to answer, but the thought never occurred to her. She was gone before Gunner could complete the motion of standing up to see her out.

Mickey Moore, the barber in whose shop Gunner's office space was located, came back to see him immediately afterward, just as Gunner figured he would. Mickey could pounce on a potential piece of gossip faster than most people could wink their left eye.

"That was Gil Everson's wife, wasn't it? The councilman over in Inglewood," Mickey said.

"Is that right?"

"Look, just give me a simple yes or no. Was that her, or not?"

"Nice weather we've been having lately, isn't it?"

"Bet she's hiring you to follow that fool's sorry ass around, catch him dippin' his wick where it don't belong."

Gunner started scooping up the photographs on his desk, got them into a drawer before Mickey could get much more than a glimpse of one.

"You got pictures of him and that girl Chelsea, huh? The one used to be a secretary over at the courthouse?"

"Chelsea?"

Mickey nodded. "Chelsea Seymour. Ain't but twenty-two years old. You tellin' me Mrs. Everson didn't already know about her? Long as those two been messin' around?"

"Mickey, I'm not telling you *anything*. What happens back here is confidential, I've told you that a thousand times."

"Councilman likes to do some weird shit in the bedroom. She tell you that?"

Gunner looked at him incredulously, overwhelmed by the depth of the man's knowledge of all things pertinent to other people's business. Mickey wasn't just a barber, he was a minister of information.

"What kind of weird shit?" Gunner asked, trying not to sound as intrigued by the subject as he was.

But the bell over Mickey's front door rang before Mickey could answer him, followed by the sound of a woman's voice calling out for assistance.

"Hello? Anyone home?"

Mickey rushed out to see who it was, and Gunner fell in right behind him, curious.

The sister they found waiting for them in the company of Mickey's three empty barber chairs was tall and slender, just a shade under six feet, and was dressed in stone-washed jeans and a dark blue sweater. The jeans fit her like a Navy Seal's wetsuit. She had rich, walnut-colored skin, pitch-black eyes, and a little girl's upturned nose, and her dark-brown hair was arranged in tight circles that fell in gentle waves to the base of her neck. Gunner suspected she was somewhere in her mid-thirties.

The sight of her nearly stopped him dead in his tracks.

"I'm looking for Aaron Gunner," she said. "The private investigator?"

Mickey turned and pointed, said, "This is him. I'm Mickey Moore, his landlord." Mickey stuck out his hand for the woman to shake.

"His landlord?"

"That's right. I rent him some space in the back. He'll invite you in there soon as he closes his mouth and stops actin' like he's never seen a beautiful woman before." He looked over his shoulder at Gunner, said, "Won't you?"

"My mouth isn't open. Yours is," Gunner said. "Twenty-four-seven, around the clock." He stepped forward, shouldering Mickey out of his way, to take his turn at shaking their visitor's hand. "Come on back, Ms. . . . ?"

"McCreary. Yolanda McCreary."

Gunner led her past Mickey to the beaded curtain that passed for his office door, held it open for her as she somewhat cautiously stepped through it. Mickey started to follow, but Gunner shook his head at him, stopped him dead in his tracks. "Stay," he said firmly.

The investigator's office, such as it was, still wasn't much more than an empty space Mickey had no use for, but after seven years of conducting his business here, Gunner had at least finally gotten around to putting some W.H. Johnson prints up on the walls and investing in a few floor lamps that made viewing them possible. The secondhand desk, couch, and two chairs he had started with remained, looking as listless and forlorn as ever.

"Can I get you something to drink? Coffee, tea . . . ?" Gunner offered, sitting down behind his desk as McCreary took a seat opposite him.

"No. No, thank you."

She quickly produced a business card from her purse, slid it across the desk for his inspection. She had yet to show him anything vaguely resembling a smile. "I believe you gave this to a man named Elroy Covington," she said. "Do you remember him?"

Gunner took the card, recognized it immediately as one of his own. "Elroy Covington?" The name was vaguely familiar, but he couldn't place it. He shook his head and said, "Sorry, no."

"I'm not certain, but I think you met him at the Million Man March. In Washington, D.C., last October. You were there, weren't you?"

The very question brought a flood of memories down on Gunner, sights and sounds captured over three days' time he would take with him to his grave. He couldn't recall the scenario that involved a man named Elroy Covington, but he did remember now why Covington's name was familiar to him. "Covington's the missing person. The one the police here were asking about a month or so after the march."

"That's right. Then you do remember him."

Gunner shook his head. "Not really, no. I only remember the police asking me about him, showing me this card, just like you are now. He was from St. Louis, right?"

"Yes."

"But he disappeared here. In Los Angeles."

"Two days after the march, yes."

"And he's still missing?"

"Yes. You really don't remember him?"

"No. I wish I could say I do, but I don't."

"But you gave him your business card."

"Where? You mean in D.C.?"

"Either out there, or here. Where else would he get it if you didn't give it to him?"

"Ms. McCreary," Gunner said, trying hard not to sound unhelpful, "I handed out a lot of these cards that weekend. To a lot of different people. Trading business cards and addresses with men you'd never met before was a constant habit at the march, as you might imagine. If your friend Covington got this card from me out *there*—"

"You'd have a hard time remembering. I understand that. But maybe it would help if I described him for you. He was about your height, weighed around two hundred and thirty pounds—"

"Had dark skin and a mustache, wore glasses. Yes, I know, the police gave me a full description when they talked to me back in December."

The detective out of the LAPD's Missing Persons Bureau had been a tall, lean Latino man Gunner had never seen before. Gunner's guess now was that his name had been Martinez. Like most cops who worked the Missing Persons detail, he had spoken to Gunner like somebody reciting a long grocery list; the redundancy of looking for people who, ninety-nine times out of a hundred, were in danger only of being found by the friends and loved ones from whom they'd deliberately fled, had rendered the cop an emotionless, uninspired drone. He had told Gunner the investigator's business card had been among the few personal effects Covington had left behind in a motel room out in Hollywood back in October, two days after the Million Man March. Had Gunner seen or talked to Covington around that time or since, Martinez asked? Gunner said no, as hard pressed to remember Covington then as he was now.

"I take it the police have stopped looking for him," Gunner said.

McCreary nodded. "They did that a long time ago. They think he just ran off on his own."

"And you don't buy that."

"No. Tommy's—I mean, Elroy's wife does, but not me."

"His wife? You mean . . ."

"Oh. Did you think Elroy was my . . . ?" She shook her head, almost seemed to blush. "Oh, no. Elroy was my brother, Mr. Gunner. His wife's name is Lydia, she's back home in St. Louis with the kids."

"I see." It was a pleasant surprise that almost made him smile.

"You probably think it's odd that I'm the one pursuing this, rather than Lydia," McCreary said, clearly thinking it odd herself.

"A little," Gunner admitted.

"Well, I don't blame you. Lydia should be the one sitting here, not me. But it's like I said. She thinks he ran away. They were having a lot of marital problems when Elroy disappeared, she just figures this is his way of avoiding a messy divorce."

"Hundreds of men go that route every day."

"Of course. But I don't believe Elroy was one of them. I think something happened to him. Something beyond his control."

"You mean you think he was murdered."

He hadn't intended the comment to take her aback, but it did; it was several seconds before she could find the words to respond to it. "Yes. Either that, or he was kidnapped. Taken and held somewhere against his will."

"For the purposes of . . . ?"

McCreary shook her head again, said, "I don't know. Certainly not for money. At least, no one's demanded any money yet."

"Then—"

"If I had all the answers, Mr. Gunner, I wouldn't be here. I'd be out there right now, trying to find Elroy myself." She paused a moment, reined in the anger she hadn't allowed him to see until now. "I'm sorry. I shouldn't have said that."

Gunner shrugged to show her no offense had been taken. In fact, he was still too busy admiring her beauty to feel any resentment toward her at all.

"It's just that I'm frustrated. And afraid. And I seem to be the only one who knew Elroy who cares enough about him to be either." She waited to see if Gunner was going to ask her to explain that, discovered he had no interest in doing so. "My brother isn't a very likable man, Mr. Gunner. I may as well tell you that right now. But he is my brother, and the father of two young children, and somebody has to do something to find out what happened to him. So here I am." She produced a little shrug of her own.

Again, Gunner remained silent.

"So? Are you available? Or can you recommend someone else who might be?"

"Excuse me?"

"I want to hire you, Mr. Gunner. Don't tell me you didn't realize that."

He had in fact *not* realized it. Somehow, at some indeterminate point in their conversation, the idea that she may have come here not merely to talk, but to retain his services, had eluded him. Probably because the prospect of hunting her brother down excited him today, nine months after Covington's disappearance, about as much as it had Detective Martinez way back in December, when the missing man's trail would have been nowhere near as cold as it had to be now.

"Actually, Ms. McCreary, I'm tied up at the moment," Gunner said. Not because he was looking forward to renewing his surveillance of Gil Everson in the hope of catching him with a limping whore or a porno star, but because a paid gig was a paid gig, preposterous or not. "As for who else I could recommend to help you . . ."

"If you're concerned about money, Mr. Gunner . . ."

"No, no. You didn't hear what I said."

"Yes, I did. I heard you perfectly. You said you're all tied up right now."

"That's right. I'm in the middle of another case."

"Case, singular, or cases, plural?"

Gunner stiffened, said, "Sorry, but I'm not sure that's any of your business."

McCreary glowered at him, then reached over to take back the business card he was still holding in his hand. "You're right, of course. Any fool could see you're a very busy man, I don't know what I was thinking."

"Ms. McCreary . . ."

"It ever occur to you that Elroy might've come out here to see *you,* Mr. Gunner? That *you* were the reason he was here in Los Angeles in the first place?"

"Me? Why the hell would he want to see me?"

"I don't know. Maybe to hire you, same as I did."

"Except that I never met him."

"You mean you don't *remember* meeting him. Same as you don't remember giving him this card."

"You suggesting I'm lying about that?"

"I'm not suggesting anything. I'm just telling you it has to be more than just a coincidence, Elroy disappearing way out here, eight hundred miles from home, only days after you—or whoever—gave him your card. It *has* to be."

"He couldn't have been visiting family in the area? Or a friend or business associate, maybe?"

She shook her head vigorously. "We don't have family out here. In fact, besides each other, we don't have family, period. I'm Elroy's only living relative, and he's mine. And as for him visiting a business associate out here, his business never took him any farther west of St. Louis than Jefferson City."

"Jefferson City?"

"In Missouri. Out in Cole County, about a hundred and fifteen miles west of Elroy's office downtown."

Gunner nodded, fell silent again. Actually thinking now about where he might look for Covington first.

"I need your help, Mr. Gunner," McCreary said. "I want you to help me find my brother. I could hire someone else to do that, I know, but I'd feel better hiring you."

"Because you think I had something to do with his disappearance."

"In one way or another, yes. I do. You say you never met him, so I guess I have to believe that. But Elroy got your card somehow, from somebody, and he held onto it for a reason. Elroy never holds onto anything without a reason."

"It's been nine months. If it was hard to find him then, it's going to be harder now."

"I understand that."

He told her what his rates were, watched second thoughts cloud her eyes, then quickly evaporate. "At those prices, I can pay you for about a week," she said.

And naturally, she wanted him to start right away.

2

Emilio Martinez had been transferred out of Missing Persons three months ago and was now working out of Fugitive. Easiest damn job he ever had, he said.

"First place you look, that's where the idiots are. Watching TV at the old lady's place, or playing fucking video games at their mother's. Hell, most times you ring the bell, they're the ones who answer the door, ask you to come right in."

He laughed, something Gunner would have thought him incapable of when last they'd met. He looked like a new man.

Fugitive did keep him busy, though, so the LAPD detective had declined Gunner's offer to feed him, suggested this meeting at the 7-Eleven on Sunset and Van Ness in Hollywood instead. A cop who only wanted coffee in return for a little information was something Gunner could easily get used to.

"See, that's the thing Joe Citizen doesn't realize," Martinez went on. "Same with the movies. Your average criminal is a moron. He isn't smart, he isn't dangerous, he's just stupid. Knows how to run, but he ain't got a clue how to hide."

They were standing out in the parking lot beside the cop's unmarked Chevy, Martinez sipping gingerly at his coffee, Gunner munching on his breakfast, a Tiger's Milk candy bar, the peanut butter and honey variety.

"Funny thing, but something told me you might end up working that Covington trace," Martinez said, seeing Gunner was ready to abandon all the small talk and get down to the business they'd actually come here to discuss.

"Yeah? Why's that?"

"Because his sister wasn't gonna let it go. Sooner or later, she was gonna pay some private ticket to pick things up where we left off, and who else would she go to but you?"

"Because Covington had my card."

"That's right."

"You didn't tell her I couldn't remember ever meeting him?"

"I told her that, sure. But I guess she took that the same way I did."

"Which was?"

Martinez shrugged. "You've got a short memory." He drank some of his coffee, added, "Or a selective one."

"You really believe that?"

"Now?" The cop shook his head. "Naw. I'm not the skeptic I used to be, Gunner. I've got the time to be open-minded about people these days. Back then, I didn't."

"And back then, you figured Covington for a runaway."

"That part *hasn't* changed. I *still* figure Covington for a runaway."

"But if you had your suspicions about *me*—"

"I had an idea you might've wanted to help him make his getaway, that's all. You met 'im in D.C., took a liking to the guy, and decided to give 'im a hand with his little problem. Something like that."

"And his 'little problem' was the wife?"

"I take it you haven't talked to the lady yet. Otherwise, you wouldn't be asking the question."

"She's all that, huh?"

Martinez nodded, said, "The hair on my ass has more personality. I'd've been Covington, I might've made my break twenty minutes into the honeymoon."

"So his old lady was a stiff. That the only reason he could've had for taking off?"

"Near as I could tell. His life was a lot like she was, as I recall. Totally unremarkable. Lookin' for somethin' out of the ordinary in his profile was like lookin' for a naked tit in a copy of *Reader's Digest*."

"No major debt, no mistresses, no enemies . . ."

"Nothin' like that."

"You ever find out what brought him out to Los Angeles, specifically?"

Martinez shook his head for the third time, said, "Nope. I spoke to everybody I could find who came in contact with 'im, both here and in D.C. The staff at his hotel, the taxi drivers who drove him around—even the flight attendants on the flight he took out here—and nobody could tell me jack. He was always alone and never said more than three words to anybody."

"What about phone calls?"

"That was a washout, too. I forget the exact numbers right now, but he made two, maybe three calls from his hotel room in D.C., and at least one more credit card call from a pay phone back there, and each time, he was callin' somebody back home in St. Louis. Either the missus, or a friend on the job, somebody like that."

"And here?"

"He made one call from the motel room where we found his effects. Went out to some literary agent in New York. Silverman, I think his name was."

"A literary agent? He was an architectural draftsman. What'd he want with a literary agent?"

"I couldn't tell you, and neither could Silverman. According to him, he wasn't in when Covington called, had never even heard of the guy before then."

"Covington didn't leave him a message?"

"He did, but it wasn't much. He had a dynamite idea for a book he wanted to write, Silverman said. Didn't say what kind of a book, just that it would be dynamite. He left his number at the motel and asked Silverman to call him back, he was interested in hearing more."

"And Silverman never did?"

"He said he didn't, and phone records backed 'im up on that. Literary agents get calls like Covington's all the time, he said, they just dismiss 'em out of hand."

"Any signs of this book at the motel?"

"Nothin'. All we found in his room was a garment bag, a matching carry-on, some clothes and shoes, and the address book your card was in. That was it."

"Any other L.A. names or places in the address book?"

Martinez shook his head one more time, gulped down the last of his coffee.

"And there was no sign of struggle in the room," Gunner said.

"No. Place was neat as a pin. From all indications, Covington stepped out for a breath of fresh air and never came back."

"Leaving no paper trail behind."

"No paper trail, no physical trail—no trail of any kind."

"So he would have had to live on cash from that point forward."

"Guess so."

"Last time he used a credit card was when?"

"At the airport, afternoon he got in. Used his bank ATM card to make a withdrawal for the maximum two hundred. Which don't sound like much, two hundred, until you consider he left St. Louis with a little over two grand. Way I remember the numbers, he could've had as much as seventeen hundred on 'im when he went away the next day."

"And you think he vanished into thin air on that? Seventeen hundred?"

"Hey. All I can tell you is, it happens. I seen people disappear on a lot less, believe me."

Gunner almost commented that the cop's attitude was shamefully cavalier, until he remembered he was talking to a man who used to work missing persons cases by the truckload, and often a dozen or so at a time. Martinez sure as hell didn't need Gunner chiding him now for treating Covington's case lightly.

"Okay. One last question," Gunner said, "then I'll leave you to it."

"Shoot."

"Assuming Covington just went AWOL like you say, no other parties were involved."

"Yeah?"

"You were me, where would you start looking for him? You given it any thought?"

Martinez threw his empty coffee cup at a nearby trash can, missed its mouth by three feet. Gunner expected him to just let it lie there, but he picked it up, dropped it into the can before answering. "I can't tell you *where* I'd start looking," he said. "But I can tell you *who* I'd have another talk with first, get to know a little better."

"Who's that?"

"Your client. The sister."

"Yolanda McCreary?"

"She wants her brother back, don't get me wrong. I never had any doubt about that. But listening to her talk about him sometimes was like listening to a stereo with one speaker missin'. You could tell you weren't always hearin' all the notes to the song."

It was funny, but now that Martinez mentioned it, that had been Gunner's sense of McCreary as well. The way she had tripped up yesterday and referred once to her brother as "Tommy" was a case in point. He had let the slip go by at the time, intending to question her about it later, then had forgotten to do so. He was going to have to bring the subject up the next time they spoke for certain now.

"Thanks for your time, Detective," Gunner said, shaking Martinez's hand warmly. "You've been a terrific help."

Martinez shrugged good-naturedly and opened the unmarked Chevy's door. "Don't mention it. I got a soft spot in my heart for any-body workin' a skip trace, I'm glad to be of service." He got in the car, started the engine, then said through the open window, "You need names and dates, stuff like that, gimme a call later, I'll pull the file for you."

"Thanks. I'll do that."

Martinez pulled out of the parking lot and sped off.

Moving to his own car afterward, Gunner made a mental note to himself: He came back in his next life as a cop, he was going to ask to work Fugitive.

Easiest damn job he'd ever have.

At seventeen, Sly Cribbs was one of the most talented photographers Gunner had ever seen, but the kid said he'd never put a tail on anyone in his life. This was going to be a new experience for him.

Sly was short and tubby, with a dark, hairless face, eyes as wide and innocent as a China doll's, and fingers so fat it was a wonder he could tie his shoes in the morning, let alone work the controls on a $600 Panaflex camera. He sat across from Gunner quietly at the Roscoe's Chicken and Waffles restaurant on Pico just off La Brea and watched Gunner look over his portfolio quietly, self-confident enough even at his early age to let his work speak for itself.

"These are damn good," Gunner said.

In truth, his feelings for the photos were much stronger than that. The young man's still lifes were haunting black-and-white images of people trapped in the prison of destitution, captured in striking, natural poses that said everything there was to say about their condition. Light and shadow were like surgical instruments to the man behind the camera; the cool, calculated precision with which he wielded them was evident in every shot.

"Thanks," Sly said.

"Ms. Serrano told me you were the best student in her class, maybe the best she's had for a long time, and I can see she wasn't exaggerating. To tell you the truth, home', you're probably way too good for this gig, I'm almost embarrassed to offer it to you."

Trini Serrano was a world class photographer in her own right, a new friend Gunner had made a little over a year ago in the course of another investigation. Gunner didn't know she taught part-time at West Los Angeles City College until he called to ask if she knew anybody good with a camera who might want to make a few dollars doing surveillance over the next few days. Connie Everson hadn't called him for an update on her husband yet, but he had no doubt she would soon; putting her case on hold until his search for Elroy Covington was over was simply not an option. He had to put the Inglewood city councilman back under surveillance, and he had to do it fast.

"Don't be embarrassed," Sly said. "A job's a job, and I can use one."

"You've got a car, right?"

"Yeah, I've got a car. Who you want me to follow?"

"Later. Tell me how you'd do it, first. I told you to follow this girl working the cash register here, for instance. How would you go about it?"

"Starting from here?"

"Yeah. Starting from here."

Sly said he'd park his car over on Mansfield Avenue, where the most commonly used exit from the parking lot was, and park it northbound so he had a view of the restaurant's back door, the one all the employees used. When the girl came out, he'd give her car a good look, take down the license plate number and any unique features of the vehicle, then let her go about half a block before starting after her. He'd try to stay in the middle lane as much as possible, so he could turn in either direction somewhat easily if she made any sudden moves, and—

Gunner stopped him right there. He'd heard enough.

"The job's yours," he said.

Sly grinned. His full first name was Sylvester, but Gunner knew now that this was why people called him Sly: the grin. "So who you want me to follow?"

"You don't wanna ask about the pay first?"

"Anything's better'n what I'm gettin' now. But okay. What's the pay?"

Gunner told him it was thirty dollars a day, waited for him to push his plate of food to the middle of the table and storm out, insulted.

"All right," Sly said. "So who you want me to follow?"

Gunner glanced around, in a low voice dropped Gil Everson's name.

"Gil Everson? The councilman? Man, that's deep."

"You haven't heard the deepest part yet."

"I gotta catch 'im with a woman, right?"

"That's part of it, yeah."

Sly's face lit up, thinking he was about to become privy to some quality dirt. "You mean . . . ?"

Gunner put a palm up to urge him to lower his voice, told him the rest of it.

He thought the kid was going to hurt himself, he laughed so hard.

"I don't know what you want me to say," Lydia Covington said less than an hour later. Over the static-free, long-distance phone line, her bland, exceptionally uninspiring disposition was coming through loud and clear.

"I'd just like you to answer a few questions, Mrs. Covington. To the best of your ability," Gunner said.

"But I don't know anything. I never did. Yolanda knows that."

"Yes, ma'am, but—"

"I don't understand why she's doing this. Throwing her money away to find somebody who doesn't want to be found. It's crazy."

"But if your husband didn't run away—"

"He *did* run away. She doesn't want to believe that, but he did. I know it."

"And you know it because . . . ?"

"Because he was my husband, Mr. Gunner. That's how. We were married for four years, had two children together. Nobody knew Elroy better than me. Nobody."

"You don't think there's any chance his disappearance involved foul play of some kind?"

She didn't say anything for a long time. Finally, she said, "Not anymore I don't. I used to think . . ." Her voice tailed off, left the thought unspoken.

"What?"

"I used to think he wouldn't do it. Leave a wife and two kids behind to start a new life someplace else. I didn't think he could be that cruel."

"But you changed your mind?"

"I realized Elroy could do anything, he really felt like doing it. That was just the kind of man he was."

"Was he seeing other women, Mrs. Covington?"

He had tried to think of a less direct way to pose the question, but nothing came to mind.

"Yes."

"Do you know that for a fact?"

"You mean, can I give you their names? No. I never asked him for any names, and he never gave me any. But he was seeing them just the same. He all but admitted as much."

"How many were there, do you think? Roughly?"

"I don't know."

"Do you know if these women were co-workers of his?"

"No. I don't."

"Could he have been meeting them at bars, or the health club? Someplace like that?"

"I don't know. I didn't care where he was finding them. I just wanted him to stop."

"Of course." He gave her a minute to calm herself, knowing she could call an abrupt end to this interview, he pushed her too hard on such a delicate subject. "Were these one-night stands we're talking about here, Mrs. Covington? Or were some of them more serious than that?"

"Do you mean, was he having an affair?"

"Yes."

"I don't believe he was, no. But what difference should that have made to me?"

"To you? Absolutely none. But I ask the question because it isn't likely your husband would have run off to California with someone he'd only been with once or twice. But someone he was having an extended affair with, well, that could have been a different story."

"All I can say about that is, Mr. Gunner, if there had been such a woman, I never knew about her. If I had . . ."

"Yes?"

"I would have never allowed Elroy to go to Washington in the first place. I almost didn't let him go as it was."

"I see." Gunner found himself wondering how many other things Covington had done in his life only because he had his wife's permission to do so.

"Listen, was there anything else? I was on my way out when you called, I really have to go."

"Of course. About this book Elroy wanted to write."

"Book?"

"Yeah. The one he was trying to place with an agent."

"You mean the agent they said he called right before he disappeared."

"Exactly. You remember his name, by any chance?"

"His name? No. I only heard it once, back when they first told me that Elroy had called him."

"You'd never heard of him before that?"

"No. Never."

"His name was Silverman." Gunner consulted the notes he'd taken during his follow-up call to Emilio Martinez a few minutes earlier. "Stanley Silverman. He's a literary agent out of New York."

Lydia Covington was silent.

"Can you tell me what kind of book it was your husband was trying to pitch to him? You ever hear the idea, or read something Mr. Covington might have already written of it?"

"Read something? Something *Elroy* wrote?" She chuckled, made just a little gurgling sound of amusement that she quickly swallowed back down, lest he discover she was actually human enough to have a sense of humor. "Elroy wasn't going to write any book, Mr. Gunner. I don't know what he called that agent for."

"He never talked to you about wanting to write a book?"

"Did he *talk* to me about it? I'm sure he did, at one time or another. He talked about doing all kinds of things."

"But—"

"He liked to dream and he liked to lie, Mr. Gunner. That agent wasn't the first person he ever called to promise something he knew he couldn't deliver, and he won't be the last. You can believe that."

"It isn't possible this was something he was working on without your knowledge? At the office, in his spare time, perhaps?"

"It's possible. But it isn't very likely. Elroy showed no interest in *reading* books, how was he ever gonna *write* one?"

"You haven't come across anything that could have been part of a manuscript he was putting together? Say, an outline? Notes? Something like that?"

"No. I haven't seen anything like that."

"Then it was all in his head. This book idea he claimed to have."

"It must have been. Is that all, Mr. Gunner?"

"Just one more question, please."

"Yes?"

"You have any idea how or why he ended up here in Los Angeles? Near as anyone can tell, he didn't know a soul out here."

Lydia Covington had to pause a moment before answering. Gunner wondered why. "I don't know why he went to Los Angeles," she said. "Except that he always talked about going there someday. Hollywood, and all that. I imagine he thought it would be an exciting place to start over."

The way she had said it, it almost sounded as if she wished he had taken her along.

3

"October? Man, that was a long time ago,"

the desk clerk at the Stage Door Motel said, shaking his shiny head. Gunner had seen Cadillacs roll off the showroom floor with less reflective sheens.

Emilio Martinez had said the Stage Door was a fine place to get blown in Hollywood, but you wouldn't want to actually get laid there, and he hadn't been far off the mark. The motel on Sunset just three blocks west of Vine was a relic, a two-story, inverted U that looked like something a film crew had started to erect, then lost interest in halfway through the process. Tourist friendly it wasn't. If Elroy Covington hadn't come here for the express purpose of having sex with one of the few desperate whores who still lingered about its entrance, Gunner couldn't imagine what he'd been thinking, choosing the Stage Door over all his other options.

"I was hoping you'd have a good memory," Gunner said, squinting into the glare coming off the obese, hairy-armed desk clerk's bald pate. Charm was hard to come by in the face of so much unattractiveness, but he was giving it his best shot.

"My memory ain't the problem, mister. I can remember last October like it was yesterday. Trouble is, I wasn't here back then. I only been here since March."

"And the clerk who was here back then? He's not still around?"

The clerk shook his head. "Never met 'im. Understand he was a nice guy, though."

Gunner cursed his luck, then said, "The manager around? Or the owner, maybe?"

"You're lookin' at the manager. The owner never comes in here. Paydays only."

"I was wondering if there might not be a file somewhere with this guy's name and address. That possible?"

"It's possible. Sure." His massive shoulders went up, fell back down. A giant's idea of a shrug.

Gunner waited.

And waited.

"You wanna cut to the chase, save us both a little time?" Gunner finally asked. "How much are you looking to make here? Give me a number."

"Going rate for names and addresses today is twenty-five," the clerk said, without hesitation.

"That's all I needed to know. Have a nice day." Gunner turned to walk out.

"Hey, what's your hurry? We're negotiating!"

Gunner never turned around, just stepped out of the office and started moving toward his car, the red Cobra convertible parked right outside the door. He was behind the Cobra's wheel, backing the car up, when the big man wobbled out to stop him, red-faced from exertion and embarrassment.

"Come on, pal! Take it easy," he said, standing in the Cobra's path like a human roadblock. "I can be reasonable."

"Yeah? Reasonable is ten dollars. Take it or leave it."

"Ten dollars?"

"You heard me. You think that's an insult, step aside, and I'll take it somewhere else."

He punched the Cobra's gas, revved the engine, hoping to bully the clerk into a quick decision.

The fat man's head was all but blinding in the sun. He released a long, disgruntled sigh, said, "Wait here."

He went back inside, leaving Gunner to slip the Cobra into neutral and throw on the parking brake, content to let the car idle right where it was. Blocking access to the parking lot was no problem; the motel was as dead as a firecracker stand on the fifth of July. At least it was until Gunner heard a door close, looked up to see a teenage boy retreat from a room up on the second floor, bare chested, alabaster skinned, his torso plastered with tattoos. He came down the stairs stuffing something deep into a pants pocket and passed Gunner's side of the car on his way out to the street. Gunner tried to count the number of silver and gold rings he had dangling from various body parts, only got as far as eight before the kid disappeared from view.

The ponderous clerk returned a few seconds later, holding a half page of lined paper torn from a yellow notepad. He handed it to Gunner and said, "The guy's name was Cong Pham. A Vietnamese guy, looks like. I didn't know he was Vietnamese 'til just now, the owner always calls him Rocky. Pretty unusual name for a slope, huh? Rocky?"

Gunner let the racist remark go, just looked the note over briefly, then folded it up and tossed it onto the passenger seat beside him. He removed two fives from his wallet, stuffed them into the pocket of the clerk's greasy white T-shirt and said, "Many thanks."

Then he made the Stage Door Motel a distant memory.

Cong Pham was indeed Vietnamese. He lived in a tiny cottage apartment on Hudson Avenue in Hollywood, less than three miles from his former place of employment, but he wasn't home when Gunner came looking for him. His wife said he was at work; he parked cars now at a professional building down in Mid-Wilshire. She had large, yellowed teeth and a cranelike neck, but she deferred to Gunner's photostatic license like it was something divinely issued, gave him the professional building's address without hesitation.

While his wife's English had merely been bent, Cong Pham's was broken through and through. He was a bone-thin man in his early forties, with an enormous Adam's apple and shoulders so square they almost touched his ears on either side. He used his hands a great deal when he spoke, and Gunner kept waiting for his watch to spin off his arm and take flight, so loosely did its band fit his left wrist.

He did a lot of nodding and shaking his head, and every now and then said "yeah" or "no" in response to a question, but beyond that, he had nothing to tell Gunner the investigator didn't already know. He hadn't seen anything, he hadn't heard anything, he didn't remember anything about Elroy Covington's last night at the Stage Door Motel. That was his story, at least, and he was sticking to it.

But he was lying.

Gunner wasn't sure what was driving him to do so; all the hand gestures and head bobbing made it difficult to get a fix on the man's eyes. But he was avoiding the truth about something, masking over it with a false blanket of ignorance, and this was usually a tactic born of fear.

"I don't believe you," Gunner told him.

"Huh?"

"I don't think you're telling me the truth, Mr. Cong. I think you know something you're not telling me."

Cong shook his head violently, like he was trying to dislodge something stuck in the space between his ears.

"Yes, you do," Gunner insisted. "You act as if you're afraid of something. Or someone."

"No, no. I tell you everything," Cong said.

"Maybe it would help if I came back with a policeman. Would you rather talk to a policeman?"

"No, no, please. *Please,*" Cong said, glancing about to make sure this last had not been overheard by any of his co-workers. He was getting highly distressed.

Gunner crossed his arms for show, said, "Okay. So tell me the truth. What happened at the motel the night Covington disappeared?"

Cong hedged a moment longer, finally said, "I don't know. I not see *anything.* I . . ."

Gunner was starting to lose patience with this guy. "Yes?"

Cong studied the black man's face for an interminable minute, trying to decide whether or not it belonged to a man he could trust. When he'd reached an apparently satisfactory conclusion, he said, "I not *at* motel that night. I stay for two hours, that's all."

"Two hours?"

Cong's head bobbed up and down. "First two hours of shift, then I go."

"Go? Go where?"

"School. I go to school, at night. Hollywood High School, I have English class."

"You were going to night school?"

"Yes." He nodded again.

"So who was watching the desk at the motel?"

Cong was loath to say the name, but he managed to spit it out nonetheless. "Blue. He always watch desk for me when I go to school."

"Blue? Who is Blue?"

"Blue." Cong nodded his head emphatically, unaware that the gesture in and of itself would not answer Gunner's question. "He the cleaning man. The . . ." He made tight little circles with his right hand, his mind busily searching for the proper descriptive term.

"Janitor?"

"Yeah, yeah," Cong said. "He the *janitor.*"

"And he was at the desk the night Covington disappeared. Not you."

"Yeah, yeah. It was Blue."

"This Blue have a last name, do you know?"

Cong shook his head and shrugged at the same time. "I don't know," he said. "I only know 'Blue.' "

Gunner started to ask why Cong had never mentioned any of this to Emilio Martinez, but quickly realized how foolish such a question would have been. Relying on a janitor to watch the front desk on nights when Cong had English class could not have been something he was doing with the motel owner's blessing.

"He still work at the motel?" Gunner asked instead.

"I don't know. I think maybe," Cong said.

He was still sweating bullets, unsure of Gunner's satisfaction with his answers. The investigator couldn't remember the last time he had seen someone so unnerved by the threat of a policeman's visit to his or her place of employment.

Figuring the poor bastard had suffered enough, though, he thanked Cong for his time and left.

The janitor named Blue, it turned out, was a finely muscled black man in his early twenties, and he was indeed still employed at the Stage Door Motel. Gunner found him on his hands and knees, buffing a brown stain out of the avocado green carpet in room twenty-one, after the investigator had decided to bypass the fat man at the front desk to look for Blue on his own.

The young man didn't strike Gunner as someone who would have warmed up to Cong, or anyone else for that matter, easily—his eyes were narrow slits of perpetual suspicion, and the corners of his mouth rarely turned up or down to create either a smile or a frown—yet he spoke of the Vietnamese man with open respect, if not actual affection. This respect aside, however, he was not happy to learn that his former co-worker had made Gunner privy to the lies they had told Emilio Martinez immediately following Elroy Covington's disappearance.

He wasn't happy at all.

"Cong is a goddamn lie," he said, speaking in a low, even tone filled with unmistakable menace.

"I don't think so," Gunner said.

Blue eyed him, trying to decide how much good it would do to continue taking Gunner for a fool.

"I call myself doing you a favor," Gunner said. "Asking you these questions myself, instead of having the police to do it for me. I personally don't give a damn that you and Cong lied to them last October, but the *cops . . .*"

"Okay. You made your point."

He wasn't going to say another word until Gunner forced him to.

"You were at the desk the night Covington disappeared?"

"Yeah. But I didn't see anything."

"You check him in, or did Cong?"

"Cong did. He was already checked in when I took over."

"Did you see him at all that night?"

Blue shrugged. "Couple times, I guess. Not for long, though."

"Tell me about it."

"He came in the office once to borrow a phone book. About an hour after that, I saw him outside his room, looked like he was going back in."

"And he was alone both times?"

"Yeah."

"This phone book he wanted to borrow. What kind are we talking about? The Yellow Pages, the White Pages . . . ?"

"White Pages. There's a Yellow Pages in every room here."

"Any chance that book's still around?"

Blue shook his head. "We get new books in here every three months. That book's long gone."

"He say anything to you other than to ask for the White Pages?"

"He asked me where he could get something to eat—that was it."

"How about visitors?"

The man named Blue paused for a fraction of a second, said, "He didn't have any visitors."

"And you know this because . . . ?"

"Because I didn't see any."

Gunner didn't say anything, waiting to see if a little silence would change the man's mind.

It didn't.

"You never saw him with anyone else that night?" the investigator finally asked.

"No."

"I think you're full of shit, Brother Blue."

The younger man's eyes lit up, the muscles in his shoulders visibly flexing, but he made no attempt to move. "If that's how you feel," he said, "you won't mind if I go back to work now. Will you?"

"The man had a family back in St. Louis," Gunner said. "A wife and two kids. Did I neglect to mention that?"

"I'm all through talking to you, Mr. Gunner. Step off."

"Just like that, huh?"

"Unless you want me to help you."

Gunner opened his arms wide, invited him to do just that.

Blue laughed as if Gunner had to be kidding, didn't see the right hand the other man was throwing until it hit him just below his left eye. The blow threw him backwards like someone falling off a cliff, sent him crashing into a wobbly-legged coffee table that exploded under his weight. He recovered instantly, rolled over and was ready to return the favor when a sudden change of heart overcame him. Gunner suspected the 9-millimeter Ruger in his right hand had a good deal to do with that.

"You're thinking I won't kill you, you're probably right," Gunner said, aiming the gun's snout in the general direction of the space between the janitor's eyes. "But I'll kneecap your ass without a second thought, that's how you want to play it."

Blue remained motionless, legs coiled up beneath him like a cobra about to strike, then slowly came to his feet again. "You're a lucky man," he said, his gaze entirely focused on the Ruger.

"You mean because I brought this?" Gunner asked, grinning. "That isn't luck. It's intelligence. Hardheads like you make this sort of thing a necessity in my business."

"It's not going to change the fact I've got nothing else to tell you."

"I'm sorry to hear that. Your friend Cong will be, too. Like I said before, he was hoping I could get the information I require without involving the police in any of this."

"Man, fuck the police. Fuck Cong. And fuck you."

"Damn. That's a real hostility problem you've got there, Mr. Blue.

I come here to ask you a few questions, and you start throwing 'fuck yous' around. Where the hell is all this anger coming from, man?"

"I don't like mixing in other people's business. You got a problem with that?"

"I'm not convinced yet Covington's business wasn't your business. In fact, I'm starting to think more and more that they might've been one and the same."

"I didn't have anything to do with what happened to that man. Not a thing!"

"So who did? You aren't buggin' like this because you don't know. You're either trying to protect yourself, or somebody else. Or maybe both."

Blue fell silent again, his attention turned once more to the Ruger Gunner was still halfheartedly training upon him. It was clearly the only thing keeping him from going for Gunner's throat, let alone becoming nonconversant.

"I tell you what you want to hear," he said finally, "it's over. For good. I don't ever wanna see you or the cops in here again asking about this man Covington. You understand what I'm telling you?"

"The cops have a mind of their own," Gunner said. "If I told you I can control where they go and who they talk to, I'd be full of shit."

"They aren't gonna come around here unless you bring 'em around."

"Okay. So I won't bring 'em around. Providing, of course, you can convince me you had nothing to do with Covington's disappearance."

"I didn't. I swear it."

"Good. Now convince me."

Blue paused one final time, sucked in a deep breath. "Some people in this world you just don't wanna fuck with. Man I saw with Covington that night, he's like that. He ever finds out I talked to you about this, I'm dead. That's guaranteed."

"I understand," Gunner said.

"He was with Covington the time I saw him going back into his room. They were going in together, it looked like Covington was inviting him in."

"Who?"

Blue shook his head. "I don't know the man's real name. All I know is what people like to call him: Barber Jack. On account of the razor he carries, the biggest fucking knife I ever saw."

"Barber Jack? You mean Johnny Frerotte?"

"I told you. I never heard the man's real name."

"Johnny Frerotte's about five-six, five-seven, weighs close to two hundred and thirty pounds. Light skin, light hair, walks like he's got bricks in his pockets."

"You know him."

"No. But we've met."

The truth was much more complicated than that, but Gunner didn't care to say so just yet.

"Then I don't have to tell you why I don't like talking to you about this," Blue said. "Do I?"

"No. You don't," Gunner admitted. Wondering if *he'd* be doing any talking, were their situations reversed.

"It might not've even been him, I don't know," Blue said. "I'd only seen the man once before. But it sure looked like him to me."

"And you only saw him with Covington the one time?"

"Going into unit five, yeah. That was the last time I saw either one of them that night."

Gunner asked him if he'd overheard any conversation between the two men, and Blue shook his head, said, "They weren't having any conversation. At least, none that I could hear, anyway."

"Then you don't know what they were doing together."

"No. I don't."

"And you weren't curious enough to find out."

"Curious? Why the hell would I be curious?"

"I just thought it might pique your interest, that's all. Seeing a Joe

Average tourist like Covington rubbing elbows with a local psycho like Barber Jack."

"My interest doesn't get piqued over shit like that. I told you."

"You don't like mixing in other people's business."

"That's right. I don't."

"I know you're never going to believe this," Gunner said, slipping the Ruger back into its holster under his left arm. "But I don't like to do it much, myself."

He was trying to be fair, giving the janitor this one last chance to rush him, but the younger man never moved. Either distrustful or merely disinterested, he just stood there and watched as Gunner wrapped a business card in a twenty dollar bill, tossed the bundle atop the bed beside him.

"The money's for the table. The card's for you," the investigator said.

Then he turned and walked out the door.

4

Barber Jack's straight razor

was eight inches long.

A winged dragon with a serpentine tail was ornately carved into both sides of its ivory handle, and its gilded, finely filigreed blade was always polished to perfection. People who claimed to have seen its owner wield it said he liked to open the razor up slowly, dazzle a foe with the light dancing off its edges before cutting him down with a single sweep of his right arm. The city was teeming with stories of those who had died at the touch of Barber Jack's uniquely horrific weapon, but few were ever told about those who had managed to survive it. Many doubted such people even existed.

Gunner knew firsthand that they did.

He had been at the Acey Deuce Bar the last night Barber Jack—whose real name was Johnny Frerotte—made an appearance there. It was nine years ago now, back when J.T. Tennell, the South-Central bar's original owner and bartender, was still around to manage the conduct of his patrons like a short-tempered prison warden. J.T. had never cared for Frerotte in the first place, never really liked having his kind around, but the squat giant with the fancy knife rarely visited the Deuce, and always managed to behave himself when he did, so the barkeep had little excuse not to tolerate his business.

On this night Frerotte had been alone, standing at the bar instead of sitting there for fear a stool might fail to bear his weight. He was smoking his customary cigar, a Cuban blend as long and fat as the leg of a chair, and was drinking Johnnie Walker Black, neat, while his eyes rolled over the near-empty house like those of an angry policeman. Gunner sat in a booth with his cousin Del Curry at the opposite end of the room, trying to pretend it didn't bother him to have Frerotte's gaze washing over him like that. A broad-shouldered black man named Adam Cowens and his date, a heavy-set sister wearing an unconvincing wig and blatantly false eyelashes, were the only other customers in sight. They sat farther down the bar to Frerotte's right, whispering various come-on lines into each other's ear, laughing and giggling like two kids at the movies. Cowens seemed not to notice the avaricious looks Frerotte kept giving his woman, but Gunner had no such problem, even from a distance.

J.T. noticed them, too. Standing behind the bar directly in front of Frerotte, watching him like he was the only living soul in the house, the big bartender could smell the blood about to flow as if it were already in evidence. His instincts told him to show Frerotte to the door, step in on him now before he could do something irreversible, but he chose instead to give the man the benefit of the doubt, worried that he might be reacting to something that wasn't really there.

It was a decision J.T. would regret for the remainder of his life.

Cowens left his woman to go to the bathroom, and Frerotte took advantage of his absence to eye his lady in earnest, all but licking his lips and rubbing his palms together as he did so. Cowens's friend, meanwhile, just sat there, doing a masterful job of ignoring his very presence in the room. Without turning her head to one side or the other, she slipped a cigarette into the right side of her mouth and began to rummage around in her purse for something to light it with. Frerotte never hesitated; he lumbered over to her, thumbing a gold-tone lighter to life, and waited for her to make use of the proffered flame.

"Here you go, little lady," the fair-skinned giant said.

The woman with the bad wig looked at him, thought for a moment about turning him away, then tilted her head toward his lighter to accept his invitation.

That was when Cowens reappeared.

"What the hell is this?" he asked. Directing the question at Frerotte, and not his friend.

Gunner sat up in his seat and wondered if Cowens had any idea who Frerotte was.

"Sister needed a light, I was giving her one," Frerotte said calmly, his shoulders lifting once in a tiny shrug. He was even smiling to show the man how innocent it all was.

"She *ask* you for a light?" Cowens asked.

"No. You always wait for a lady to ask before you give her somethin'?"

J.T. started moving toward the pair, said, "All right, all right, chill out a minute."

"He was just lighting my cigarette, Adam, that's all," the woman said. "Don't make a thing out of it, please."

"Fatboy's the one makin' a thing out of somethin'," Cowens said. "Ain't that right, fatboy?"

"I said that's *enough!*" J.T. bellowed.

"I am fat, that's true," Frerotte said, the smile still visible on his face. "But that ain't no reason to be insulting."

The closed straight razor was in his right hand now. No one had seen him reach for it, it had just *appeared* there.

"Put that goddamn thing away, Jack," J.T. said.

"You better do what the man says," Cowens agreed. More respectful of Frerotte, perhaps, but still not smart enough to be afraid of him.

Gunner eased his way out of the booth and stood up, finally convinced that Cowens was oblivious to Frerotte's identity.

"You know what your problem is, brother?" Frerotte asked Cowens, not even showing J.T. the courtesy of a glance. "Too much muscle. Shit's got you thinkin' you're indestructible."

No one Frerotte's size should have been so capable, but he flicked the razor at Cowens' face and withdrew it again almost faster than the naked eye could register the motion. A huge chunk of flesh took flight and landed at J.T.'s feet on the other side of the bar, as Cowens howled and brought both hands to his face, trying to stanch a flow of blood his fingers could barely abate.

"But see? You ain't indestructible," Frerotte said, smiling now not to disarm Cowens, but to torment him.

"Goddamnit, Jack!" J.T. shouted, before bending over to pick up the bloody brown nub that had once been the better half of Cowens's nose.

Cowens was still screaming in horror, tears and blood running down his hands, as his woman rushed over to him, begging somebody, anybody, to go get her a towel. J.T. scrambled around the bar, ushered her and Cowens into the back where his office and private bathroom lay. That left Gunner and Del alone to watch Frerotte clean his razor with a bar napkin, performing the task as nonchalantly as a man setting the proper time on his watch.

"Put that fucking thing away, Jack," Gunner said.

Frerotte looked up to see the investigator standing just outside of his reach, eyes set hard like somebody braced for war. His cousin Del stood right beside him, his expression equally determined, the two of them creating a united, if unimposing, front. The grin that had left Frerotte's face momentarily returned, only a little lighter and less venomous than before.

"You talkin' to me, Gunner?" Frerotte asked.

"Yeah, I am. Fold the goddamn machete up and put it in your pocket. May take the cops a while to get here, and I don't feel like looking at that thing while we're waiting."

"You ain't gonna have to. I'm leavin'."

Gunner shook his head.

"Oh, I see. You gonna make me stay, is that right? You and your little brother there?"

"That all depends on you. I don't want to mix it up with you, Jack. We aren't friends, but we aren't enemies, either. I'd like to keep it that way, if we can."

"Then stay the hell out of my business."

"You mutilate a man in my presence, I figure that *is* my business."

"Then you figure *wrong*. What the hell you thinkin' about, gettin' in my face like this? Are you strappin'? Is that it?"

"Put the knife away, Jack," Gunner said again. Knowing even as he did so that evading Frerotte's question was as good as answering it: No, he wasn't carrying a gun tonight.

"I tell you what," Frerotte said. "I'm either gonna see what you had for breakfast this mornin', or what you got for me. One or the other."

The big man took a step in Gunner's direction.

"Stop right there, motherfucker," J.T. said.

He was back behind the bar, training the shotgun he always kept anchored to a shelf beneath it on Frerotte's ample gut. Even in his agitated condition, Frerotte could see that this man of little patience had no more patience left for him.

"Get the fuck outta here, and don't come back," J.T. said. "I ever see you in my place again, I'm gonna empty this motherfucker on you first, and ask you to leave later. You hear what I'm sayin'?"

Frerotte examined the barkeeper's face for a moment, searching for some indication that the threat was insincere, only to discover just the opposite was true. He would die if he ever set foot in the Deuce again. He had never been so sure of anything in his life.

"All right. Have it your way," Frerotte said, trying to portray a man too big to be affected by so small a defeat as this. He turned to face Gunner one last time, said, "Until next time, my brother."

He closed the razor in his right hand lovingly, slipped it into his back pocket, and was gone.

Nine years later, the "next time" Frerotte had referred to still had not materialized.

Gunner had done everything in his power to avoid the big man, and Frerotte had never come looking for him, at least to the investigator's knowledge. Gunner didn't know why, and he didn't much care; he was just glad to see Jack had lost interest. Cowens, meanwhile, left Los Angeles for good not long after his mutilation, some said for Atlanta, others Memphis, taking his girlfriend and a badly reattached nose with him. Gunner saw him once before his departure, pumping gas into a Lincoln at a station on Hawthorne Boulevard, and had a hard time not staring at the misaligned mass of flesh and bone Frerotte's butchery had left him to live with. Neither one of them said a word about Barber Jack.

After years of not doing so, it would have suited Gunner just fine to never speak the man's name again, but now that was impossible. A janitor named Blue had seen to that.

"What the hell you wanna ask me about him for?" Lilly Tennell asked Gunner, spilling Wild Turkey all over the Acey Deuce's bar as she tried to pour him a shot and scold him at the same time. The big woman with the red smear of a mouth hadn't been there the night her late husband had banned Frerotte from the premises, but it was a move she had always been strongly in favor of. She despised Frerotte with a passion and had been riding J.T. to close the Deuce's doors to him from the moment she first laid eyes on him.

"I need to talk to him, Lilly," Gunner said. "For a case I'm working on."

"Ain't a case in the world that important. Do yourself a favor and leave that motherfucker alone. You'll live longer."

"I hear what you're saying, and I feel the same way. But I don't have a choice, I really have to talk to him."

"And you think I know where you can find him?"

"I was hoping you might've heard something about that, yeah."

"His name don't come up around here, Gunner. You know that."

"Doesn't mean he hasn't dropped in at least once since J.T. passed, just to see if he could get away with it."

Lilly laughed at the very thought. "Shit. I wish to God he had. He'd've lost more than his goddamn nose, he'd've tried comin' in here."

"Then you *don't* know where I can find him. That what you're saying?"

J.T.'s widow stared at him, two massive, meaty arms crossed in front of her chest, trying to decide if he was man enough to handle the information he was asking her to divulge. Gunner just let her look, knowing from experience how useless it was to press her when she was determined to be deliberate about such things.

"Man came in here a while ago, said he an' Jack was in the joint together once," Lilly said eventually, her tone full of disdain and disapproval. "Talked about the time they did together like it was a vacation on the Riviera, or somethin'."

"And?"

"And he said he just run into Jack a couple days before that, first time since he got out, over at one of them casinos over on Normandie. Jack's a security man there, he said, you can believe that shit."

"Which casino was this?"

"The Royalty Club, I think it was. I'm not sure."

"The one across the street from the Queen of Hearts."

"Yeah. But I could be wrong, like I said. Man was talkin' to Benny Abbott that night, not me, so I'm only tellin' you what I overheard."

"Sure. How long ago did this happen?"

Lilly thought about it, said, "Two, three months ago. Maybe a little longer."

Gunner asked her if that was it, and Lilly nodded her head, said she'd told him everything there was to tell.

"I guess you goin' out there now, huh?" she asked, as Gunner slipped off his stool and pushed a ten-dollar bill toward her side of the counter.

"Yeah. You wanna tell me to be careful?"

"I wanna tell you to bring somethin' for his ass this time. That's what I wanna tell you. You go messin' with that fool again without a gun in your pocket, you *askin'* to get cut up."

"I hear you, Lilly."

"Don't hear me, Gunner. Just do what I'm tellin' you, all right?"

The giant black woman snatched the ten off the bar, shoved it into an apron pocket, and left him to take care of another customer.

"Well, well, well," Johnny Frerotte said. "Ain't this somethin'."

He'd gained a few pounds in nine years, and the only hair left on his head was growing long and unmanageable in the back, but other than that, he was the same smooth, fearsome character Gunner remembered. He had an office overlooking the gaming tables up on the Royalty Club's second floor, and Gunner had been shown to it only after a guard downstairs had called ahead to announce his arrival. What the hell the Gardena card casino called itself doing, hiring a sociopath like Frerotte to head its security staff, Gunner couldn't imagine, but there the big man sat: feet up on his desk, a drink in his right hand and a TV remote control in his left, eschewing the huge observation window at his back for a talk show playing on a television set just off to his right.

"What's up, Jack," Gunner said, making a herculean effort to be polite.

Frerotte sat up in his chair, used the remote control to turn the television off. "Aaron Gunner. Man, I thought I'd never see your tired ass again." He smiled.

"Yeah, I know. I was beginning to think the same thing about you."

"Been what? Ten years since we last saw each other?"

"Nine or ten. Something like that."

Frerotte laughed, said, "That was the night I cut that boy's nose off, huh? Over at the Deuce."

"Yeah, it was. Look, Jack—"

"What was that fool's name again? Somethin' with a C . . ."

"Cowens," Gunner said.

"Yeah, that was it. Cowens. I heard the doctors put his shit back on. You hear that?"

Gunner just nodded his head, finally realizing his host wasn't going to hear anything he had to say until he was all done reminiscing.

"Somebody seen him after, I don't remember who, told me they fucked it up. Boy's nose was all crooked an' shit. My man said he'd'a been better off leavin' the fuckin' thing on the floor where he found it." He laughed again.

Gunner watched him and waited.

When Gunner's silence became too much for him, Frerotte said, "So. What you want with me after all these years? You ain't lookin' for a job, are you?"

Gunner shook his head, said, "I've already got one, thanks. As a matter of fact, that's what brings me here today."

"Oh, wait a minute. You were some kind'a investigator, right? A private investigator?"

"Yeah. You remember."

"Yeah, I remember. I remember a lot of things." He showed Gunner his teeth again.

"That's good. Maybe you remember a brother named Elroy Covington, then."

The grin froze on Frerotte's wide face, betraying an effort on the big man's part to project unfamiliarity. "Who?"

"Elroy Covington. He disappeared from a Hollywood motel last October, I've been hired to find out what happened to him."

"Covington?" Frerotte shook his head. "Never heard of nobody named Covington."

"Maybe it would help if I told you the name of the motel. The Stage Door. It's on Sunset, just west of Vine, the south side of the street."

"Don't know it. Somebody said I been there?"

"At least a couple of people, yeah," Gunner lied. "They both said you were the last person to see Covington the night he disappeared. You were in his room, they said."

"Bullshit. I don't hang in Hollywood."

"Maybe you did back then. Just this once."

"You ain't hearin' me, Gunner. I said I don't know the man, an' I don't know the place."

"Then these people I talked to were lying, I guess."

"I guess they were. People are funny like that."

"Sorry, Jack, but I don't think so."

"You don't think so?"

"I think you're the one doing the lying. Question is, why?"

Frerotte pushed himself to his feet, reached behind him with his right hand to withdraw the eight-inch straight razor with the ivory handle, his eyes never leaving Gunner's own.

"I wondered when I'd see that," the investigator said.

"You tax a man's patience, motherfucker," Frerotte said. "Same as always."

"Let's not do this again, Jack. Please."

Frerotte grinned. "What? You don't wanna dance with me, Gunner? Just 'cause J.T. ain't around this time to save your sorry ass?"

"I didn't come here to dance with you, Jack. I just want some answers, that's all."

"You should'a left well enough alone. I gave you a break once, lettin' you slide for gettin' in my shit that night at the Deuce. But I guess you don't know how lucky that was, do you?"

He opened the knife, gave Gunner a good look at its gleaming silver blade.

"Put it away," Gunner said simply.

"Fuck you," Frerotte said. Certain beyond a shadow of a doubt that Gunner had the same problem now that he'd had nine years ago at the Deuce: He was unarmed. Frerotte's people wouldn't have let him up here, otherwise.

"Suit yourself," Gunner said. He picked up the heavy upholstered chair in front of Frerotte's desk and rushed the big man with it.

Frerotte hadn't expected this, was too slow of foot to get out of the way before Gunner had him pinned between the chair and the giant window behind him. Grunting like a stuck pig, he tried to wave the razor in his right hand at the other man's throat, but for naught; his right arm was trapped directly beneath a chair leg and the window frame, limiting its range of motion severely.

"Somebody needs to remind you you're a very fat man, Jack," Gunner said. "Your hands may be fast as hell, but you can't move your feet worth a damn."

Frerotte tried to say "fuck you" again, but he couldn't find the breath to do so; Gunner was pressing the chair into his chest like somebody trying to push a car up a steep hill.

"All right. Listen up. I can't hold you like this for long, so we're gonna have to make this fast. I want you to drop that knife and answer some questions for me. Otherwise, I'm gonna lean on this chair a little more, see how much pressure that glass behind you can take. Understand?"

Frerotte opened his mouth to shout something, but Gunner hunched over, leaned harder into the chair to cut the big man's air off before he could make a sound.

"Make up your mind, Jack," Gunner said. "You wanna fly, or you wanna talk to me?"

Frerotte strained to turn his head sideways, trying to peer out the full-height window Gunner was threatening to force him out of. On the other side of the one-way glass rendering them all but oblivious to his plight, the hundred or so people down below looked to be a long way off; the fall might not kill him, Frerotte knew, but it could easily leave him a cripple for life.

He dropped the razor in his right hand to the floor.

"Good. First question," Gunner said. "You were at the Stage Door Motel the night Covington disappeared, weren't you?"

"I can't . . ." Frerotte said, too short of breath to finish the thought. He was sweating profusely now, and looked like he might lose consciousness any minute. Gunner couldn't have been happier.

"Don't try to speak. Just move your head to indicate yes or no," the investigator said. "Were you at the Stage Door with Covington, or not?"

Frerotte shook his head.

Gunner put his back into the chair again. "Come on, Jack . . ."

Frerotte changed his tune, showed Gunner a feeble nod.

"All right. Next question. Is he still alive?"

The big man paused a moment, then shook his head a second time.

Gunner absorbed this, tried not to let Frerotte see his disappointment. He had expected to learn that Covington was dead from the moment the man named Blue dropped Barber Jack's name; it was, after all, the logical result of someone as ordinary as an architectural draftsman from St. Louis mixing with a big city predator like Johnny Frerotte. But now that his suspicions about Covington had actually been confirmed . . .

His mind had been off Frerotte for all of a tenth of a second, but that was all the time the big man needed to make his move.

Gunner heard him scream like a madman in an asylum, his gaping mouth spraying the air with strands of saliva, then the chair and Frerotte both were coming at him like a brakeless Peterbilt charging downhill. Gunner was flat on his ass before he knew it.

Frerotte could have killed him right there, brought the heavy chair down on his head and then done with him whatever he wanted, but that wasn't the way Barber Jack had built his reputation. Frerotte wanted his razor, so all he did with the chair was throw it down at Gunner's head before turning around to find it.

Gunner caught the brunt of the chair on his right shoulder, heaved it off of him just as Frerotte was bending over to pick his beloved knife up off the floor. The investigator scrambled to his feet, watched as the man mountain before him straightened up and started lumbering toward him, the razor held out in front of him like a beacon lighting his way. The door was only ten feet from Gunner's back, but he knew that wasn't close enough. Not by a long shot.

He had maybe two seconds to scan the room, find something, anything, with which to slow Frerotte down.

A black floor lamp stood to his left, but was too far out of reach;

on his right was a coffee table, long and low. Parts of a newspaper were scattered upon the latter, along with an empty coffee cup, a sugar bowl, and a spoon. Gunner reached out quickly with his right hand, snatched up the larger of the two porcelain objects—the coffee cup—and slung it sidearm at Frerotte's head as hard as he could, hoping there was still enough distance between them to make the toss effective. There was. Frerotte tried to duck, even as he continued his advance, but the heavy cup glanced off his left eyebrow with a solid thud and stopped him in his tracks. As Frerotte backpedaled once, eyes blinking frantically to fight back tears, Gunner went to the floorlamp on his left, ripped its cord out of the wall and proceeded to use its body like a lance to drive the giant backward, his legs churning for all they were worth. By the time Frerotte recognized his intentions, it was too late: His massive frame was already crashing through the observation window behind him, leaving him nowhere to go but down to the gaming room below.

His arrival caused quite a stir. With an almost deafening boom, he fell on the edge of a large poker table, landing on his back, and sent two people sitting there sprawling amid a shower of cards, poker chips, and glass. A woman across the room had been screaming from the first, was still screaming now over the excited murmurs of the crowd. Gunner stood in the gaping hole of the shattered observation window, watched as a ring of people slowly formed around Frerotte's motionless body and the ivory-handled straight razor still clutched in his right hand.

Then he sat down behind the big man's desk and waited for Frerotte's friends to descend upon him.

5

"You know this guy?"
Detective Fred Saunders of the Gardena Police Department asked
Matt Poole, a homicide detective with the LAPD.

Poole was an old friend of Gunner's, had been for many years, but
today he looked at the black man seated before him as if the two had
never met. "If this were a courtroom, I'd take the Fifth," he finally
said. "But since it ain't . . . yeah, I know him, I guess."

The three men were up in Johnny Frerotte's disheveled office at
the now nearly empty Royalty Club. Frerotte had been rushed to
the hospital almost an hour before, looking more like a corpse than
a man still clinging to life, and the club's customers and most of its
staff had been sent home shortly thereafter. Only a handful of Saunders's GPD associates and the club's entire security force—sans its
leader, Frerotte, of course—roamed the floor below, cleaning up the
mess Frerotte's graceless skydive had left behind.

Gunner, meanwhile, had been answering every question Saunders
and his partner, an older, indifferent white man named Clooney,
could throw at him, trying to erase their suspicions that his attack on
Frerotte had somehow been part of a botched attempt to rob the
casino. They were a relatively polite and undemanding pair, as cops
went, but after forty minutes in their company, Gunner felt no more
in their good graces than he had when they arrived. That's when he
suggested they call Poole.

He hadn't really expected the LAPD detective would show up at
the scene; he thought he might agree to say a few words in Gunner's
defense over the phone and leave it at that, and then only that if he
wasn't too busy turning a *Playboy* vertical or something. Yet here

Poole was, in the flesh: weary eyed, flabby cheeked, dressed like a man who'd stayed out in a hurricane too long.

It had to be a slow day for homicide down at Southwest, Gunner decided.

"You see?" he said to Saunders. "Didn't I tell you we're like brothers, this man and me?"

Saunders just frowned, said to Poole, "We were pretty much through with him when we called you, but we didn't want to let him go until we were sure he hasn't just been jerking us around. Frerotte's pretty badly hurt, after all."

"I hear you," Poole said. They'd already told him what Gunner's account of the day's events was, and it all sounded just typical enough of Gunner to be true. He'd seen the investigator have similar misadventures before.

"So I'm free to go now?" Gunner asked, standing up.

"Yeah, you can go," Saunders said. "But if we try to call you and the phone rings more than *once* . . ."

"I know, I know. You'll have the dogs on me before I can blink. Or some other smart and witty threat to that effect."

He started for the door, never turned once to see if Poole was following him or not.

"Boy, you got serious trouble," Poole said a few minutes later, returning to his and Gunner's table at the Baskin-Robbins ice cream shop on Rosecrans and Crenshaw from the parking lot outside. He'd just used the radio in his car to check on Johnny Frerotte's condition, and the smile on his face said the news couldn't have possibly been better. "Ol' Barber Jack's in critical condition over at Martin Luther King, his list of injuries is longer than the Old Testament."

"If that means he's not dead yet, I'm sorry to hear it," Gunner said dryly.

Poole laughed, dug back into his cup of mint chocolate chip. A favor from Poole usually cost Gunner a full meal, but he was getting off light today. Ice cream was all the remuneration Poole desired.

"I thought you needed him alive," the cop said.

"Actually, I do. Think you could get me in to talk to him?"

"Not a chance. This ain't my party, Gunner."

"Come on, Lieutenant. I need to talk to the son of a bitch."

"And you think he's gonna talk to you now? After your makin' a human cannonball out of his ass?"

"He knows what happened to Covington, Poole, and he might be the only one who does."

"Even if that were true, and I doubt it, he's in no condition to help you. Or didn't you just hear me say how fucked up he is?"

"But if he was the last one to see Covington alive—"

"Like I said. You ask me, he wasn't. Jack's a neighborhood head case with a violent temper, nothing more, and nothing less. He doesn't make people disappear, he cuts 'em to ribbons and leaves the pieces all over the sidewalk."

"Yeah, I know, but—"

"Forget the buts. You go over to see Jack at the hospital and he picks that moment to croak, our friends with the Gardena PD are gonna show you a *real* vanishin' act. The next twenty-five years of your life, *poof!*, gone in sixty seconds. You don't believe me, you're outta your mind."

But Gunner did believe him. The chance Poole was describing was very real.

"All right. So I can't talk to him. But I can do the next best thing."

"Show you what a sport I am, Gunner, I'm gonna act like I'm too stupid to know what that means," Poole said.

He took his cup of ice cream and walked out, not wanting to be a party to whatever the investigator intended to do next.

Returning to his office at Mickey's to make a few phone calls, Gunner walked into a full-blown discussion regarding his need to own a pet. Both Mickey Moore and Winnie Phifer had people in their chairs, and four other customers were waiting their turn, everybody talking and laughing like revelers at a New Year's Eve party. Among the customers, only Drew Taylor and Joe Worthy had faces Gunner recognized, but that didn't matter; the good will of the hour could not be undone by unfamiliarity.

"You could use a companion, seems to me," Winnie told Gunner. "It ain't healthy, bein' all alone all the time."

It seemed she had a ten-week-old Rhodesian Ridgeback puppy she was trying to find a home for, and the investigator was the only person left who hadn't explained to her satisfaction why the dog would be miserable living with them.

"I'm not alone all the time," Gunner said.

"What? So you bring some woman into the bedroom two or three times a month. What's that do for you?"

All the men in the house started laughing.

"Shit, I'll tell you what it does for 'im," Mickey said. But before he could go on, Winnie swung her left arm out as if to slap him, missed on purpose.

"You know what I'm talkin' 'bout!" she said, chuckling despite herself. "I mean, what the hell good is somebody you only gonna see two or three times a month? All the rest of the time they ain't around, you're lonely?"

"I'm not lonely," Gunner insisted.

"You alone six days out of every week, you're lonely," Winnie said.

"And you think a dog would solve that problem."

"It could. A dog or a cat. *Somethin'.*"

"Ain't you ever had a pet?" Joe Worthy asked. It was his head Winnie was shearing down to the scalp on both sides, her clippers buzzing around his skull like an angry bee.

"I had a goldfish once," Gunner admitted.

"A *goldfish?*" Mickey said, obviously unimpressed.

"Yeah. I called it Spike. Little Rocky Bythewood was selling 'em door-to-door for a dollar one day, so I bought one."

"Rocky Bythewood? That boy used to live over on Fifty-fourth Street?" Drew Taylor asked.

Rocky Bythewood had been a pint-sized con man who could sell a

Malcolm X T-shirt to the grand dragon of the Ku Klux Klan. If he was alive somewhere today (and it was doubtful), it was only because his family had moved to Chicago before his legion of victims could band together to lynch him in the street.

"Yeah," Gunner said. "You remember him?"

"I remember him. Man, I'll bet that fish was dead in a week."

"Try a *day*. That was the sickest damn goldfish I ever saw, I could've kicked Rocky's narrow little ass."

Taylor just shook his head.

"And that was the only pet you ever had?" Worthy asked.

"That was it," Gunner said.

"You got your feelings hurt," Winnie said.

"Hell, yes, I did. I couldn't flush the toilet for a year without thinking about that fish."

He tried to keep a straight face when he said it, but he couldn't. One look at him, and everybody cracked up again. Worthy fell out of Winnie's chair, he was laughing so hard.

Finally remembering what he was doing here, Gunner headed for his phone in the back, paused on his way to ask Mickey if he had any messages.

"Mrs. You-Know-Who's called you twice," Mickey said, a little smile on his face. "She wants to know what's goin' on."

Gunner knew "Mrs. You-Know-Who" was code for Connie Everson and was sharp enough not to waste his landlord's uncharacteristic use of discretion by speaking her name out loud. It had been almost two days now since her last visit to his office, and he hadn't spoken to her since. Maybe a little impatience on her part was understandable at this point.

"Anybody named Sly call?" Gunner asked Mickey, hoping his new field assistant had something to report.

"Sly? Who's that?"

"Kid I hired to do some work for me."

"He ain't out watchin' the councilman, is he?"

So much for discretion, Gunner thought. "I don't know what the hell you're talking about. Did the boy call or not?"

Mickey shook his head, said the only calls Gunner had received were from the lady he'd already mentioned.

Gunner put a call in to Sly as soon as he reached the phone on his desk, but the boy's mother said he wasn't home, she hadn't seen him all day. She sounded like the worrying type, the kind of mother who would disapprove of her son shadowing a city councilman for the sole purpose of capturing his adulterous activities on film, so Gunner just left his name and number and said a quick good-bye before she could grill him. He didn't feel up to lying to anyone's mother today.

His next call was a more painful one to make. He would have preferred to put Connie Everson off until he had something of substance to tell her, but he'd been doing that now for two days and she was obviously tired of being avoided. And since it wasn't too late to stop payment on her last check . . .

"That's impossible," Everson said after he'd told her he was still waiting for her husband to hook up with the woman she wanted him found with.

"Impossible?"

"Yes, impossible. He was with her *yesterday,* Mr. Gunner. How could you not know that?"

"Yesterday? Where?"

"I have no idea where. But they were together, I assure you. And if you didn't see them—"

Gunner didn't know what to say. Why the hell hadn't he heard from Sly Cribbs if what Everson was telling him was true?

"Believe me, Mrs. Everson, if they had been together yesterday, I'd know about it. You must be mistaken."

"I am *not* mistaken. Although I may very well have been mistaken in hiring you for this job."

"Mrs. Everson . . ."

"No more excuses, Mr. Gunner. I told you two weeks ago that I wanted this done quickly and efficiently, and you assured me then that you would handle it that way. Now, I don't know if you were feeding me a line, or exaggerating your capabilities, but either way, you're going to get me the photographs I require by this time tomorrow, or issue me a full and complete refund of my retainer. Do I make myself clear?"

"A refund? You—"

The line went dead with a loud click before he could accuse her of joking.

Which she hadn't been, of course. Connie Everson wasn't the kind of lady who went around making threats just to get a laugh. She was going to try and get her money back if Gunner couldn't produce the desired results tomorrow, and a fight would ensue when Gunner told her he'd put two weeks into her husband's surveillance and that amount of his time was going to cost her *something,* fruitful or not.

An ugly lawsuit seemed to loom on the horizon unless Sly Cribbs already had the pictures Gunner's client was so anxious to get her hands on. But Gunner had hired Sly primarily because he seemed so responsible; surely the investigator would have heard from the kid by now if he had seen, let alone photographed, any tryst between Gil Everson and the strung-out, gimpy black prostitute his wife was somehow convinced he was seeing.

All the same, Gunner would have gone out looking for Sly personally had he not had more pressing matters to attend to. Like finding out what motive a character like Johnny Frerotte could have possibly had for kidnapping, and perhaps even murdering, Elroy Covington. Gunner already had an idea how this might be accomplished, just as his friend Poole had suspected, but he wanted to talk to someone first, give her a chance to address the question before he tried something illegal that could conceivably cost him his license.

And he wanted to see Yolanda McCreary again, in any case.

———

They ended up eating a late lunch at a sports bar and restaurant called the Grand Slam, down in the lobby of the Airport Marriott where McCreary was staying. A midweek lunch hour crowd was waiting for them, creating a wall of sound that left them little to do but make small talk during their meal. Having to defer any meaningful conversation until they could retire to the hotel bar was an inconvenience Gunner hadn't counted on, but he wasn't really complaining. McCreary had come down from her room looking radiant and relaxed, even more alluring than when the investigator had last seen her, so the patience to put off the questions he had come here to ask was not particularly hard to find.

She was something called a "LAN administrator." Thirty-two years old, divorced, no children. Graduated from Michigan State with a BA in computer science in '85. Liked to read Nikki Giovanni on rainy days, and never saw an Arnold Schwarzenegger movie in her life. She was dating someone back home in Chicago, a fireman named Ken, but the relationship didn't seem to be going anywhere, she couldn't—or wouldn't—say why. She laughed once in forty minutes, reacting to something Gunner said about the food, just to show him she knew how.

He could feel himself being drawn to her like an infatuated schoolboy.

When at last their meal was over and they had moved to the more quiet environs of the hotel bar, where Gunner nursed a Wild Turkey neat, and McCreary a 7&7, Gunner asked her if the name Johnny Frerotte meant anything to her.

McCreary said it didn't.

"How about Barber Jack?"

"Barber Jack? What kind of name is that?"

Gunner gave her some background on Frerotte, asked her again if the name sounded familiar.

"No. God, no," McCreary said. "Why do you ask?"

Cushioning the blow as best he could, Gunner said, "It's beginning to look as if Frerotte might've had something to do with your brother's disappearance. A witness saw him visit Elroy at his motel room, he was apparently the last person Elroy was with that night."

"Oh, my God."

"But I wouldn't read too much into that just yet. All we know right now is that they were together."

"But you said this man—"

"Is dangerous. Yeah, I did. But that doesn't necessarily mean Jack harmed him in any way."

McCreary nodded, not the least bit reassured.

"You wouldn't have any idea what Frerotte might've wanted with your brother?" Gunner asked.

"Me?" She shook her head. "No. I couldn't begin to guess."

"Because Jack's not a thief by reputation. Snatching a tourist with a fat wallet and then making him disappear afterward doesn't sound like his kind of action."

"So?"

"So I don't think it was money that brought them together. At least, not Elroy's money. Jack must've been after something else."

McCreary didn't say anything, seemingly unaware that he was looking to her for some response.

"But you don't know what that something else could have been," he finally said.

McCreary looked up, drawn from a sudden reverie, and shook her head again. "No. I don't. I'm sorry."

Gunner studied her face, remembering how Emilio Martinez had said he'd start his search for Covington with her, if he were Gunner. Not calling McCreary a liar, exactly, but reinforcing Gunner's own odd sense that she wasn't always saying everything there was to be said.

"Who is Tommy?" Gunner asked directly.

"Who?"

"You called your brother Tommy once. In my office, when you first came to see me. Remember?"

"I did?"

"Yeah, you did. I meant to ask you about it earlier, but the thought slipped my mind."

McCreary avoided his gaze for a brief moment, said, "Tommy's what we used to call Elroy when we were kids. We almost never use that name for him anymore, I'm surprised to hear I did."

"And you called him Tommy because?"

"It's a nickname, Mr. Gunner. We had an uncle named Tommy whom Elroy strongly resembled, one of our father's older brothers, so Dad liked to call Elroy 'Little Tommy.' It's what we all used to call him, right up until his senior year in high school." She paused to let Gunner absorb this, then said, "Any more questions?"

She was daring him to ask one more, strangely tired of a line of discussion less than five minutes old. He had every reason to believe she'd get up and return to her room if he refused to back off, but he was willing to take that chance. He was already jumping through hoops for one client, he wasn't going to do it for another.

"Look, Ms. McCreary," he said. "What's your problem, exactly? You wanna tell me now or wait until I figure it out on my own?"

She looked stunned. "Pardon me?"

"There's more to your brother's disappearance than you're telling me, and I'd just as soon not get blindsided trying to find out what it is."

McCreary glared at him, said, "I don't have the slightest idea what you're talking about."

"Sorry, but I don't believe that. If Jack Frerotte had an interest in him, the odds are good your brother was involved in something deep, something outside the realm of the ordinary joe you've been describing."

"Something like what? What are you accusing Elroy of, Mr. Gunner?"

"I'm not accusing him of anything. I'm only saying it doesn't fit, a head case like Frerotte targeting a nobody out of St. Louis, Mo, for an impromptu kidnapping."

"A '*nobody*'?"

"You know what I mean. Somebody with no discernible flaws or hang-ups. No fortune to demand as ransom, no enemies who might've wished him harm."

"But that's who Elroy *was*. I don't know what kind of business this Frerotte person could've had with Elroy any more than *you* do."

"You're sure about that?"

"Of course I'm sure. You want to know what they were doing together, you should be talking to Frerotte, not me."

"I tried that."

"And?"

"And I didn't get a whole lot out of him, I'm afraid."

"You mean he wouldn't talk to you?"

"I mean he had an accident. Just as the subject of your brother was coming up, as a matter of fact."

"I don't understand."

"I went to see him to ask him about Elroy this afternoon, and his reaction was to try cutting me up like a Christmas goose. Naturally, I objected."

"You killed him?"

"No, not quite. But he's in the hospital, in no condition to talk to anybody. Which is why I'm here, bothering you with all these silly questions I'd otherwise be asking him."

"I see."

"But if you don't know anything, I've just been wasting my time. *And* yours."

McCreary held his accusatory gaze this time, aware that he was offering her one last chance to come clean with him, and said, "I wish I could help you more, Mr. Gunner, but I can't. I've told you all I know, I'm sorry."

Gunner considered this a moment, then nodded his head and gave her a little smile, his willingness to alienate a woman he desperately wanted to know more intimately fully exhausted. Which was not to say his doubts about her honesty were gone, by any means; he simply understood that she had told him everything she was going to at this moment.

And he would know soon enough if she was lying to him, in any case.

Mickey was always complaining that his life lacked excitement, so Gunner gave him a little job to do to liven it up.

Naturally, all his landlord did was try to beg off.

"If it was anybody but Barber Jack, I wouldn't mind," he said. "But anything that's got to do with that fool, I want no part of. I'm sorry."

"The man's fucking comatose, Mickey," Gunner said. "He won't even know you're in the room."

"That's what *you* say."

"It'll take you five minutes. You sit by the bed, mumble a few words, then grab his keys and get out. Come on, man."

"That nigger's crazy. I could be sure he was gonna die without ever gettin' outta there, I might consider it, but since I ain't . . ."

It took Gunner almost thirty minutes to break him down, convince him he wouldn't be risking his life to take the mission on. Gunner drove him out to Martin Luther King, the hospital in Inglewood where Johnny Frerotte was taking up space in the ICU, then sent him inside and waited for his return out in the parking lot, hoping and praying his landlord could handle the menial task he'd been assigned without messing something up, bringing the wrath of God down upon both their heads. Gunner wasn't normally comfortable involving other people in his business, but this time it couldn't be helped; he needed Frerotte's house keys, and he couldn't go get them himself. At least, not without daring the fates to make good on Matt Poole's prediction that Frerotte would go flat-line on him the moment Gunner came calling. The investigator had seen worse luck than that before.

Mickey was gone for nearly forty minutes. By the time he emerged from the hospital's lobby again to approach Gunner's car, Gunner was already choosing the words he would use on Ira "Ziggy" Zeigler to convince his lawyer to come bail the two of them out of jail. Mickey was sweating like he'd just run a marathon, but the smile on his face had been visible from over twenty yards away.

"I got 'em," he said, getting in the car. He dropped a small ring of keys into Gunner's open palm and grinned wider still, immensely proud of himself.

"And the address?"

"Fifteen-twenty-one Sixty-sixth Street. Got it right off his driver's license, just like you said."

"What the hell took you so long?"

Mickey frowned. "You said act like the man was a friend of mine, so I acted like he was a friend of mine. I said a prayer over 'im."

"A prayer?"

"Wasn't nothin' fancy. Just a few words askin' the Lord to ease the poor man's sufferin'. Man looked like you run his ass over with a truck."

"Anybody see you take the keys?"

Mickey shook his head. "I don't think so. Nobody cares about no hospital full of black folks and Mexicans, man." He laughed. "Hell, I probably could've stole a patient during a goddamn operation, I'd'a wanted to."

Gunner had to laugh at that himself. Sometimes, the truth hurt too much to be dealt with any other way.

Johnny Frerotte's place on 66th Street was a white, two-story frame house sitting on a short rise of grass between Normandie and Hall-dale Avenues. At just after 10:00 P.M., it looked like the home of a grandmother, clean and quiet and dark as the insides of a closed casket, but Gunner knew different. What it was was the hiding place of a monster, the inner sanctum of a knife-wielding sadist who might not ever darken its doors again.

Gunner got out of the Cobra and walked briskly up to the front door.

Over the years, he had learned to pick locks with some alacrity, but the practice still made him too uneasy to resort to it often. Every minute it took to solve the myriad puzzles of a lock felt like an hour to him, and the fear of getting caught, of having someone train a flashlight on his face before blowing him off their front porch with a hunting rifle, was always with him. So tonight he'd enlisted Mickey's help in getting Frerotte's keys, hoping to use and return them to Frerotte's hospital room before anyone even realized they were gone.

As far as Gunner knew, Frerotte was a single man who lived alone, but he rang the bell twice anyway before using Frerotte's house key to slip quietly inside the big man's lifeless house, behaving like somebody who had every right in the world to do so. Experience had taught him that bold straightforwardness often drew less attention than stealth; look both ways before climbing in a window, and neighbors would call out the National Guard to have you arrested, but do a cartwheel through a pane of broken glass without hesitation and they paid you no mind, reassured by your air of confidence that you were unworthy of their concern.

Gunner stood motionless in the foyer of the big house and listened to a long, hard silence that never broke. Not a single footstep did he hear; no water running in sink or tub, no stereo nor television blaring. He was either alone or in the company of someone who liked to bed down early. His instincts told him it was the former.

Nevertheless, he proceeded to creep through the dark house like a mine sweeper, using his penlight selectively, making as little sound as possible. He went through the living room, examining the titles on a wall of bookshelves, fanning through the pages of assorted magazines atop a coffee table, slipping his hands under the cushions of a matching couch and chair. He found nothing. Moving on to the kitchen, he scanned the contents of cupboards and drawers, checked the underside of a kitchen table and its two chairs for objects that may have been taped there, but weren't. He noticed that there was enough food in the room to feed three men, but that was hardly unexpected; Frerotte hadn't become the behemoth that he was by eating light.

Gunner inspected the dining room next, made quick work of the scarred wooden table and four chairs at its center, and a tall china cabinet with beveled glass doors set against one wall. Again, he came across nothing out of the ordinary. In the drawer of a rolltop desk, however, he discovered a cloth-bound ledger book and an envelope filled with receipts and canceled checks. He examined both carefully, hoping to find something he could connect to Elroy Covington, but he saw no mention of Covington's name anywhere. The only thing that caught his eye at all was a pair of entries Frerotte had made in the ledger just before, and then right after, Covington's disappearance. Recordings of cash monies received from a "DOB"; first $2000, then an additional $3000.

Frerotte's price for making Covington go away?

Nowhere else in the ledger, nor on any of the documents contained in the envelope, were the initials DOB inscribed. Gunner sat before the desk for a moment, trying in vain to fit the three letters to a name, then returned the ledger and envelope to their original places and closed the drawer. He was turning away from the desk when he remembered something, withdrew the drawer again and used his right hand to feel around its underbelly.

This time he found something.

It was a plain white envelope, sealed closed and taped to the drawer's bottom. Even before opening it, Gunner could see that it contained a single photograph. He opened a pocket knife, gripping the penlight between his teeth, and slit the envelope open. Inside was a Polaroid snapshot someone had taken at night: a large man's lifeless body laid out on its back in some heavy, moonlit underbrush. His throat was apparently cut, blood painting the front of his white shirt a dark crimson. The black man's head was turned to one side, removing his face from the somewhat distant camera's view, but his size and shape made him a good bet for only one man.

Elroy Covington.

Gunner felt a brief pang of empathy for his client, then put the snapshot and the envelope into his jacket pocket and closed the desk drawer. He went out into the foyer, intending to check the second floor . . .

. . . and heard something.

What it was, or where it was coming from, was not immediately clear. An arrhythmic clicking of some sort, like the chattering of a windup pair of false teeth, the sound was too faint and intermittent to get a good fix on. And it was gone as soon as he took note of it. He waited at the staircase landing to hear it again, but he never did, leaving him to wonder how real it had been.

He had taken two steps up the stairs when he caught sight of a cellar door's reflection in a wall mirror and stopped.

It was just a six-foot, three-inch slab of white-painted pine set into the wallpapered side of the staircase. Nothing about it was worthy of his attention, but he was drawn to it all the same. Its wooden face was cold against his ear as he listened to a dead silence standing on the other side, then gingerly tried the knob with his right hand. It turned freely, unlocked. He swung the door open and aimed the narrow beam of his penlight down a steep set of stairs, into the black pit below, able to see nothing but an icy concrete floor and the lower third of a washing machine.

Gunner slipped the 9-millimeter Ruger from its holster under his arm and started slowly down the stairs.

It was a small room with unfinished walls and high windows that afforded it a ground-level view of the outside world. A naked light bulb in a simple fixture dangled from the ceiling like a spider on a strand of web, but nothing happened when Gunner tried to turn it on. With only his penlight to defend against the darkness, he examined his surroundings as best he could, generally catching only glimpses of objects before moving on to the next: the washing machine he had seen from above and the twin dryer sitting open-mouthed beside it; a file cabinet missing the bottommost of four drawers, and a mop handle protruding from a paint-stained metal bucket; a wicker basket full of dirty clothes, a rust-encrusted bicycle standing on two flats, and a giant oil painting unsuitable for framing propped up against a mound of cardboard boxes.

And against one wall, near the open door of a tiny water closet, a small cot covered by a pair of green army blankets.

Gunner moved in for a closer look, saw a lozenge-shaped, flowery throw pillow lay at one end of the cot, a collection of newspaper clippings and open magazines at the other, all of the latter splayed out on top of each other like bodies engaged in an orgy. Gunner sifted through the pile, held a few pieces up close to his face where the penlight made reading possible. He recognized immediately that the subject of each article was the same: the rise and fall of a black newspaper reporter out of Chicago, Illinois, named Thomas Selmon. Selmon's story was old news, a scandal that dated back at least five years, but Gunner remembered it well.

"Jesus," he said under his breath.

All the pictures of Selmon accompanying the articles were those of a dark-skinned black man in his early thirties, standing approximately six feet tall and weighing around two hundred pounds. He wore glasses, but no mustache. Gunner recognized him anyway.

Nine months earlier, he'd been sitting two stools down from Gunner at a crowded hotel bar in Washington, D.C., on the most peripheral edge of a conversation Gunner was having with the bartender and two other black men drinking there. He hadn't said more than three words the entire evening, so it wasn't really surprising that Gunner had had no recollection of him until this moment—but now Gunner remembered him clearly, reaching across the bar to take one of the business cards the investigator was dishing out to anyone who would have one . . .

Gunner looked up from the last magazine on the cot, pointed the needle of light emerging from the instrument in his right hand into the little bathroom off to his left. Both the seat and the lid on the toilet were down, and something stood just before the bowl he couldn't quite see from this angle. He circled closer, saw the penlight's flash reflect off a shiny, rectangular surface hovering just above the legs of a typewriter stand . . .

. . . and then he felt something hit the back of his skull like a frozen wrecking ball.

Everything after that was just a thick soup of dulled sensation. Pain. Dizziness. Nausea.

And finally, the ice cold embrace of unwanted sleep.

6

H e   c a m e   t o   c o u g h i n g ,
his throat and lungs burning like he'd swallowed a lit road flare.

He opened his eyes, discovered that they, too, were burning, but
he kept them open stubbornly, blinking back tears to focus on the
pair of blurred ovals that were floating back and forth before him.
Faces. Two men he didn't recognize, one white, one black, both serv-
ing as foreground to a starry night sky streaked with smoke. The
white man spoke first.

"Take it easy there, buddy. You're gonna be okay."

He was a paramedic. He was wearing the yellow turnout gear of a
fireman, sans helmet, and the clear plastic mask of an oxygen tank
was gripped tightly in his right hand. His similarly attired partner
stood behind him. The black man on Gunner's opposite side appeared to be just a fireman, though the orange helmet atop his head
carried a clear suggestion of authority. To this man's right was a
fourth, yet another fireman, this one older than the rest, wearing a
white helmet and a grim, inimical expression on his face.

All four men were looking down at Gunner as if he were a baby in
a bassinet.

The investigator realized now that he was on his back, lying on the
damp bed of Johnny Frerotte's front lawn. He turned his head to
one side and tried to sit up, saw Frerotte's house engulfed in flames,
the smoke escaping from its blackened roof turning slowly gray as a
company of firemen poured water into the heart of the inferno.

Instinctively, Gunner reached into his right-hand jacket pocket,
felt around inside . . . but the Polaroid snapshot he'd placed there
only minutes ago was gone.

"Shit," he said, only to start up coughing again.

"You'd better lie back down a while," the first paramedic told him, "have another taste of this."

Gunner shook his head to decline the proffered oxygen, looked around to see that a number of Frerotte's neighbors had come out of their own houses to watch Frerotte's burn down, their faces aglow from the colored lights winking on the roofs of the four Los Angeles County Fire Department vehicles parked at conflicting angles in the street. A few people began to point in Gunner's direction as he continued to stir.

"What happened?" Gunner asked.

"You're a very lucky man, that's what happened," the man in the orange helmet said. "This fellow here saved your life."

He was referring to a black man standing sheepishly off to one side on Gunner's right. Potbellied and fortyish, he was wearing a sleeveless white T-shirt and an oversized pair of green sweat pants, and he was standing on Frerotte's wet grass in bare feet.

"You got me out of there?" Gunner asked him.

The other man just nodded his head.

"Thanks. I owe you one."

"You don't owe me nothin'. I seen smoke an' come runnin', that's all. You just lucky I seen you down there."

"He says he found you in the basement," the black fireman said. "Where it looks like the fire started."

He waited for Gunner to confirm or deny this, looking more like a cop now than a fireman. Gunner could see now that the silver badge on his helmet was that of a captain, while the one on his grim-faced friend's was that of a chief.

"I couldn't tell you," Gunner told them both, becoming more and more aware of a throbbing pain at the back of his head. "I was out when the fire started."

"Out?"

"Somebody coldcocked me."

"They what?"

"I was struck from behind and knocked unconscious."

"By whom?"

"I have no idea. But I'd imagine it was the same person who torched the place afterward, wouldn't you?"

The black fireman watched Gunner massage the base of his skull with one hand for a while, then said, "Mr. Martin here says you're not the owner of the house. That he's never seen you around here before."

"That would be right. He probably hasn't."

"So what were you doing in there, Mr. . . ." Having finally spoken, the man in the white helmet consulted an open wallet that Gunner instantly recognized as his own. ". . . Gunner?"

"I wasn't playing with matches, if that's what you're thinking. I'm a private investigator working a missing persons case. You want a look at my license before handing the wallet back, be my guest."

The chief accepted his offer, examined the license carefully before closing the wallet and passing it down to his subordinate, who in turn placed it in the palm of Gunner's extended right hand. "All right," the chief said, asserting himself fully now. "So you're a private investigator. That still doesn't explain what you were doing in the house." When Gunner started to respond to that, he said, "I tell you what. Hold your answer to that for a moment. I'm sure these guys are gonna wanna hear it as much as I do."

Gunner turned, following his gaze, watched as two uniformed police officers stepped out of a cruiser to begin moving slowly toward them.

The uniforms ended up detaining him for forty-five minutes. His explanation for his presence in Frerotte's home was woefully slight—he told them the front door had been ajar upon his arrival, and a loud noise had lured him down to the basement—but all the evidence at the scene seemed to corroborate his assertion that the arsonist they were looking for was someone other than Gunner himself. The paramedics had to admit he did indeed have a nasty bump on the back of his head, and the position of his body when Frerotte's neighbor found him had been inconsistent with that of a pyromaniac who'd stumbled and hit his head trying to flee the scene.

Still, the two cops had grilled him long and hard before sending him on his way, asking all the questions he had been asking himself ever since he'd regained consciousness on Johnny Frerotte's front lawn: Who would have wanted to knock Gunner cold in Frerotte's basement and then set fire to the entire house? A burglar who liked to cover his tracks with arson? Or an arsonist who liked to mix a little murder with his fires from time to time? And why would either man take a photograph of a dead man out of Gunner's pocket before fleeing the scene?

Gunner didn't know. There was no logical explanation for a burglar being down in Frerotte's basement looking for something worth stealing, nor for an arsonist choosing to make Frerotte's humble home the site of his next bonfire.

So Gunner was left to believe only one thing: He owed his present headache to neither a burglar, nor an arsonist, but to someone who merely wanted him dead. Someone he'd spooked into committing an impromptu arson by connecting Frerotte to the central figure in an all but forgotten newspaper scandal that was now half a decade old.

He didn't have a name for this someone yet, but he had a pretty good idea who might. And just as soon as the uniforms became comfortable enough with his flimsy explanations to release him on his own recognizance, he angrily fired his red Cobra up to go have a little talk with her.

"I don't know what you're talking about," Yolanda McCreary said for the second time.

"Don't say that again," Gunner warned her.

"It's the truth."

"It's a goddamn lie. You don't slip and call your brother Tommy every now and then because he resembled some dead uncle of yours as a kid. You call him Tommy because that was his *name* once, Tommy. Tommy *Selmon.*"

McCreary shook her head. "No."

"Before the hounds on his heels forced him to start a new life in Missouri as a mild-mannered family man named Elroy Covington."

"No!"

She tried to edge past him to the door of her hotel room, no doubt intending to order him out, but he caught her by the arm, pinned her to the spot. "Look," he said, "the game is *over.* I know who your brother was, and what he was running from, so stop playing stupid and start leveling with me for a change."

She ripped her arm out of his grasp, went to the door, and opened it for him. "Get out of here, Mr. Gunner," she said, closing the baby blue terry cloth robe she was wearing even tighter around her waist. "You're fired. I don't want your help anymore."

Gunner stayed where he was, said, "It's too late for that now. I'm in too deep. There's no going back."

"I said I want you to *leave!*"

Gunner went to the door, clinging to the last shred of his expiring patience, and closed the door himself. "You're not paying attention. I said I'm in too deep to walk away now. Your brother's dead. I saw a snapshot of his body tonight."

McCreary was visibly shaken. "What?"

"Jack Frerotte had taped it under a desk drawer in his home. The body's face wasn't visible, but it looked like your brother to me."

"I don't believe you."

"It's true. I would have brought the photo along, but somebody relieved me of it after knocking me out, then trying to burn Frerotte's house down with me still in it. I thought it might've been Jack himself, but it wasn't. I called the hospital he's been staying in before I came over here, they say he's resting comfortably."

McCreary examined his disheveled condition more closely, realized he wasn't just making the story up. "Oh, my God," she said quietly.

Gunner saw her list to one side, said, "Maybe you'd better sit down to hear the rest of this."

McCreary nodded, drifted over to the couch nearby, and sat down. Taking a seat himself in the armchair across from her, Gunner watched silently as his client began to cry.

"I saw something else besides that photograph tonight," he said after a while. "Jack had a pile of newspaper and magazine clippings about the Thomas Selmon scandal down in his basement. The man in all the accompanying photographs wasn't quite as heavy then as he was last October, and he hadn't yet grown his mustache, but he was your brother just the same. Wasn't he?"

McCreary continued to sob, acting like she hadn't heard the question.

"I'll take that for a yes."

"All right." McCreary looked up to meet his gaze, suddenly angry again. "So Elroy's real name was Thomas Selmon. You think I should have told you that from the beginning, I suppose."

"It would have been a nice piece of information to have, yeah."

"You would have never taken my case, Mr. Gunner. You know it, and I know it."

"You didn't think I'd find out who he was eventually?"

"I didn't know if you would or not. I just knew you'd never agree to help me if you knew who Tommy was up front."

"So you lied to me."

"I took a chance that whatever happened to Tommy last October had nothing to do with his troubles back in Chicago. That you'd be able to find him without ever learning who he was or what he had done." She wiped her eyes with both hands, shook her head forlornly. "In retrospect, I can see that I must have been dreaming."

Gunner didn't say anything for a long time, letting her squirm while he decided what to do. "Okay. Now that we both know the score, let's start over. I'm going to need you to tell me everything you can about the scandal. Everything you can remember."

It wasn't what McCreary had been expecting him to say. "I don't . . ."

"As it sounds like you've just figured out, whatever happened to your brother probably didn't happen to Elroy Covington, Ms. McCreary. It happened to Thomas Selmon. The internationally disgraced newspaper man. And right now, all I know about Selmon is what the media were saying about him five years ago."

"But I thought—"

"That I'd walk on you once I found out who he was. Yeah, I know, you said that."

McCreary appraised him skeptically, said, "You're saying you still want to help me? Even though Tommy's *dead?*"

"Call me stupid, but yeah. I do. But not just because I'm a prince among men. I've got reasons of my own for sticking this thing out."

"Really? Like what?"

"Like the job you paid me to do's not finished yet, for one thing. And it won't be until I find your brother's body, prove for a fact that he's dead, just as that photo tonight suggested."

"And?"

"And this thing is personal with me now, needless to say. Somebody tried to kill me tonight, remember?"

"I'm sorry, but I still don't understand. Most black people *hate* Tommy for what he did, Mr. Gunner. Why don't you?"

"Hate Thomas Selmon?" Gunner shook his head. "I don't have that kind of energy to waste. Your brother wasn't evil—he was sick. To run the game on people he did, he would've had to be."

McCreary turned her gaze downward, onto the hands folded gently upon her lap, and nodded almost imperceptibly. "Yes. That's very true."

Gunner gave her a moment, then said, "Tell me about him, please."

Of all the things Thomas Roosevelt Selmon was good at, nothing came easier to him than lying.

From the age of four, he could lie about himself, his family, even strangers on the street with total and complete alacrity, and he could

do so for reasons of supreme importance, or for no reason whatsoever. Mostly, as his big sister Yolanda now recalled, it was the latter.

Selmon didn't mean anything by it; it was just his way of getting
by. Truth could open a lot of doors, Selmon knew, but a well-told lie
often opened them wider and faster than the mere truth alone. So
lies were simply tools to him; devices with which to make his life easier, more hassle-free. And trying to acquaint him with the immoral-
ity of the practice was an exercise in pure futility.

In his youth, Selmon lied spontaneously and impulsively, with little or no regard for consequence. But later, as he began to understand the value of timing and discrimination, he learned to reserve
his fabrications for only those occasions when there was something
tangible to be gained. An honor or a prize he could not win honestly,
or a punishment he was desperate to escape.

By the time he was twenty, Tommy Selmon was a master of the big
lie. Having graduated from Illinois State with honors, embarking on
a promising career in journalism as a cub reporter for a small black
newspaper in Rockford, he was one of the world's greatest purvey-
ors of falsehood and deceit—and only those closest to him knew it.
Which was the true test of a liar, after all: invisibility. The lack of a
liar's crippling reputation. For all the empty promises and counter-
feit history that had fueled all but a few of his successes, Tommy Selmon was looked upon by almost everyone who knew him as a man
who could be trusted—and that made him very dangerous indeed.

Still, his potential for destruction wasn't fully realized until he
reached the age of twenty-six, fifteen months after he was hired to
cover the inner city for the *Chicago Press Examiner*. A brilliant,
gut-wrenching series of stories Selmon had written about a black,
twenty-something Chicago drug dealer named Zero had won the
Press Examiner the coveted Pulitzer Prize for investigative journalism for 1991—then brought the paper endless shame and ridicule
when Selmon was forced to confess the stories had no basis in fact.
Zero had been a figment of Selmon's imagination, his knee-jerk re-

action to the growing pressure the paper's editorial staff had been placing on him for months to deliver hard-hitting urban crime stories. In the fallout of Selmon's confession—made only after his employers had amassed enough evidence of his deception to all but render a confession moot—Martin Keene, the highly respected *Press Examiner* editor who had personally hired Selmon, was fired, a second editor resigned in disgrace, and Selmon himself was publicly flayed and vilified by news media around the world.

No one attacked him with greater fervor and tenacity, however, than his fellow African-American journalists.

For Selmon's incredible fraud had shamed them all. In the arena of American journalism, where the abilities and credentials of black newswriters were already under constant scrutiny, Selmon's deception served only to reinforce the popular notion that writers and reporters of color could not be counted on to deliver the goods. That their work was not only subpar, but of dubious integrity and reliability. Selmon's winning of the Pulitzer Prize had promised to free black journalists from the shackles of this myth forever, and when it was stripped from his grasp like the colors from the breast of a court-martialed war deserter, it was stripped from them all.

Had Selmon only been able to acknowledge this, to understand it enough to offer his wounded peers some form of apology, the call for his blood might not have been so resounding. But Selmon could do neither. He could not openly regret the damage he had done to others because he could not fathom it. The idea that his fate was tied to that of other black men and women like himself was not only against his wishes, but completely beyond his comprehension. Because Tommy Selmon didn't *want* to be black, and never thought of himself as such. The Selmon family's upper-middle-class existence had always allowed him to gravitate toward the white man's side of the world—white schools, white friends, white lovers—and the experience had rendered him all but blind to the reality of his own ethnicity. He didn't reject his blackness, exactly—he simply erased it from his consciousness, like a physical defect he chose to ignore.

It was this crime of self-delusion and insensitivity, in the end, that finally drove him into hiding.

For once the scandal he had created made him the focus of national and international attention, and his life became the subject of endless newspaper stories and magazine articles, his misguided disinclination to accept what he was—a black man in a white man's world—was exposed for all to see, bringing the wrath of black America down upon him like a rain of fire.

Twenty-two days after his highly publicized firing from the *Chicago Press Examiner,* Tommy Selmon went underground, where he disappeared from public view forever.

Two weeks after that, in a small motor vehicle office in St. Louis, Missouri, a man named Elroy Covington was created to take his place.

"Well, I guess now we know what kind of book he was thinking about writing," Gunner said when Yolanda McCreary's story had come to an end.

"What? Oh, yes. I guess we do, don't we?"

"His side of the story would have been worth a few dollars on the open market, even after five years. That poor literary agent he called in New York should've been in to take his call."

McCreary just nodded silently.

"Who all knew about your brother's new identity besides you?"

"Besides me? No one. I was the only one who knew. Tommy wrote me a letter from St. Louis right after he got there, telling me how he'd changed his name and where he could be reached, but he made me promise not to tell anyone else. Reporters, especially."

"And you never did?"

"No." She shook her head slowly from side to side, looking as sad and tired as an abandoned child.

"What about other members of the family? You said earlier you were Tommy's only living relative, but was that the truth, or . . . ?"

McCreary shook her head again, embarrassed, and said, "We have a baby sister, Irene. She lives in Springfield. Springfield, Missouri. But I'm sure she never knew anything about Tommy's whereabouts. She didn't want to know. Like our father did before he passed away, she despises Tommy for what he did, she doesn't want anything more to do with him."

"Maybe she felt that way before. But it's been five years. People's minds change."

"Not Irene's. That girl's as bitter now as she ever was."

"You don't think Tommy ever tried to contact her anyway?"

"No. Irene would have told me if he had."

"What about old friends? Somebody Tommy worked with at the paper, perhaps?"

"Those people weren't Tommy's friends, Mr. Gunner. When he needed their support, they all turned their backs on him. None of them could be trusted to keep his new life a secret, and he knew it."

"Still, he must have been tempted. After five years . . ."

McCreary shook her head, said, "Tommy was very comfortable with his life in St. Louis. He wasn't at first, of course, but in time he learned to be. He wouldn't have jeopardized it all just to get in touch with some old friend at the newspaper."

"Just the same, I don't suppose you'd know if any of the people we're talking about ended up here in Los Angeles, would you?"

"I wouldn't have any idea about that, no. I never knew any of those people myself. But why—" She cut herself off, answering her own question before she could even voice it. "Oh. You're thinking maybe that's what brought Tommy out here from D.C."

Gunner shrugged. "It's a thought." He thought McCreary might want to expand on the idea, but she showed no interest. He decided to let it go. "And Tommy's wife? Does she know who he really is?"

"Oh, yes, of course. After they'd been married a couple of years, he told Lydia everything. They were about to have their first child, and he wanted to be sure she wouldn't run out on him if she found out on her own."

"So how'd she react?"

"About the way you might expect. Tommy said she was horrified. But fortunately, she loved him, and she was pregnant with his baby, and she believed him when he told her that he wasn't the same person he used to be, that more than his name had changed since he'd moved to St. Louis. And that was really true, Mr. Gunner. Tommy *was* a changed man. It might have taken him too long to see it, but he finally understood how wrong his actions had been in Chicago, and how many innocent people he'd hurt with his lies."

Good for him, Gunner wanted to say, but didn't. Instead, he shifted gears, asked McCreary if the initials DOB meant anything to her.

"DOB? No." She shook her head again. "Why do you ask?"

"Apparently, Jack Frerotte received five thousand dollars from somebody with those initials about the time your brother disappeared. Two grand before, and three right after. There may be no connection, but I'm inclined to believe there is."

"DOB?" She stopped to think, eyes focused straight ahead on nothing in particular, then shook her head one more time. "I'm sorry, no. I can't think of anyone with initials like that."

"What about an acronym? For an organization, or a group of some kind?"

Again, McCreary considered the question in silence for a moment, then shook her head. "No," she said. "You think this DOB paid Frerotte to murder my brother, is that it?"

"It's beginning to look that way, yeah," Gunner said.

"Why? For what reason?"

"I won't know that until I know who or what this DOB is. Or until Frerotte recovers enough from his injuries to talk to either me or the police, if he's so inclined."

"But you think it had something to do with Tommy's problems in Chicago, you said."

"That seems like a safe bet, doesn't it? Unless there was more to your brother's role as Elroy Covington than anyone's made me aware of yet."

Recognizing a thinly disguised question when she heard one, McCreary said, "As far as I know, Mr. Gunner, Tommy's life in St. Louis was just as innocuous as it appeared to be. Tommy liked it that way."

Gunner nodded, reviving the headache he'd been presented with down in Jack Frerotte's basement. Watching him rub the back of his head with one hand, wincing, McCreary asked if he'd like her to go get him some ice.

"No thanks. I'm on my way out." He stood up.

"What are you going to do?" McCreary asked, getting to her own feet.

"Go home and get out of these clothes, for one thing. Shower and get some sleep, for another. After that, I don't know. I'll have to get back to you on that."

McCreary walked him to the door, held it open for him as he stepped out into the hall. "If you want, I can call Lydia and Irene, ask if either of them knows who this DOB could be," she said.

"That would be helpful, thanks," Gunner said.

"You said you couldn't see the face in the photograph. The one you said you found in this man's house—Frerotte, was it?—before it burned down." She paused. "Should I take that to mean there's still a chance my brother's alive?"

Gunner had hoped she wouldn't ask the question, disliking the answer he knew he would have to give her. "You want my professional opinion, or a more optimistic one?"

"I'd prefer the professional one, of course. But I think I just heard it, didn't I?"

Gunner nodded, grateful that nothing more needed to be said. He was hurting and needed sleep, and the anger he had come here with was all used up, leaving him drained and listless.

"Thank you for your honesty, Mr. Gunner. Good night," McCreary said.

Gunner watched her close the door on him, then quickly walked away.

On the long ride home, he thought about her terry cloth robe, and the smooth, well-rounded body it enveloped.

It was a small pleasure, and one that he could only now enjoy. Lusting after his client while breaking the news of her brother's death would have been inexcusable, the conduct of a boor. And had he allowed himself to contemplate what she looked like in such a partial state of dress, how badly he was starting to want her, while she was still within *reach* . . .

Better that he go to bed tonight with the mere hope of someday being with her, than the knowledge that he never would.

Proud, then, to have proven himself yet again a man of tremendous moral character, he drove straight home, went directly to his lonely bedroom, and found two messages waiting for him on his answering machine there. The first one was from Mickey, informing him that Sly Cribbs had been looking for him, and that Mickey had given the kid Gunner's number at home—he hoped that was okay. The second message, predictably, was from Sly himself.

"Yo, Mr. Gunner. I got 'em. I got the pictures." Sly laughed. "Wait 'til you check this shit out. You're not gonna believe it. Man, it is *wack!* I'm havin' the prints developed now, I'll bring 'em by your office first thing in the mornin'. Peace."

Gunner wasn't sure he could wait until morning to hear the details, but the clock on his nightstand said it was well after midnight, no time to be calling the kid's household and raising his mother out of bed. Sly was probably in enough trouble for disappearing on his moms earlier as it was.

So Gunner just showered and went to bed as planned, unaware that neither Sly nor his mother would have been available to take his call, even if he had chosen to make it.

7

Mickey said, "Tell me what I heard this mornin' ain't true. Tell me Jack Frerotte's house didn't burn down last night."

"We'll talk about it later, Mickey. I'm busy right now."

"I'm the one got you the keys to the man's house, Gunner. If I'm about to go to jail for that—"

"Nobody's going to go to jail, Mickey. Now, get the hell out of here, please, I'm waiting for somebody."

"You're waitin' for somebody? That's why you're sittin' back here in the dark? Because you're waitin' for somebody?"

"That's right. If Sly Cribbs comes in, send him straight back, will you?"

But Sly Cribbs never did come in, and he didn't call, either. Gunner waited for him patiently right up until 10 o'clock, then tried to reach the kid by phone at home. It was like trying to get someone to answer the pay phone in a boarded-up gas station.

Gunner didn't get it.

Then Matt Poole called, and it all made sense.

"You're on some kind of roll, partner," the cop said dryly.

In no mood for his repartee, Gunner said, "Every phone call has a point, Poole. You wanna tell me the point of this one?"

"You've got another friend in the hospital, Gunner. That's what."

Gunner sat upright in his chair, said, "Not Sly Cribbs."

"Then he *is* a friend of yours. She isn't just makin' it up."

"Who?"

"The kid's mother. Charlotte Cribbs."

"Tell me what happened, Poole. No more bullshit, all right?"

"You better come down here and see for yourself. Kid's in a pretty bad way."

"Where?"

"Daniel Freeman ICU. Just follow the red stripe on the floor, you can't miss it."

Gunner said he was on his way.

In a contest of who had the most medical hardware keeping them alive, Sly Cribbs would have undoubtedly beaten Jack Frerotte by a landslide.

In the dark, silent spaces of his room in ICU, the kid looked like something out of a sci-fi movie: smothered in gauze, encircled by instruments, wires and tubes and IV lines fanning out from his body like the tendrils of Medusa's crown. The only indication that a living being lay at the center of all this chaos was the languid beeping of the machines tracking Sly's vital signs.

"Kid took two hits from a forty-five at close range," Poole said before Gunner could ask, standing outside the observation window looking onto Sly's room. "One was a through-and-through that entered his right shoulder, went clean out his back. The other shattered his left collarbone on its way to a kidney. Doctors had to go in and get that one soon as they brought 'im in."

"When was that?"

"Just after eleven P.M."

"So what happened? Who the hell did this?"

"Looks like a carjacker. Over on Exposition and Vermont, less than six blocks from his home."

"A carjacker?"

Poole nodded. "Perp fled the scene on foot, he's still at large."

"Anybody get a description?"

"He was a big guy with a ski mask on his head. The one witness we've got thinks he was black, but he says he can't be sure."

Gunner turned away for a moment, suppressing the need to curse aloud, then regarded Poole again and asked, "How bad is it? They expect him to make it?"

The cop shrugged, said, "Doctors say his chances are a little better than fifty-fifty. He lost a shitload of blood, apparently."

Gunner nodded solemnly, fell silent for a moment. "You say the 'jacker left without his car? After shooting him twice?"

"Yeah. Seems kind of ass-backwards, doesn't it? But it happens."

"Cribbs's car have a stick shift in it?"

"Yeah. A 'ninety-four Olds Ciera with a manual five, gotta be the first I've ever seen. You know about these assholes and sticks, huh?"

Gunner nodded again to say that he did. As a general rule, professional car thieves could drive anything with four wheels, but not every carjacker was so versatile. More than a few of them only knew automatics, they were lost behind the wheel of anything with a manual transmission. And time and again these idiots would make a move on a car, pop a cap in its driver if the driver complained, and only *then* see the five-speed stick rising up between the seats, rendering the car all but useless to them.

"I guess by now you must be wondering why I asked you down here," Poole said.

"Come on, Lieutenant. Don't even go there, all right?"

"Take it easy, cowboy. I know you didn't do this. But seein' as how Cribbs has been under your employ for the last few days, I thought you might have an interest in his condition. Maybe I was wrong."

"Under my employ? Where'd you get that?"

"From his mother. Remember? She's been with him ever since they brought 'im in, she should be back from the cafeteria any minute now." He fixed his eyes on Gunner's own and left them there, waiting.

"Okay. The kid's been working for me, sure," Gunner admitted.

"On the Covington case?"

"No. This is something entirely different."

"Any chance what he was doin' for you had somethin' to do with this?"

"No. No way."

"Why don't you tell me what he was doing, just for the record."

"Surveillance. A simple tail-and-shoot, nothing fancy, nothing dangerous."

"A tail-and-shoot on who?"

"You don't know?"

"How the hell would *I* know? You and I aren't psychically connected, right?"

"Then you didn't find any photographs in his car."

"No. We didn't find any photographs in his car. And we didn't find a camera, either, in case you were wonderin'. It was a tail-and-shoot on who, Gunner?"

Gunner looked around, suddenly aware of all the hospital personnel moving busily about them, and waited to satisfy the cop's curiosity until no one was within easy earshot. "A local politician with a jealous wife," he said, his voice just above a whisper.

"Yeah? Which one?"

"I tell you what, Poole. The minute I find out that question's relevant to this, I'll answer it for you. Gladly. But right now, I don't see a connection."

"Look, Gunner—"

"Give me a break, Lieutenant. You want my client's name, I have to give it to you. We both know that. But if the job I had Sly doing landed him in here, I'll bring you the people responsible myself, inside of forty-eight hours. You've got my word on that."

Poole pondered the offer, said, "You don't trust me to be discreet? Is that what I hear you sayin'?"

"Don't take it personal, Poole. But no, I don't. Not in this case, anyway."

The cop took a long time to grin. "It's that juicy, huh?"

"Like a mango fresh off the tree, yeah."

Poole started to laugh, then his expression changed, his eyes catching sight of something at Gunner's back. Gunner turned around, saw a diminutive black woman in blue sweatpants and a matching hooded pullover inching slowly toward them, a lidded Styrofoam cup in her left hand, a leather-bound Bible in her right. Her eyes were as red as her skin was dark and smooth.

"Mrs. Cribbs," Poole whispered to Gunner. "And maybe I should've warned you, but—"

"Are you Mr. Gunner?" the black woman asked, stepping right up to glower at the investigator from point-blank range.

"Yes, ma'am," Gunner said, saving his apologies for later.

"You tryin' to get my child killed? Is that what you're doing?"

"No, ma'am. I don't think this—"

"Sylvester told me he's been workin' for you. Takin' pictures of some kind. You got no business usin' a boy his age to do your dirty work, Mr. Gunner! That child ain't but *seventeen years old!*"

"Yes, ma'am, I know he is. But Sly—"

"He should've been at home with me. Instead've out in the street, where all them crazy fools are!"

Poole stepped forward to put a hand on her shoulder, said, "Come on now, Mrs. Cribbs. Don't go gettin' yourself all worked up again, huh?"

"That's my only baby in there! He's all I've got! If that boy *dies . . .*" She burst into tears, offered no resistance as Poole gently guided her away, past a doctor and a pair of nurses who had been moving forward to silence her.

Poole glanced over his shoulder, said, "You've got forty-eight hours, Gunner. We don't have a shooter by then, I'm gonna need your client's name."

Gunner nodded, sealing the deal, then stole one final look at Sly Cribbs's body before making his way over to the elevators.

So now he had *two* cases to work.

With Sly Cribbs laid up in the hospital with only a fifty-fifty chance of pulling through, it seemed logical to pursue the Everson case first, but Gunner had a more personal and immediate interest in the Elroy Covington/Thomas Selmon affair. It had been that piece of business, after all, that had almost cost him his own life at about the same time that someone had been trying to put an end to Sly's.

But he'd given Poole his word he'd make Sly's shooting a priority, and that was what he intended to do. He was far less ready to accept the blame for the kid's fate than Sly's mother was to brand him with it, but he had to admit the timing was curious: Sly leaves him a message saying he's got the pictures Gunner hired him to take, then gets himself shot full of holes by a carjacker who jets without taking his car. And the photos Sly had been so excited about taking earlier were missing, along with the camera with which he had taken them.

Still, the photographs in question hardly seemed the stuff homicides were made of, providing they had been of the nature Connie Everson had insisted they would be. Councilman Gil Everson and a lady of the night. Was that a tableau Everson would have killed to keep secret? Gunner was certain that it wasn't—except for one small detail: the councilman's bodyguard. A giant black hulk Gunner had watched follow Everson around for ten days before handing the councilman's surveillance over to Sly Cribbs. Sly's assailant had been a big man in a ski mask, Poole had said. Give Everson's bodyguard such a mask, and he would have fit that description just fine.

It was a stretch, and a big one at that, but Gunner had no choice but to look into it. He had to find out what happened to Sly, and he had to do it inside of forty-eight hours.

He started by paying Connie Everson a little visit.

Ladera Heights wasn't Inglewood, but Everson and her councilman husband could see Inglewood just fine from there. Their spacious home at the pinnacle of the Heights had a spectacular southbound view of Inglewood and the communities beyond, and Gunner figured the Eversons probably felt that was as close to actually residing in Inglewood as any fair-minded person could expect them to get.

Ladera Heights was the little Bel Air of Los Angeles's black upper-middle class, a hillside haven just west of Baldwin Hills and north of Inglewood that was populated by degreed professionals and public servants like Gil Everson who either lacked the wealth to escape the 'hood altogether or were content to exist only on the distant fringes of it. There were Benzes and Lexuses in every other driveway, and no home seemed complete if a pair of stone lions perched upon brick pedestals wasn't guarding its front entrance.

It wasn't Beverly Hills, but as wannabes went, it wasn't bad.

Gunner parked the Cobra in the Eversons' circular driveway, just behind a pearl white, late-model BMW with personalized license plates that read CON E E, and rang the bell at the front door. An Hispanic maid wearing an apron and everyday clothes appeared to greet him, no surprise there whatsoever, and looked him over like someone had sent the pool man to the house wearing the wrong uniform.

"Yes?"

"I'm here to see Mrs. Everson. The name's Aaron Gunner."

"Señora Everson es no' home. You wan' to leave a message?"

Her face was a mask of fear and guilt, and she couldn't keep her feet still beneath her. Gunner thought it was nice to see there were still some people in the world who couldn't tell a bald-faced lie in comfort.

"Sure," the investigator said. "I would like to leave a message. Tell Señora Everson that if she doesn't bring her fine ass to this door in five minutes, she's gonna be the top story in the Metro section of the *Times* tomorrow. You got that? Go give her that message now, por favor."

Everson's maid blinked at him, engaged in the exhausting process of assimilating what she'd just been told, then went to go get her employer. The councilman's wife didn't take the whole five minutes Gunner had given her to appear, but it was close. And when she reached the door, she looked Gunner over like something she couldn't trust to be real.

"You shouldn't be here," she said, looking like something less than the cool, unflappable beauty Gunner had come to know and love. Her clothes seemed haphazardly thrown on, and her face was amazingly ordinary, devoid of all the makeup she generally used to such striking effect.

"I would have called, but I had a feeling you wouldn't have been in," Gunner said.

"I'm sorry, Mr. Gunner, but my decision is final. I'll pay you for time invested, but that's all."

"Excuse me?"

Everson studied him, confused. "You didn't get my message?"

"No. What message is that?"

"I don't want my husband followed anymore, Mr. Gunner. I want you to stop the surveillance you're doing on him immediately."

"What?"

"I mean it. I don't want you following Gil around anymore. Just send me a bill for whatever I owe you, and I'll mail you a check. Now, if you'll excuse me . . ."

She tried to close the door in his face, but he put a hand out to stop her, said, "Wait a minute. What the hell are you talking about? Twenty-four hours ago, you were riding my ass because I couldn't follow your husband fast enough. Now you want me to *stop*?"

"Yes. Please."

"I don't get it. Did you hire another investigator?"

Everson shook her head emphatically, said, "No! I don't *need* another investigator. Gil explained everything to me. I should have never hired you in the first place."

"But the photos you said you wanted. I thought—"

"I don't care about the photos, Mr. Gunner. You aren't hearing what I'm saying. This was all a big mistake, there was never anything to take photos *of*."

"That's bullshit. The photographs have already been taken, they were shot yesterday evening."

Everson's surprise was beyond her abilities to disguise. "What?"

"You heard me. The pictures you were so hot to get your hands on were taken yesterday, by a seventeen-year-old kid named Sly Cribbs. *He's* been working the surveillance on your husband for the last two days, not me."

Everson started to speak, decided to hold her tongue instead.

"He's out at Daniel Freeman. Somebody shot him twice and left him in his car to die around eleven o'clock last night, over on Exposition and Vermont. Doctors say his chances of making it aren't good."

Finally finding her voice, Everson said, "That's terrible."

"Yeah. It is. Especially if you and I are responsible."

"Me? How could I—"

"We put Sly up to taking those photos of your husband and his girl-friend, Mrs. Everson. You and me. And now he's close to death, and the photos he took are missing. What the hell do you make of that?"

Everson worked her mouth around nervously for a minute, then said, "I don't make anything of it. Whatever happened to your friend had nothing to do with me."

"You sure about that?"

"Yes, I'm sure. I'm *very* sure. And that's all I have to say about the matter. I want you to leave, Mr. Gunner. Right now. Before Gil comes home and finds you here."

"Yeah? I think I'd like that. It'd save me a trip down to City Hall."

"You stay away from City Hall, you hear me? Leave my husband out of this!"

She was snarling now, finally exhibiting the firebrand spirit she had always shown Gunner in the past.

"My, my," the investigator said. "Look who's got her claws back."

Unamused, Everson said, "Get out of here, Mr. Gunner. I don't ever want to see you again. If you ever come back here, or attempt to talk to my husband, *for any reason whatsoever,* I will sue you for every dime you could ever *hope* to make. Do you understand me?"

For a long time, Gunner didn't say anything. Then, just before she seemed ready to repeat the threat, he said, "Perfectly."

And finally, Everson closed the door on him.

8

"You got a message," Mickey said the minute Gunner walked through the barber's front door. He picked up a notepad nearby, read his own writing aloud. "Yolanda McCreary called. Said she talked to Lydia and Irene, and neither one of 'em knows anything about no 'DOB' What's a DOB?"

"Never mind that," Gunner said, eyeing the little brown puppy trotting in circles around Mickey's feet. "What the hell is *that*?"

"That's your dog," Mickey said.

"Shit. I thought I told you guys I didn't need a dog."

"I heard you say that, yeah, but I guess you weren't too convincin'."

The little male Ridgeback scurried around to Gunner's end of the floor, started sniffing playfully at the cuffs of his pants. He had paws the size of a grown man's fists and a long patch of hair along his upper spine that ran counter to the rest of his short coat, creating the "ridge" his breed was known for. "So where's Winnie? She's gotta take him back."

"Winnie's off for the day. He's all yours."

Gunner reached down, picked the animal up with one hand. "Damn, Mickey," he said.

"I know. You got enough trouble just tryin' to feed yourself."

It was Mickey's late lunch hour, the *closed* sign was facing the window, and the two men were alone in the shop. Gunner lowered himself into a chair and patted the little dog's head as his landlord cleaned some scissors and clipper blades in a big bowl of alcohol.

"So? What's a DOB?" Mickey asked again.

It was all the excuse Gunner needed to unload. He told Mickey everything, from his near immolation in Jack Frerotte's basement to the conversation he'd just had with Connie Everson. He didn't much give a damn about the ethics of sharing his clients' business with his landlord; what he needed most now was someone to bounce ideas off, to ask questions he might neglect to ask himself, and Mickey was always happy to fill that role.

"So you think it was this DOB who hit you upside the head and set fire to Jack's house?"

"For lack of a better suspect, yeah. I do. Still doesn't ring any bells for you, huh?"

"No. I know a D-*A*-B—Darren Allen Baker, he's one of Coretta Baker's boys—but no D-*O*-Bs. You sure it was D-*O*-B?"

"Yeah."

"And you're sure Selmon's dead?"

"I'm not sure about anything, really. But the body in the photo looked like Selmon's, and there's no other reason for Jack to have a photo like that except to prove that the man in it was dead."

"You told his sister that yet?"

"More or less."

"And she's still payin' you?"

"Maybe. Maybe not. Doesn't matter to me one way or the other, now."

Mickey grunted and shook his head, vigorously drying a pair of scissors with a white towel.

"You think I should just drop it, huh? After damn near being flambéed last night?" Gunner asked.

"Let's just say, if it wasn't for that, I'd find somethin' else to do with my time, I was you. I sure as hell wouldn't bust a gut worryin' about where Jack buried that asshole's body, or how many pieces he cut it up in beforehand. That much I know."

"That's kind of harsh, don't you think?"

"It was meant to be harsh. What that boy Selmon did was dead wrong, Gunner. He hurt a lot of people."

"So if he was kidnapped and murdered, no one should give a damn."

"I don't remember sayin' that. But I will say *this:* If I had a choice between findin' that nigger's body, and findin' the people responsible for shootin' that poor boy Cribbs up last night, it wouldn't be no contest."

"It's not. I already told you, Sly's shooting is all I'm working on right now."

"Good. You said a prayer for 'im yet?"

"In my way."

"That means you ain't. So we gonna say one right now, you and me. Together."

"Mickey—"

But Mickey had already started praying, and Gunner had no choice but to join in. Because one, he didn't feel like arguing with the barber, and two, a little prayer was good for him now and then.

"He's gonna be all right, Gunner," Mickey said when they were done. "All you gotta do is believe that."

"Sure," Gunner said.

"You really think Gil Everson had somethin' to do with him gettin' shot?"

"If it weren't for the councilman's bodyguard, and the way his wife was acting twenty minutes ago, I'd say no. Not a chance. The photos Sly took of him might have cost him a few dollars in divorce court, maybe, but they would have hardly spelled the end of his career. Assuming there was nothing more to them than what Mrs. Everson had been asking for, anyway."

"And if he didn't wanna *give up* those few dollars in divorce court?"

"He has his man Friday pop two forty-five caps into a seventeen-year-old kid's chest to keep the photos from ever reaching his wife's hands. That sound logical to you?"

"No."

"It doesn't to me, either."

"So where are the pictures, then? You said they weren't in the boy's car, right?"

"Right. They weren't."

"Well, why not? If Everson didn't have the boy shot, the pictures should have been in his car."

"Unless Sly didn't have them on him, or the carjacker snatched them along with his camera."

Mickey nodded, agreeing, then cleaned his scissors and combs in silence for a while. "Are you sure he really took them?" he asked shortly.

"Am I sure he really took them? Who? The carjacker?"

"Not the carjacker. Sly. Are you sure he really took the pictures like he said?"

It was a possibility Gunner had never considered before. "Am I sure? No, I'm not *sure*. I'm not sure about anything, remember? But the kid *said* he took the pictures. His message on my machine said—"

Gunner never completed the thought, frozen by a sudden realization.

"What?" Mickey asked.

"Damn," Gunner said.

"*What?*"

"I just remembered what his message actually said. It said he was having the pictures *developed* somewhere. That he'd bring the prints over here in the morning when they were done."

"You mean—"

"They could still be there, yeah. Wherever, or to whomever, he took them to be developed."

He stood up, scanned the room for the dog he'd allowed to hop from his lap only moments before, but didn't see the little guy anywhere.

"So how you gonna find out where that is?" Mickey asked.

"Talk to his mother, I guess. See if she might know who usually does his photo developing."

"But you said—"

"She blames me for what happened to her son. Yeah, she does. I'm gonna have to try and talk to her anyway." He went to the door and opened it. "In the meantime, Mick, I think you'd better go get a paper towel or something. Looks like *my* dog just took a shit on *your* floor."

Mickey turned, started cursing as Gunner gleefully fled the scene.

"You've got a lotta nerve, comin' here," Charlotte Cribbs said.

"Yes, ma'am. I know that," Gunner agreed. He was standing on the porch of the Cribbses' clean but tiny duplex apartment on Leighton Avenue near Exposition Park, wondering if he was ever going to be invited inside. "I called the hospital before I came over. They told me you were probably here. They say it looks like Sly's turned the corner, he's going to be all right."

"Yes, thank the Lord Jesus. And no thanks to you."

"No, ma'am. No thanks to me."

"What do you want, Mr. Gunner? Say it and leave, I'm very tired."

Gunner told her, leaving the Everson name out of the telling, and describing the subject matter of the photographs he was after in very general terms. He knew if he told her too much about the work her son had been doing for him, he'd be in even more hot water with her than he already was.

"You want to know where Sylvester gets his pictures developed?"

"Yes, ma'am. If you happen to know."

"After what happened to my boy, you're still worried about that? About those fool pictures you had him taking?"

"Yes, ma'am, I am. You see . . ." Gunner paused, hoping he wasn't about to make a huge mistake. "I don't know if the police told you this or not but . . . there's an *outside* chance what happened to Sly last night had something to do with his work for me. That it wasn't just a carjacker who shot him."

Charlotte Cribbs stared at him, not knowing what to say.

"And if that's the case—if Sly was shot because of something I had him doing, and not just because he was in the wrong place at the wrong time—then it's my job to find out who shot him, and why. His blood is on my hands, and no one else's."

"You're damn right it is," Sly's mother said, her eyes now aglow with the anger Gunner had been dreading he might see.

Still, he stood there and absorbed her wrath contritely, waiting for her to decide how worthy—or *un*worthy—he was of her help.

"I'm sorry, Mr. Gunner, but I can't help you," she said finally. "I don't know where Sylvester goes to get his pictures developed."

"Is it possible he has a receipt lying around somewhere that could tell us? Say, in his room, maybe?"

"He might. But I don't like to go into my son's room when he ain't here, if that's what you was about to ask me to do."

"I'm sure you don't, Mrs. Cribbs, and I admire you for that. But I think Sly would forgive you just this once, under the circumstances, don't you?"

Charlotte Cribbs considered this briefly, then said, "All right. I'll go look. You wait right here."

She disappeared inside the apartment, left Gunner to fidget on the other side of her screen door for several interminable minutes. When she returned, she stepped outside to join him on the porch, a large yellow receipt in one hand.

"Sylvester had quite a few of these, so I guess this is where he usually goes, I don't know."

Gunner took the receipt when she offered it to him, saw that it had come from a One Hour Foto-Stop franchise on Jefferson and Hoover, in the University Mall complex across from USC.

"Sly didn't happen to have a receipt like this on him when they brought him into the hospital, did he?" Gunner asked.

"I couldn't say. Why? You can't use that one?"

"No, it's not that. I just thought if I had the actual receipt Sly received last night, they might be more inclined to cooperate with me over there, that's all." He gestured with the receipt. "But this will do just fine. Many thanks."

"Only thanks I want from you is you keepin' your word, Mr. Gunner. Whoever shot my boy is an animal don't need to be out on the street. You find him and see he don't never shoot nobody again, hear?"

"Yes, ma'am. I hear you."

She didn't look like she believed him, but she allowed him to leave her porch without questioning him any further.

The manager at the One Hour Foto-Stop shop in the University Mall was a skeptical, mop-topped brunette named Jenny Palmer, and she gave Gunner the runaround for nearly thirty minutes before letting him have the developed prints Sly Cribbs had indeed brought in the night before.

"I don't mean to be difficult," she kept saying, "but I could lose my job here. Because you don't have a receipt, number one, and we're really not supposed to turn over a customer's prints to anyone but the person who brought them in, number two, unless of course we receive instructions to do so beforehand."

Gunner's photostatic license had impressed her, and she seemed to have nothing but respect for his authority, but it was only after he resorted to a little exaggeration—he told her the life of a bullet-riddled Sly Cribbs literally hung in the balance of her decision to assist him—that the overly conscientious shop manager abandoned her hard-line stance to find Sly's prints and turn them over to him. With the fear of God on her face all the while, like she just knew she'd been tricked into doing something that could only get her fired later.

Gunner waited until he was out in the parking lot, behind the Cobra's wheel, before sliding the prints out of their envelope to look them over.

There were twenty-four in all. Gunner's usual success rate for surveillance photos was about seventy percent—meaning three out of every ten shots he took turned out to be useless—but Sly, beginner that he was, had batted a thousand here. Every one of the twenty-four color prints in Gunner's hands had captured the desired goods: Inglewood City Councilman Gil Everson and a thin, provocatively dressed black woman, sharing a particularly hot and graphic sexual interlude. The woman didn't have to be either a prostitute or a porno star, as Connie Everson had insisted she would be, but she definitely had the look of both: the cheap, titillating clothes, the detached expression of a professional making love by rote. And if she wasn't addicted to one drug or another, as Everson had also suggested, her appearance again did little to indicate it; she had the telltale scrawny build of someone who was often too strung out to eat.

Taken from a bird's-eye view at night, suggesting Sly had either stood on a balcony, or perched on a rooftop to take them, each photo depicted Everson and friend making love on a garden patio somewhere, either at someone's home, or perhaps a luxury hotel, the apparent conclusion to a candlelight dinner they had just enjoyed outdoors. Amid a mess of dirty dishes cluttering a patio table, they moved from heavy petting to industrial-strength foreplay, foreplay to all-out intercourse, in a broad array of colorful and explicit steps, before Everson finally lifted the nude woman into his arms and took her inside, past a pair of open patio doors where a bedroom presumably awaited them.

Gunner went over the prints three times, studying each carefully and patiently. But in the end, he was looking for something that wasn't there. The photos were exactly what Connie Everson had said she wanted, physical and indisputable proof of an illicit affair her husband was having with a younger woman, very possibly a prostitute—but that was all they were. A perfect EXHIBIT A in just another celebrity divorce, as unusual in the City of Angels as capped teeth.

It didn't seem possible that Sly Cribbs had been gunned down to suppress this.

Connie Everson had warned him to keep his distance, but Gunner decided to approach her husband anyway. He couldn't see where he had any other choice.

Though he never actually saw the councilman himself; he just saw the man's car. It took a little surreptitious maneuvering to get into the private, underground parking lot beneath Inglewood City Hall where all city employees like Everson parked their cars, but he managed to do so with alarming ease. He found Everson's marked space in the lot, slipped a heavily sealed manila envelope under the left wiper blade of the gold-tone Jaguar XJ6 sitting there, and got out, making a blip on the radar screens of the building's security systems that apparently no one noticed, or cared enough about to investigate.

Gunner had to know whether or not Everson had been the driving force behind the brutal assault on Sly Cribbs the night before, and this seemed to be the only way to find out. If all went according to plan, his client's name would never enter the mix, but if he had to sell Connie Everson out to nail the gunman he was after, he would do so, however reluctantly. Such trade-offs were part of the job.

Of course, it helped to know that Connie Everson would feel the same way about him, were their situations reversed.

9

"His name is Pharaoh Doubleday,"

Little Pete Thorogood said. "Pharaoh, like the Egyptians. Doubleday, like in baseball. Ain't that some shit?"

He cracked up laughing, his head turned toward the man pouring Eggy Jones a drink down at the far end of the Acey Deuce's bar. Lilly Tennell was off at a table somewhere, scolding somebody for spilling a beer. The bartender to whom Little Pete was referring was a tall, delicate black man with fair skin and a freckled face, whose every move was made with slow, deliberate grace, like he was afraid he might break something if he moved too fast. As far as Gunner could remember, he was the first person Lilly had hired to help her at the Deuce since J.T.'s death eight years ago.

"Gay?" Gunner asked Little Pete.

"Oh, yeah. Doesn't make any bones about it, either. Why? You have a problem with that?"

"Me?" Gunner shook his head. "But some of the knuckleheads who come in here . . ."

"Yeah. I hear that. They say Lilly had to set one of 'em straight already." He grinned.

"Don't tell me, let me guess: Baxter Peale."

"That's the one. I guess he's a regular in here, huh?"

"We call him Bonehead Baxter. Lilly has to throw him out on his ass more often than she does you."

Little Pete chuckled, taking no offense at the remark. The diminutive black man with the baby face was the neighborhood's most notorious street corner arms merchant, and Lilly had never much cared to have him around her place of business. In actual truth, she had never formally asked him to leave, but her treatment of him on those rare occasions when he dropped by generally had the same effect. Either ignored like a fly on the wall, or badgered unmercifully from the moment of his arrival, Pete invariably felt compelled to flee the Deuce hours before he was ready. That he was mildly amused by this, and continued to look upon Lilly with genuine affection, was as inexplicable to Gunner as lottery winners who refused to quit their day jobs at the refinery.

Inevitably, the conversation between the two men turned to other matters, and Little Pete got around to asking Gunner what he was working on these days. Having hoped the subject would come up, Gunner told him in the broadest terms possible, then asked him the question he'd been spreading elsewhere around the bar since he'd entered it two hours ago.

"You must be talking about the Defenders of the Bloodline," Little Pete said. Like Gunner couldn't have asked him about anything more glaringly obvious.

"The what?"

"The Defenders of the Bloodline. DOB. You've never heard of 'em?"

"No. What the hell is a 'Defender of the Bloodline'?"

"A crazy nigger who likes to trash-talk Uncle Toms, I guess. I've never met one myself, but I see their flyers around all the time."

"What do you mean, they like to trash-talk Uncle Toms?"

"I mean that's what they say they're all about: ridding the black race of all Uncle Toms. Brothers and sisters who have backstabbed their own people. Defenders of the Bloodline, get it?"

"And so, what? The Defenders advocate the killing of these people?"

"They don't just advocate it, man. They say they've been *doin'* it. But personally, I don't think they've been doin' *shit*. I think it's all just a lot of talk."

"Why's that?"

"Because I ain't never met a Defender, number one, like I said. And number two, I've never heard of anyone they're supposed to've whacked. Have you?"

Gunner thought about it, said, "I may have. On both counts."

"Yeah?"

"I can't tell you who the victim might've been. But I think the Defender was Johnny Frerotte."

"Johnny Frerotte? You mean Barber Jack? Is that right?"

"Somebody with the initials DOB paid Jack five thousand dollars to commit a kidnapping, and possibly a murder afterward, last October," Gunner said. "And the victim would have met a lot of people's criteria for a so-called Uncle Tom."

"Damn. So Jack's gone and gotten political on us, huh?"

"Maybe. But I think it's much more likely he was just a hired gun. Otherwise, he'd have done the victim for free, right?"

Before Little Pete could answer, Gunner heard his name being called, turned to see Pharaoh Doubleday addressing the house with the telephone in his hand. "We got an Aaron Gunner in here?" the big man asked again, his voice no less commanding than that of an agitated professional wrestler.

Gunner raised his hand to attract his attention, and said to Little Pete, "These flyers you say you've seen. Where do you think I could find one?"

"They're all around, like I said. On telephone poles, and bulletin boards, places like that. I saw one yesterday over on the board at Will Rogers Park, in fact."

"You Aaron Gunner?" Pharaoh asked, reaching Gunner's place at the bar.

"Yeah. Thanks." The investigator reached up and plucked the cordless phone out of the bartender's hand, then slipped off his stool and addressed Little Pete once more. "Sorry, Pete, but I've gotta take this. Do me a favor and ask around a little, see if you can turn one of these Defenders up, huh?"

"Be glad to," Little Pete said.

Gunner started to walk away with the phone, saw that Lilly's new employee was still standing there, waiting to be either properly acknowledged or properly dismissed, one or the other.

"I'm just going to take this over there, all right, partner?" Gunner asked, pointing to an empty booth near the door.

The big man named Pharaoh eyed him with stonelike stoicism, giving no thought whatsoever to looking to Lilly for help, then broke down and nodded his head. "Go ahead," he said.

Gunner and Little Pete exchanged a quick glance—this guy was going to be fun to have around—before the investigator removed himself to the empty booth as promised.

"Good evening, Councilman," he said into the phone as soon as he sat down.

There was a long pause as the party on the other end of the line gathered enough resolve to speak. "Who is this?" Gil Everson asked.

"You already know my name. And the rest we can get into later. But not over the phone."

"Look. What do you want? If this is some kind of extortion attempt—"

"It's not. But to find out what it is, you're gonna have to see me in person. Tonight, right here, in one hour. Would you like directions?"

"You must be insane. I'm not meeting you anywhere tonight."

"Okay. Whatever you say."

Gunner hit the flash button on the phone to hang up on him.

Lilly came over to his table, having finally taken notice of him, and said, "What've I told you about tying up my phone, Gunner? Huh?"

"This is only going to take a minute, Lilly. Relax."

"I'll relax when I'm dead. Right now, I got a business to run, and I can't run it without a phone."

The phone began to ring.

"Just let me take this one call," Gunner said. "I'll keep it short, I promise."

The big woman eyeballed him, pursing her crimson lips in disgust, then walked away.

"That you, Councilman?" Gunner asked, speaking into the phone again.

And this time Everson spoke right up, said, "This 'Acey Deuce' where you're at. I take it it's a public place?"

"That's right. But nobody from the local press is likely to spot us here, if that's what you're worried about."

"We can't meet someplace more private?"

"Sorry, but I'm afraid not. Not that I don't trust you, but I'd feel safer if we met right here, in the company of a few friends. You understand."

Everson didn't say anything for a good length of time. Then: "How do I get to this place?"

After Gunner told him, he gave Lilly her phone back and ordered himself another drink.

The trouble with baiting the hook for sharks with one's own flesh was, sometimes you actually got a bite.

Gunner had been waiting forty minutes in a dark, distant booth in one corner, his Ruger P-85 pinned flat between the cushion of his seat and his right thigh, when Gil Everson and his ubiquitous bodyguard entered the bar. The investigator was relieved to see the councilman here himself—his presence made it all but a certainty that no violence toward Gunner was in his immediate plans—but his sizable black friend was not so reassuring. Though Gunner had seen him many times before during his own surveillance of Everson, it was still highly unsettling to be faced with him here again, in such close quarters, and Gunner couldn't help but wonder if Sly Cribbs hadn't felt the same way almost twenty-four hours earlier.

He watched Lilly point him out for the big man, then fingered the Ruger nervously as the two men slowly approached him.

Everson reached him first, his companion hanging just behind so as to better watch the councilman's back, and said, "You Aaron Gunner?"

"Yeah. Thanks for coming down, Councilman."

Everson took the seat opposite him in the booth on his own initiative, gestured for his man to do likewise at an empty table nearby. The flat-topped bodyguard in the crisp, double-breasted green suit obeyed the command without so much as blinking. "Let's cut the bullshit here, Mr. Gunner," Connie Everson's slightly graying, though still strikingly handsome, husband said. "I'm not your councilman, and you're not one of my constituents. Our business here tonight is all about money, so why don't you just name your price and get the fuck on with it?"

"Because I'm not a blackmailer. I told you that before."

"I know what you told me. And I'd like to believe you. But it's for damn sure you didn't take those photographs of my friend and me just to try out a new camera, now, isn't it?"

"Actually, I didn't take the photographs. They just happen to be in my possession. The person who did take them is over at Daniel Freeman, recovering from a couple of gunshot wounds he received late last night." He slid his eyes over to the councilman's bodyguard, saw no discernible reaction. "Maybe you heard about it."

"No. I'm afraid I didn't."

"He's just a seventeen-year-old kid. Goes to college, lives with his mother. Wants to be a photojournalist some day."

"That's fascinating."

"But somebody nailed him in his car on his way home, just around eleven o'clock. Shot him twice with a forty-five caliber automatic while he was waiting for the light to change over on Exposition and Vermont. The cops think it was a carjacker, but I have a theory of my own."

The big man in the green suit remained as expressionless as ever.

"Get to the point, Mr. Gunner," Everson said.

"Somebody was after the photographs you're so interested in. They thought he had them on him, but he didn't."

"And you think that somebody was me, is that it?"

"You or your goon over there. He does have a handgun under all that fabric, doesn't he?"

He'd said it just loud enough for the big man to hear him, as was his intention, but the councilman's friend only winked at him in response, no easy man to rile, apparently.

"Rafe was with me at eleven o'clock last night," Everson said. "He wasn't anywhere near the intersection of Exposition and Vermont."

Gunner smiled, nodded his head. "That's a great alibi. He was with you, and you were with him. You two should rob banks."

"Look. I don't know what the hell this is all about, but if you don't start making some sense quick, I'm going to the police. And what you do with the photographs after that is your problem."

He seemed completely sincere. He was more frustrated than angry now, and Gunner's little game of cat and mouse was getting on his nerves.

"All right, Councilman. Settle down," Gunner said.

"Settle down, my ass. Are the photographs for sale or not?"

"For sale? No." Gunner shook his head. "They're not for sale. But I might be willing to exchange them for something."

"Exchange them for something? Like what?"

"Like information. A few simple answers to some questions I'd like to ask you and your friend here."

"And my questions? What about *them*?"

"You mean like, who am I, and who am I working for? That sort of thing?"

"Exactly."

"The answer to the first question is, I'm a private investigator. As for the second—"

"A private investigator?" He was far more surprised than he should have been, Gunner thought. His wife had told Gunner just hours earlier that she and the councilman had discussed everything, and that all of her suspicions about a street hustler with a limp had been laid to rest. But if that were true, her husband should have figured Gunner for his wife's private investigator from the start.

Fifteen seconds went by before the councilman shook his head, a small grin crossing his face. "That goddamn Connie . . ."

"Who?"

"My wife, Mr. Gunner. Your client."

"You think your wife is my client?"

"Of course she is. I must've been an idiot for not seeing it sooner. Not every attack upon me is politically motivated, after all."

"No, probably not. But you're a black city councilman with a promising future. You think your wife's the only person who could want photographic evidence that you've been having an affair with a prostitute?"

Everson bristled at this, said, "You trying to say there's something perverse about that?"

"It doesn't matter what I have to say about it. But if someone looking to derail your re-election wanted to put that particular spin on it . . ." He let a simple shrug complete the thought.

"All right. To hell with who you're working for, for now. All I care about are the photographs. You give me those, and the rest won't matter."

"Fine. All I want is my friend's shooter. You help me nail him, and the photos are yours."

"Your friend's shooter? I don't know who shot that kid!"

"You didn't know he was following you around last night?"

"No."

"Or about the photographs he'd taken of you and the lady?"

"No! I didn't know anything about the photographs until this afternoon, when I went down to my car and found that goddamn envelope on my windshield."

Gunner nodded toward the silent big man seated nearby. "What about him?"

"Rafe? He's a security man. Not my mother. His job is to protect me from physical harm, not do damage control."

"All the same—was he really with you last night around eleven o'clock? Or was that something you said just to make conversation?"

Everson took too long to answer the question, rendering his reply all but unnecessary. "I don't say *anything* just to make conversation, Mr. Gunner," he said.

"Then he was with you when the photographs were taken."

"You mean at the hotel? Yes, but—"

"All night."

"Yes, goddamnit, all night! He was in the suite right next to ours, he was there the whole time we were."

"He couldn't have spotted the kid taking the photos and followed him afterward?"

"No. I *told* you—he's a bodyguard. Not a hitman." When Gunner failed to pursue the matter further, he said, "I'm sorry, Gunner, but it's really very simple. I didn't have anything to do with your friend getting shot, and neither did Rafe, or anyone else under my employ. I'm sorry it happened, of course, but it had nothing to do with me."

"I see. You think maybe I should be talking to your girlfriend, instead?"

"No! You leave Shelby—" He stopped, instantly aware of his mistake, and started again. "You leave the lady out of this, Gunner. She couldn't possibly help you."

"Couldn't she? She's the second adulterer in the photographs, Councilman. And depending on who she is and what her circumstances are, she could have just as much to lose if they were to go public as you do."

"She doesn't. You can take my word for that."

"And if I don't?"

"Then you and I are going to stop talking and start swinging. Both figuratively and literally."

"What, here? Right now?"

"You know what I mean. You go anywhere near the lady in those photographs, and I'll nail your ass to the cross, so help me God."

It wasn't just an idle threat; Everson meant every word. Gunner could see that in his eyes alone.

"Now," the councilman went on. "Do I get the photographs, or not?"

Gunner let him wait a long time for his answer, carefully thinking things through before choosing his next move. "The kid shot a full roll of twenty-four. One print is already in your possession. I'll messenger you another twenty-two tomorrow, plus the negatives, and keep one print for myself."

"What? Like hell you will!"

"You have my word it won't be used against you in any way. No one will see it, or know about it, but me."

"Fuck your word! The deal was, I answer your questions, and you give me the photographs. *All* the photographs!"

"I know what the deal was. But if you want me to trust you about the lady, you're going to have to trust me about this. It's a two-way street, Councilman."

"Bullshit!"

"I told you: I don't care about anything but finding the person who capped my friend last night. As long as that isn't you or your boy Rafe, you've got nothing to fear from me, with or without the photographs."

"And your client? What about her?"

"You mean what about *him*?"

"Him, her, whatever!"

"I guess I forgot to mention. I don't have that client anymore. I was fired earlier today."

"And you never—"

"Showed my client the photographs? No. I didn't."

Now Everson was the one thinking things through, trying to decide what to do next. He was in a tight spot, and he didn't like it there one bit.

"I don't know anything about you, Gunner. Why should I think I can trust you?"

"The short answer? Because you don't have a lot of choice. The long answer's that, plus the fact you know who I am and where you can find me. Neither of which I'd've allowed you to know if my intent all along was to fuck you over, right?"

Everson fell silent, discovered he had no rejoinder for this argument. "I want that last photo, Gunner. If you think I'm going to let you hold onto it forever, you're crazy."

"I tell you what. As soon as the cops make an arrest in my friend's shooting that looks like it's gonna stick, you can have the photograph. I'll put it in a nice frame for you and everything."

"Forget the frame. Just get me the photograph. *All* the photographs."

He slipped out of the booth and stood up, gestured without turning for Rafe the bodyguard to follow suit. Naturally, the big man did.

"I'll be watching for that messenger tomorrow, Gunner," the councilman said, smoothing the wrinkles from the front of his coat with both hands. "Please don't let me go home empty-handed."

"It was a pleasure meeting you, too, Gil," Gunner said. He got to his own feet as Everson began to storm out, hiding the Ruger he'd been sitting on behind his back, and called out to the security man rushing to fall in behind the councilman. "Yo, Rafe!"

The big man stopped, turned.

"Satisfy a little human curiosity, huh? Let me see the piece. Just a peek, black, come on."

The bodyguard actually grinned, opened the left side of his coat to show Gunner the brown leather holster affixed to his belt. It was hard to tell for sure in the Deuce's dim light, but Gunner thought the weapon in its embrace looked like a 9-millimeter SIGarms, either the P226 or -229. Neither of which, to his knowledge, could handle .45 caliber ammo.

"Wow. Very nice," Gunner said, giving the big man the thumbs-up sign.

"Let's go, Rafe," Everson said, waiting.

Rafe closed up his coat, treated Gunner to another wink, then followed his employer out to the street.

10

"What's the latest?" Gunner asked Matt Poole

the first thing Friday morning.

"Not a hell of a lot. Your boy Cribbs is improving rapidly, he was able to give us a statement this morning. And that wraps it up for the good news. The bad news is, his statement ain't worth a shit."

"He couldn't add anything to the description you already had of his assailant?"

"He told us the guy was wearing a blue sweatshirt and pants to go with his matching ski mask. And that the guy was indeed a brother. 'His voice sounded black,' he said."

"The shooter talked to him?"

"Oh, yeah. I forgot to mention. Cribbs said he got shot because he put up a fight. He was told to get out of the car, and he didn't."

"Suggesting our man might've been just a carjacker after all."

"Yeah. Though I remain unconvinced."

"What about his camera?"

"The shooter took it, just like we figured. Either because he couldn't take the car, and the camera was the next best thing, or because the camera was all he was really after in the first place. Take your pick."

"And the weapon?"

"No weapon yet. If the shooter doesn't still have it, he must've dumped it where we haven't been able to find it."

"You didn't come up with anything in the car?"

"Like some prints other than Cribbs's, you mean? Afraid not. Face it, partner, we're stuck at square one. Our shooter was a big black guy with a forty-five auto."

Gunner thought of Rafe the giant bodyguard again, said simply, "Yeah."

"What about *you*? You don't have anything to tell me this morning?"

"Not yet, Lieutenant. Maybe soon."

"How soon is soon, Gunner? Your forty-eight hours is halfway up."

"Yeah, Poole, I know. I'm working on it, man."

"Okay. You do that. Now, if you've got no further questions for me, I've got a cup of java gettin' cold here, so . . ."

"What do you know about the DOB, Poole?" Gunner asked, catching the detective completely unprepared for the question.

"The what?"

"The DOB. Defenders of the Bloodline. Don't tell me you've never heard of 'em."

"Oh, yeah. *That* DOB. Are *they* mixed up in this?"

"No, no. This is something different. But . . . They really do exist, huh?"

"I don't know. Do they? All we've ever seen of those clowns around here are those fuckin' flyers they're always puttin' up somewhere."

"You're telling me you've never seen one, either?"

"A Defender? Not that I know of, I haven't. And that's usually the first thing I ask a guy, too. 'Are you a Defender of the Bloodline?' "

Gunner could see the subject for Poole was nothing more than a joke, told him to go put his java in the microwave before hanging up the phone. Then he sat at his desk in his makeshift office, eyeing the little Ridgeback sleeping peacefully on his couch, and tried to decide which of two roads he should travel for the remainder of the day.

For as urgent as the need was for him to determine whether or not Gil Everson and/or his associate Rafe had been involved in the attack on Sly Cribbs, Gunner still felt compelled to search for the man or woman who had tried to burn him alive in Johnny Frerotte's basement Wednesday night.

It should have been an easy choice to make. Matt Poole and the considerable resources of the LAPD were hard at work trying to solve the former crime, while no one at all, save for the Los Angeles Fire Department's arson detail, was investigating the latter one. That Gunner was tempted to place his own attempted murder above that of another was nothing if not understandable.

And yet, in the end, he was unable to put Sly's shooting aside for his own self-interests. Because Sly hadn't driven into the path of those two .45 slugs by accident: Gunner had positioned him there. And the nagging guilt that came with this awareness could not be assuaged by letting someone else seek justice for him. Finding Sly's assailant was Gunner's responsibility, and no one else's, just as he had told the kid's mother yesterday, and he came back to this realization soon enough.

So he rubbed his new puppy's head on his way out the door and left, fully intending to do what Poole had just strongly suggested he do: get on with the business of determining what connection, if any, his work for Connie Everson could have possibly had to the near execution of a seventeen-year-old boy.

After, that is, he made one little stop to visit an old friend.

He was heavily sedated and strapped down to his bed like a madman in a psycho ward, but Barber Jack Frerotte was conscious when Gunner walked into his room at Martin Luther King Memorial Hospital.

His left arm was bound to his torso in a heavy elastic sling, and a neck brace was fastened around his massive throat, making it all but impossible for him to turn his head. Gunner walked around to the foot of his bed where Frerotte couldn't miss seeing him and showed him a warm smile.

"How're you feeling, Jack?" he asked.

Frerotte blinked his eyes several times, not sure he could believe what he was seeing, and tried to make his mouth work. It was a long, arduous process.

"You're a dead man," he finally said, his voice a barely audible expulsion of air.

"Yeah. I knew you'd say that," Gunner said. "But that's okay. A little resentment's only natural, I guess."

Frerotte tried to tell him to get out, didn't do a very good job of it. Gunner moved closer, up on the left side of the bed near the big man's head, and said, "But look. I can't stay long, so I'd better get to the point. I want the name of the Defender of the Bloodline who hired you to kill Thomas Selmon."

Frerotte attempted to turn his head toward him, nearly blacked out when his injured vertebrae rebelled against the move.

"Take it easy, brother," Gunner told him. "It's just you and me in here. No one has to know we had this little talk but us."

Frerotte felt around with his right hand, trying to find the electronic control pad dangling from its cord on the bed's railing on that side, but Gunner took it, moved it out of his reach. "I saw the photograph, Jack. The one you took of Selmon's body just before you buried it. It was taped to the bottom of the drawer in that rolltop desk in your dining room, the same drawer you keep your ledger book in."

"You been in my *house*?" the big man managed to rasp. He almost looked more frightened than anything else.

"Yeah. I don't suppose you've heard it burned down."

Frerotte's lips moved, but he couldn't speak.

"I was down in the basement, looking over all those articles you had on the Selmon newspaper scandal, when somebody hit me from behind and set fire to the place. I'm afraid the crib's a total loss, partner."

. The big man's eyes rolled around in his head, a sure sign of incredulity. "I don't . . ."

"Believe it. It's true." Gunner waited for a nurse passing by the open door of Frerotte's room to disappear down the hall, then went on. "I don't know who your friend with the match was, but I think I can guess. And I'll bet you can, too."

Frerotte's eyes were blinking back tears now. He wanted nothing more than to rise from the bed and disembowel Gunner with his bare hands, but all he could do was lie there playing captive audience, instead. It had to be frustrating as hell.

"It's all right there in your ledger book," Gunner said. "Five grand from the DOB. Two to snatch Selmon, and three to murder him afterward. The photograph was your way of proving you'd done both."

Frerotte didn't say anything, just went right on blinking at the white wall in front of him.

"Now, you can lie there playing deaf, dumb, and blind if you want. That's your prerogative. But if I were you, I'd talk to me. While you still have the chance."

"I ain't . . . tellin' you *shit,*" Frerotte said.

"Come on, Jack. I'm giving you a chance to do yourself some good here. I'm gonna find Selmon's body, and the man who put you up to killing him, with or without your help, but if you force me to do it without, the law's gonna come down on you like a solid-gold Cadillac."

"Fuck you, Gunner." The big man tried to call for a nurse, but he couldn't make his broken voice reach that far.

"Cooperation with the authorities always looks good to a jury, Jack. You sure that's your final answer?"

Frerotte's eyes rolled toward him. "You . . . heard me, mother . . . fucker!"

Gunner smiled, stepped back away from the bed. "Okay, champ. If that's your call, that's your call. But let me leave you with a little something to think about, huh? Your DOB homeboy tried to light me up like a fireplace log two nights ago, and I'm not happy about it. Anybody who gets in the way of my returning the favor is going to get hurt, and you just did.

"So take your time getting well. Kick it in here as long as you can. Because there's not gonna be anything waiting for you when you get out but a cellmate in San Quentin who's just itchin' to see what your fat ass looks like bent over at the waist. I promise you that."

He flipped Frerotte's control pad onto his lap and walked out.

"Councilman Everson's office," a matronly voice said after the phone had rung in Gunner's ear three times.

"I'd like to speak to the councilman, please. Is he in?"

"No, sir, I'm afraid he isn't. He's in Sacramento today. May I take a message for him?"

"Actually, it's the councilman's bodyguard I really need to speak with. Rafe . . ."

"Rafe Sweeney?"

"That's it. Would he be around, by any chance?"

"No. He's in Sacramento, too, Mr. . . . ."

"Gunner. Aaron Gunner. When do you expect Mr. Sweeney to return?"

"I'm afraid I'm not at liberty to—"

"I don't need an exact time. I just need to know the day of the week. Will he be gone the entire weekend, or . . . ?"

"Mr. Sweeney and Councilman Everson should be back in their offices on Monday, Mr. Gunner. If you'd like to leave a message on Mr. Sweeney's voice mail, I'd be happy to connect you."

"I'd appreciate that very much. Thank you."

Everson's secretary transferred his call, and a taped greeting from Rafe Sweeney played on the line. Gunner doubted he'd ever heard a more succinct one.

"This is Rafe Sweeney. Leave a message, and I'll call you back," it said.

But Gunner declined the offer, just hung up the pay phone instead. He'd heard what he wanted to hear: Sweeney *did* sound like a black man.

And if Poole would give him just a few more days to work with, Gunner would find out Monday if the bodyguard was the right one.

Sometimes, what a person *didn't* say was far more revealing than what they did.

And Jack Frerotte had never said he didn't know who the hell the Defenders of the Bloodline were. In fact, he hadn't denied a thing. Which wasn't exactly proof that all of the allegations Gunner had made in Frerotte's hospital room less than thirty minutes ago were on the money, but it certainly seemed to reinforce the idea.

Unfortunately, knowing the Defenders had hired Frerotte to murder Thomas Selmon and finding the actual Defender he'd been dealing with—or *any* Defender, for that matter—were two different things. The flyer Gunner had just picked off of the community announcements bulletin board over at Will Rogers Park, where Little Pete Thorogood had said Thursday night Gunner could find one, was no help in actually identifying the mysterious group at all. It was an ideological outcry, and little more, printed in plain block letters on yellow paper:

This is to Serve Notice

To the serpents among us. The liars and sinners in blackface who work in legion with the white Devil to shame our proud people. The defenders of the bloodline will purge you from the house of Africa until none of you remain. Some have already met the sword of righteousness. Many more will follow. Your hour is close at hand. Allah, the most merciful, is on our side.

That was it. Short, spare, and completely uninformative. Gunner couldn't decide which told him less: the text or the physical flyer itself. It could have been printed anywhere by anybody. But he held onto it nonetheless, afraid to discard anything that could prove useful to him later.

With Rafe Sweeney and Gil Everson out of town until Monday, he had nothing else to do with his time but pursue the Thomas Selmon disappearance case again, once a single piece of Everson business had been dealt with. He left Will Rogers Park for a messenger service office in El Segundo, and sent the negatives and twenty-two of the last twenty-three photographs he had of Everson and his girlfriend to the councilman's office as promised, keeping the most potentially damaging print of the set for his own protection. Everson had said he'd be waiting with bated breath for the photos to arrive at his office today, and he could do that just as easily from Sacramento as anywhere else. Gunner wasn't so sure turning the photographs over to him was the smartest thing to do, but he'd struck a deal with Everson and the councilman had held up his end of it, as fruitless as this gesture had proven to be. Gunner had to follow suit now, or risk having word get out that he was a welsher, a reputation few private investigators could ever overcome.

From the messenger service office, Gunner drove out to the Central Library downtown. The 105 Freeway, still relatively undiscovered at only two years of age, was its usual anomalous self—a Los Angeles thoroughfare that wasn't clogged with traffic—but reality kicked back in as soon as he made the exchange to the northbound Harbor. The drive from there, even in the open-air Cobra, was an uninspiring crawl through an automotive morass. Only the sun on the investigator's face kept him from going slightly insane.

At the library, Gunner spent a good hour and seven dollars in change at a copying machine, copying every newspaper and magazine article he was able to find chronicling the Thomas Selmon/*Chicago Press Examiner* Pulitzer Prize scandal. By the time he was through, he had everything he'd seen down in Jack Frerotte's basement, and more. He sat down to skim through the copies briefly, underlining the names of all the story's principal players, then retreated to his office at Mickey's.

His landlord was sitting in one of his own waiting chairs, petting Gunner's salivating dog, when the investigator walked in. Winnie Phifer was etching a part into a teenage boy's hair with her clippers, being as meticulous about it as a safecracker trying to evade an alarm. Gunner tried to get past the trio without conversation, figuring he could ask Mickey for messages later, but it didn't happen.

"When you gonna give that dog a name?" Winnie demanded. She stopped what she was doing and turned her clippers off to face him.

"A name? When I get around to it," Gunner said.

"Dog can't be trained, it don't have a name. And it's goin' on eleven weeks old. You gonna give it a name, or am I?"

Gunner didn't feel like being bothered, but this last gave him reason to pause. Winnie's two grown children were named Beaumont and Celestine, and she had personally named them both; what kind of moniker the woman would come up with for a dog, he didn't want to know.

He looked at the muscular little Ridgeback in Mickey's arms for a minute, became suddenly inspired. "Dillett. His name is Dillett," Gunner said.

"Dillett?" Winnie squinched her nose up. "What the hell kind'a name is *Dillett?*"

"He's a bodybuilder. Paul Dillett, a Canadian brother. Makes Arnold Schwarzenegger look like a little girl."

"You must be kiddin'," Mickey said.

"No. The brother's huge. Just like that dog's gonna be, I can find a way to keep feeding him."

"Dillett," Winnie said again, trying to warm up to the idea. She looked over at the puppy, said in her best mommy-to-baby voice, "That what you wanna be called, boy? You wanna be called Dillett? Huh?"

The dog sat up in Mickey's lap, started yapping and slobbering excitedly in her direction.

"Guess that settles that," Mickey said.

"Can I go now?" Gunner asked.

"Go ahead," Winnie said, turning her clippers back on. She'd said it like her permission had really been necessary.

Gunner went back to his desk, hit the power switch on the new $3000 IBM computer sitting there. He'd been getting by without a computer just fine up to now, but he decided two weeks ago to stop pressing his luck. As rapidly as the rest of the world was incorporating the machines into their everyday lives, both professional and personal, he knew he couldn't afford to fall any further behind the learning curve than he already was. Information was at the heart of Gunner's business, after all, and the way information was both distributed and assimilated today was via Pentium processors, 2-gig hard drives, and modems that could move data across normal telephone lines at 33.6 thousand bytes-per-second.

At least, that was how the salesman who sold Gunner the machine had put it.

While the computer booted up, Gunner reached for the phone and paged Little Pete. Pete was a hard man to track down, as mobile businessmen always were, but if you were privy to his pager number, you could usually reach him inside of an hour. Gunner couldn't remember exactly when Pete had honored him with it, but he was glad to have the number now. Next, Gunner called Daniel Freeman Memorial Hospital, asked the nurse who answered the phone in the ICU if Sly Cribbs was receiving visitors yet. She said yes, but only from immediate members of his family. Gunner thanked her and hung up, thinking he'd call Charlotte Cribbs later, see if she'd care to take him along the next time she checked in on her son.

Finally, Gunner turned to the black-skinned machine before him and powered his way onto the Internet.

What he knew about the so-called Information Highway wouldn't have filled the voice bubble in a comic strip, but that wasn't much less than what he cared to know. After two weeks behind a keyboard, he was able to use search engines competently and could send e-mail to anyone with an address, and that probably made him as dangerous as he would ever need to be. In fact, the website he was tapping into now—the Law Professional's National Resource Center—was where he expected to do all but a fraction of his future "net-surfing."

Originating from a server in Hartford, Connecticut, the LPNRC was a mammoth database intended for the exclusive use of licensed skip tracers and private investigators like Gunner, and there was little in the way of non-government classified information the site could not either provide itself or offer a dynamic link to. Once the site was satisfied with the validity of a visitor's credentials, it was the closest thing to one-stop shopping a PI could ever hope to find.

While most of the White Pages–like services on the Internet excluded individuals and/or companies not listed in already existing telephone directories, the LPNRC's did not. Drawn from a vast array of disparate databases, from magazine subscriber listings to health club membership rolls, the LPNRC's White Pages were the state of the art in skip-tracing mechanisms. Gunner had only experimented with the system once before, running searches on himself and Lilly Tennell just to see what would happen, but today marked the first time he would be using it in earnest.

He spread the copies he had made at the Central Library out on his desk and, one by one, ran searches on the people whose names he had underlined:

Sandra March, the *Chicago Press Examiner* senior editor who had distrusted Thomas Selmon from the first.

Karen Whitlaw, the white feature writer for the *Press Examiner* with whom Selmon had been rumored to be having an affair.

Martin Keene, the *Press Examiner*'s managing editor who, in the wake of Selmon's fall from grace, was publicly ridiculed for having hired Selmon in the first place.

Gregory "Zero" Gates, the sociopathic black drug dealer with the Mensa-grade intellect Selmon had admittedly manufactured for his Pulitzer Prize–winning "investigative report."

And *Leonard Sloan,* the whistle blower, a talking head in the

Press Examiner's legal department who had found all the holes in Selmon's story, and then lobbied for a heavy *Press Examiner* lawsuit against him.

That the LPNRC's White Pages were able to produce addresses and phone numbers for four of the five people Gunner had inquired about was not surprising; he had expected nothing less than this result. Zero Gates, of course, had been the one person for whom no data had been found, nonexistent as he allegedly was. But it wasn't mere mailing addresses Gunner had been hoping to find here; rather, it was a specific *kind* of address. One Gunner could pay a visit to without putting much more than a handful of miles on the Cobra parked outside.

Martin Keene had such an address.

According to the LPNRC's listing for him, Keene now lived in Los Angeles, at 2404 Hidalgo Avenue, out in Silver Lake. It didn't seem logical that Selmon would have made his impulsive detour to L.A. last October just to see the one man in the world who, it could have been argued, had reason to despise him most, but it was certainly possible. And if Gunner could find some link between Keene and the Defenders of the Bloodline . . .

He made a printout of Keene's address, as well as those of the other three people he had run his search on, and terminated his Internet connection. Less than thirty seconds later, his phone began to ring.

It was Little Pete.

"Listen here, Gunner," he said. "When you page somebody, you're supposed to keep the line clear so they can call you back. Hasn't anybody ever told you that?"

"Sorry, Pete. I was on-line."

"On-line? *You?*"

"I'm a man, brother. Not a stegosaurus. Given time, I can adapt."

Little Pete laughed, said, "Go ahead on then, black. What can I do for you?"

Gunner asked him if he'd found a Defender of the Bloodline for him yet.

"Not yet. But I'm workin' on it. I have a partner out on the westside—he says he knows a friend who's got a friend. That sort of thing."

"Okay. Let me know as soon as you hear something, huh?"

"Sure. But, hey," Pete said, before Gunner could hang up the phone. "I think you ought to know that it hasn't been easy. In fact, it's been a bitch."

"Nobody wants to talk to you, huh?"

"Oh, they talk. But they don't really say anything. Few people who say they've heard of the Defenders talk about 'em like they're ghosts, or somethin'."

"Ghosts?"

"You know. Supernatural. Able to walk through walls and shit."

"You're not serious?"

"Man, I'm just tellin' you what I'm hearing. I never thought the boys were for real, but I had one brother tell me this mornin' he knows of at least two people the Defenders have killed already, and more are on the way."

"What two people were these?"

"He didn't mention any names. He just said they were Oreo cookies back east somewhere. A radio DJ and someone else, he couldn't remember who."

"How about a newspaper reporter?"

"A newspaper reporter? That might've been it, I guess. But the man couldn't remember the second person, like I said. He only remembered the DJ."

"Maybe I should talk to this guy, Pete," Gunner said, pencil and notepad at the ready.

"You can if you insist. But I just told you everything he knows. We've been 'boys a long time, this brother and me. If he knew a Defender, or where we could find one, he would've told me, I think."

Gunner thought that over, decided Pete was probably right. And questioning his friends' judgment in such matters was never good for business in any case.

"Okay, partner. Whatever you say."

He thanked Little Pete and hung up.

11

Silver Lake was the Los Angeles capital
of schizophrenia.

It was Caucasian and Hispanic, gay and straight, young and old. It
was picturesque, and it was garish; quaint and charming here, plastic and phony there. It had outdoor cafés and 7-Elevens; health food
stores and porn shops; three-story Tudor houses that dated back to
1911, and two-story towers of glass and steel that weren't yet a year
old. In short, Silver Lake was a multilingual, multicultural, architec-
turally diverse community that offered a little something for everybody. Including the dumb and the dumber.

Much of the community stood on a hill overlooking the city reservoir for which it was named, but no one had a better view of this
glistening pool of blue than Martin Keene. His single-story, redwood-
sheathed home halfway up Hidalgo Avenue's steep climb into the
hills sat on the west side of the street, where its perspective on the
reservoir below and the Hollywood Hills beyond was completely un-
obstructed. Gunner could see that much just from the carport, a
white, gable-roofed addition to the house that was functional, perhaps, but wholly unaesthetic.

He had thought about calling ahead, but decided to just drop in on
Keene instead. Sometimes it was better to make a wasted trip than
be rejected outright over the phone, or worse, talk to somebody
who'd had time to rehearse all their answers to his questions. But it
looked like this particular trip hadn't been wasted; the two cars in the
carport—a late-model Ford Taurus and an eighty-something Jeep
Cherokee—suggested Keene was home.

A handsome-looking woman in her early forties answered the doorbell the first time Gunner rang it. A fine-boned redhead with a freckled complexion and dignified demeanor, she opened the door wide, unafraid, and smiled at him like she'd known he was coming all along.

"Yes?"

"Is this the Martin Keene residence?" Gunner asked.

"Yes. Mr. Keene is my husband. How can I help you?"

Gunner showed her the photostatic license in his wallet, said, "My name is Aaron Gunner, Mrs. Keene. I'm a private investigator here in Los Angeles, working a missing persons case. Your husband wouldn't be around this afternoon, would he?"

Her smile lost something, never quite regained it. "He's out back, on the patio. What's this all about, Mr. Gunner?"

"Nothing serious, really. Someone your husband used to work with a few years ago has turned up missing, and the family's hired me to find him. I was hoping Mr. Keene might be able to give me a lead or two."

"Who is this person you're looking for?"

"Actually, Mrs. Keene, I'd rather not say. If Mr. Keene would care to share that information with you later, I'd have no objection to that. But right now I think it would be best if I left that decision up to him."

"I see. This is about Thomas Selmon, then."

It wasn't often that Gunner was caught flat-footed, but this was one of those rare occasions. Suddenly, Keene's wife didn't look so friendly, after all.

"That's right," Gunner said. Unable to see how lying now would do him any good. "But—"

"My husband has no interest in talking about that man ever again, Mr. Gunner. If your name really *is* Gunner. That's a part of Martin's past the two of us would just as soon forget. Now, if you'll excuse me . . ."

"Please, Mrs. Keene," Gunner pleaded, as she started to close the door. "I didn't come here to upset either you or your husband. But Selmon disappeared here, in Los Angeles, nine months ago, and no one seems to have any idea how or why."

"And you think Martin does?"

"I think I owe it to my client to ask him about it. As near as I've been able to determine, your husband's the only reason Selmon could have had for coming out here to L.A. in the first place."

"Well, that may very well be, but—"

"He left a wife and two small children behind in St. Louis, Mrs. Keene. I'm really here on their behalf, not Selmon's."

He would have thrown Selmon's "heartbroken" sister into the appeal for good measure, but he feared that might be overkill. As it was, the pitch led Martin Keene's wife to hesitate indecisively, if nothing else.

"Five minutes. That's all I'm asking for," Gunner said.

The redhead studied his face, his eyes in particular, looking for something there that might tell her what to do. "I'll ask him if he wants to see you. Forgive me if I don't ask you in."

She closed the door on him and locked it.

She returned more than five minutes later, looking somewhat tired and worn out, like she'd just lost a grueling test of wills. "He wants me to make sure you're not a reporter," she said.

Gunner shook his head and smiled. "I'm not a reporter. I'm a private investigator. If he wants to see my license himself . . ." He started to reach for his wallet again.

"That won't be necessary. Please, come in." She opened the door wider for him, closed it when he stepped inside. He was saddened to see the inside of the house was every bit as outmoded and incongruous as the outside: chrome floor lamps and wrought-iron bookcases, white leather beanbag chairs and a glass-topped, cable spool coffee table.

She walked him straight through the living room and past the kitchen to the wood deck patio out back. Martin Keene was sitting there in one of two blue-and-white deck chairs, watching sunlight shimmer off the water in the reservoir below, a narrow glass of ice tea in his left hand. He was a healthy-looking man in his early fifties, with a head of thinning gray hair combed back on his visible scalp, and he was dressed like he had either just finished putting, or was about to tee off.

"This is Mr. Gunner, Martin," his wife said.

Keene looked up, made no move to rise. He had slate-gray eyes that shone with fire, but little else. "Thank you, Pat. Would you care for some ice tea, Mr. Gunner?"

"No, thanks."

Keene's gaze turned to his wife.

"I'll leave you two alone, then," she said, going back through the sliding screen door to disappear into the house. Gunner couldn't help but feel badly for her.

"Sit down, Mr. Gunner, please," Keene said. Unlike his wife, he had yet to find the need to smile.

Gunner positioned the open deck chair to his liking and did as he was told. The umbrella stemming from the patio table between them held the sun at bay over their heads as they talked.

"So Tommy Selmon's disappeared again, eh?" Keene asked.

"Again?"

"That is to say, he's fallen out of view again. Gone into hiding. Choose whatever euphemism for making himself hard to find that you like, Mr. Gunner."

"I suppose 'disappeared' is as good as any. Last time anyone saw or heard from him was last October, here in Los Angeles. I don't suppose *you* saw him back then?"

"As a matter of fact I did. Yes."

Gunner was taken aback. The Keenes were just full of surprising proclamations today.

"You did?"

"Certainly. First in Washington, D.C., then here in Los Angeles. I think he followed me here from the Million Man March, but I'm not sure."

"You were at the Million Man March?"

"Yes. I did a story on it for *Harper's*. One white man's take on the event, the subtitle might have been."

"And you saw Selmon there."

Keene sipped his ice tea and nodded. "I was having dinner out in Dupont Circle. It was Sunday evening, the end of a long weekend. I just looked up and there he was, standing before my table."

"And?"

"He asked if he could sit down. He seemed genuinely happy to see me. If I hadn't been in such a state of shock, I would have told him to go fuck himself. But I must have just nodded feebly, instead."

"He approached you?"

"Yes. Do you think I would have approached *him*?"

"What did he want?"

"To talk about old times, of course. At the paper in Chicago, before the roof caved in. I assume that requires no explanation, Mr. Gunner, or else you wouldn't be here."

Gunner nodded.

"We spoke for all of fifteen minutes. As you might imagine, I didn't have much to say to the man. After about his third straight apology, I paid my bill and left. I didn't see him again until he showed up here at my home two days later."

"He came here?"

"Yes. Unannounced and uninvited, much like you just did." He smiled again.

"You gave him your address in D.C.?"

"No. He got my address from the hotel, he said. He wouldn't say how, exactly, but I suspect he called the reservations desk pretending to be me, got the clerk there to 'verify' my mailing address.

It's an old reporter's trick, Mr. Gunner. I used to use it all the time myself."

"But how did he know what hotel you were staying at in Washington?"

"I would assume he called around and asked for me. Isn't that what you would have done?"

Gunner ignored the rhetorical question, said, "So he shows up here at the house two days later."

"Yes."

"To offer more apologies?"

Keene hesitated for the first time, uncomfortable with the question. "No. He had a business proposition for me," he said.

"Involving a book he wanted to write."

"Yes. 'The Devil's Byline: The Thomas Selmon Story.' You know about that?"

"He made a call to a New York literary agent from his motel room here in town before he disappeared, said he had this great idea for a book. What else could it have been but 'The Thomas Selmon Story'?"

"He wanted me to co-author it with him. He said it wouldn't work any other way. No one would touch the autobiography of a world-renowned liar, he said, but if someone else were to write it, someone an editor could trust to be totally objective . . .'"

"You'd have a best-seller on your hands."

Keene nodded. "Yes. That was his theory, anyway."

"You didn't think so?"

"On the contrary. I was certain he was right. But I wasn't going to help him write his goddamn book." He poured himself a fresh glass of ice tea from a pitcher on the table, then went on. "Tommy Selmon ruined me as a newspaper man, Mr. Gunner. Forever. Twenty-seven years in the business, and it was all gone after one story. How he thought I could ever forget that is beyond me."

"You haven't been able to get work since?"

"Work? Oh, I can get all the work I want. But as a writer, not an editor. People took the *Press Examiner* scandal as proof I can't be trusted to *oversee* a newspaper story, not that I can't write one. Which is pretty fortunate for me, wouldn't you say?"

"So you told him you weren't interested in his offer."

"Yes. He wasn't happy with that answer, of course, but my answer was final, and I told him so. When he finally decided to believe me, he left."

"Did he say where he was going?"

"He left me a number at the motel you mentioned, I believe. But I never used it."

"And you didn't see him again after that?"

"No. That was the last I ever saw or heard from Tommy."

Gunner looked out over the blue water before him, said, "I wonder if the subject of his family ever came up?"

"His family? Oh." Keene smiled. "You mean the one in St. Louis you told Pat about at the door." He shook his head. "No. We never talked about that at all."

"You didn't ask him where he'd been keeping himself all these years?"

"That would have suggested an interest in such matters I didn't have then, and do not have now, Mr. Gunner."

"What about Elroy Covington? That name ever come up in conversation?"

"Elroy Covington? No." Keene shook his head again. "Who is he?"

"That's the name Selmon's been using in St. Louis for the last few years. Elroy Covington. In fact, he was registered under that name at his motel in town. You don't remember?"

Keene's expression was as blank as a crash test dummy's. "Remember?"

"If he left you his number at the motel, he must have told you what name to ask for at the desk. Otherwise, the clerk there wouldn't have known how to direct your call."

Keene smiled again, commending Gunner on his perceptiveness. "Ah. I see your point."

"Do you?"

Keene stopped smiling, said, "Tommy may have mentioned something about changing his name, but I don't remember now if he did or not. Like I said before, I wasn't really hearing what he had to say. I was just letting him talk." He glanced at his watch, showing an interest in time he hadn't exhibited before now. "Forgive me, Mr. Gunner, but are we about done? Despite all appearances to the contrary, I really do have some work to do this afternoon."

"Of course. I'm down to my last question."

"Good."

"What can you tell me about the DOB?"

"The DOB?" Keene thought about it for a moment, then said, "Oh. You don't mean that group of crazies that was supposed to be murdering black conservatives out in New Hampshire a few years ago? 'The Defenders of the Brotherhood,' was it?"

"Actually, it was 'Bloodline.' But those are the crazies I mean, yeah."

"What about them?"

"Did Selmon ever mention them when you talked to him? Either here, or back in D.C.?"

"The Defenders of the Bloodline? No. Why—" He stopped himself short, having the answer to his question before he could even ask it. "Oh. You think they had something to do with Tommy's disappearance, is that it?"

"If they really exist, I think it's possible, yes. You say they murdered some black conservatives in New Hampshire?"

"Allegedly. I don't remember all the details now, but the way I remember it, they took responsibility for a pair of homicides back in ninety-four that were never solved. A few arrests were made, but that was it."

"Was one of the victims a DJ?"

"A DJ? No. He was a radio talk show host. The other victim was a political columnist, I believe. A woman named Eddie Orville." He watched as Gunner jotted the name down in a little notebook. "But I'm not sure I understand. Tommy was politically conservative, that's true, but not so anyone would really notice. Why would the DOB target him?"

"The way I understand it, the DOB aren't just after political conservatives. They're after anyone they believe has betrayed the African-American community in some form or fashion. For lack of a better term, Mr. Keene, I guess I'm talking about Uncle Toms."

"And they see Tommy as an Uncle Tom?"

"They wouldn't be alone in that opinion if they did. His colleagues at the *Press Examiner* weren't the only people he humiliated five years ago, after all."

Keene nodded, following his reasoning.

"But again, I'm not even sure the Defenders are for real. The only evidence I've been able to find of them out here are some flyers someone's been posting around town bearing their name."

"So what makes you think they killed Tommy?"

"It's a long story. And I seem to recall I was on my way out when this subject came up. Maybe I'll bore you with it some other time."

Keene didn't like that, Gunner being evasive with him in his own backyard, but he didn't make an issue of it. He simply stood up when Gunner did and shook the black man's proffered hand.

"In the meantime, I'd like to thank you for your time today, Mr. Keene. You've been very helpful."

"Have I? I can't imagine how."

Gunner smiled and said, "You're too modest. I think you'd be surprised how much I learned here today."

He let Keene see the smile a full three seconds longer, then left him to guard the Silver Lake reservoir alone.

———

Gunner went back to Johnny Frerotte's house next.

The fire he had escaped two nights before hadn't burned the home to the ground, but it had gutted it like a fish, leaving only the charred remains of its basic two-story frame behind. Everything within— furniture and clothing and electronic appliances—was soot covered and disfigured, drowned in water and buried by debris. Had anyone else but Frerotte lived here, Gunner would have found the wreckage a sad sight to behold.

Roaming through the ruins in broad daylight was asking to be mistaken for a thief, Gunner knew, but that couldn't be helped. He wanted another look around the place before Frerotte could get out of the hospital and clean things up, and he had no desire to do so at night. He had tried that tack once before, with disastrous results, and tempting the fates had never been one of the investigator's favorite pastimes.

It was the basement he wanted to see, of course, but the basement was all but impossible to reach. Because the fire had started there, everything above it had collapsed upon it, reducing it to a caved-in bomb shelter that could barely be seen, let alone visited. The best Gunner could do in the way of investigating its remains was stand at the edge of a gaping hole in the faltering floor above it and look down, an approach that garnered him little more than a glimpse of the room he had only two nights ago been left to die in. The washing machine and the dryer, that was all of the basement he could really see, save for the toilet in its small water closet. That, too, was clearly visible, though the typewriter stand Gunner had thought he had seen standing just before it was not. It was either buried under the mound of blackened wood and waterlogged plasterboard that now stood in its place, or it was missing altogether—Gunner wasn't sure which. Maybe it had never been there at all.

He didn't know what he had come here hoping to find, exactly, but he knew this wasn't it. Whatever clues Frerotte's home still held to the man or woman who had chosen this place to try and murder him less than two days earlier, they were far beyond his mortal reach now, and that should have been obvious to him before he'd even parked his car out front.

He would have to find the Defenders of the Bloodline some other way.

Gunner called Mickey's from a pay phone on Normandie and Florence to check for messages, and Mickey told him that Little Pete had come through for him. Sort of.

The number he had left for Gunner was an unfamiliar one, but he answered the phone himself when Gunner dialed it.

"Sorry, Gunner, man, but this was the best I could do," he said.

"What's that?"

"This ain't no Defender, it's just the guy who's been printing up all their flyers for 'em. He wouldn't talk to me, but he might talk to you."

"Who?"

"Man's name is Pritchard. Clive Pritchard. He works over at a printing shop called Empowerment Printing. You ever hear of it?"

Gunner said that he hadn't, told Pete to hold on while he got out his pen and notepad. When he was ready, Pete said, "It's supposed to be over on Hoover and Seventy-sixth Street. Seven-Seven-Oh-Five Hoover. I've never been there myself, but they tell me it's where all the community activist types go to get their printing done cheap. They're one of those nonprofit operations."

"I know the kind," Gunner said.

"Word I hear is that he's doin' the Defenders' shit on the side, at night, without his boss's knowledge. Man might be more inclined to talk to you if you let him know you know that right up front."

"Yeah. He might at that. What do I owe you, Pete?"

Pete tried to go the humble route, declining payment on the grounds that he hadn't delivered the information Gunner had actually requested, but he was just being polite. Like any smart businessman, he never did a damn thing for nothing, and Gunner understood that about him completely.

"How about I get back to you later, let you know how things turn out," Gunner said. "You can tell me what I owe you then."

"That'll work," Pete said, satisfied.

Because he, like Gunner, had a strange feeling things out at Empowerment Printing were going to turn out just fine.

12

Clive Pritchard looked like a black gargoyle.

He was short and broad shouldered, with a ratty gray beard and small, rodentlike eyes. He came out of Empowerment Printing's back room wearing an ink-smeared blue apron over a substantial beer belly, an expression of grave impatience on his battle-scarred face, but he didn't really make Gunner feel unwelcome until he heard what the investigator wanted with him.

"You got the wrong place," he said, turning to go back to work.

"That's not what I was told," Gunner said.

Pritchard stopped, turned around to face him again. "I'm supposed to give a fuck what you been told?"

"You're not supposed to do anything. I just thought you might want to talk to me before I talk to your boss, that's all. What time do you think he'll be in?"

Pritchard glared at him without moving, unsure of himself now. "Mr. Angelo don't come in until late," he said.

"So I'll go get a cup of coffee and come back. What time is late?"

Pritchard remained motionless for a few seconds longer, slow to concede that his visitor had him by the short hairs. Finally, he walked back to his original place behind the order counter, directly in front of Gunner, and said, "You a cop or somethin'?"

Gunner showed him his license without comment.

"So what you wanna know about the flyers for?"

"I'm looking for the people behind them. The notorious DOB. Any idea how I could get in contact with them?"

"No."

"You're the one running the flyers, aren't you? At night, when Mr. Angelo isn't around?"

"Who the hell told you that?"

"I've got spies everywhere. Costs me a small fortune. Where can I find the Defenders?"

"I told you, man. I don't know."

"Explain to me how that's possible."

"It's possible 'cause I don't *wanna* know. All right? I know what I need to know to get paid, and that's all."

"So how do you get paid?"

"Look. I don't think you understand. You don't wanna fuck with these particular brothers, man. They're some of the most pissed-off niggers you ever wanna see. They find out I been talkin' to you—"

"They won't. Tell me how you get paid, Clive."

Pritchard kept looking at the shop's front door, terrified that someone would step through it any minute. Finally, able to see no escape from the corner he'd been backed into, he sighed and said, "I get paid through the mail. A money order every month, along with an original for the flyer. I run two hundred copies, ship 'em to a post office box, and wait for the next money order to come in. That's all I know."

"Whose name is on the money order?"

" 'The Burghardt Institute.' Same as the name on the P.O. box. I think it's somethin' they just made up."

"B-U-R-G-H-A-R-D-T?"

"Yeah. That's it. What kind of fuckin' name is that, Burghardt?"

Gunner had to grin at the small joke. To Pritchard, he said, "That's what the B in W.E.B. DuBois stood for. Burghardt. It's Dutch, I believe."

Pritchard didn't seem to give a damn what the name was.

"So how'd you get the gig in the first place?" Gunner asked him.

"A man comes into the shop one day, says he's got some flyers he wants printed up, two hundred a month. Only nobody can know about it but me. He don't want no receipts written up, no order forms filled out, nothin'. He tells me about the money orders and the P.O. box, asks me if I want the job. I say yeah, why not? I could use a little somethin' extra every month, right?"

"How long ago was this?"

"About a year ago, maybe. Could be longer, I don't know."

"And you never got this brother's name?"

"No. He didn't give it to me, and I never asked him for it."

"Describe him."

"Describe him? Man, I just told you. I seen the brother *once,* a year ago. How the hell am I supposed to describe him?"

"It's simple. Start with his age, and go on from there. Was he young, or old? Fat, or skinny? Light skinned, or dark skinned?"

"He was young. In his twenties, maybe. Not fat, but not skinny, either. Boy was buffed. Looked like he hits the weights. And . . . what was that other one?"

"His skin coloring."

"Oh, yeah. His skin was dark. Maybe darker'n you and me put together. I guess now you gonna wanna know how tall the nigger was."

Gunner nodded, though by now the man's height wasn't really in doubt. Gunner already thought he knew who Pritchard was talking about.

"He was about your height. Or maybe a little taller," Pritchard said.

"And his hair was cut close to the scalp."

"Yeah. That's right."

Gunner nodded again, searching his wallet for a couple of business cards. Finding them, he handed the pair to the other man and said, "One of these you can keep. The other I want back, after you've written the address of the P.O. box you mentioned on the back of it. I've got a pen if you need one."

"I can't do that, man. I've done too fuckin' much for you already."

"And I appreciate it. But I need the address, anyway."

"I can't do it. I *told* you. These niggers ain't nobody to fuck with."

"How do you know that? If the only contact you've ever had with them is this brother who initially hired you—"

"I know it 'cause I know a crazy-ass motherfucker when I see one, that's how. And if the rest of 'em is anything like *that* boy . . ." He shook his head. "Then the whole fuckin' world needs to be afraid of 'em. Includin' you and me."

Maybe the fear in his eyes had been there all along, Gunner didn't know.

He only knew that he was beginning to feel it, too.

Unless the label on his mailbox was wrong, the full name of Gunner's old friend at the Stage Door Motel—the muscular, angry young black man he had previously known only as "Blue"—was Byron Scales. He had found Scales's place of residence—a two-story apartment building on Stocker Avenue, between La Brea and Crenshaw Boulevards on the southern slope of Windsor Hills—thanks to Scales's co-worker, the fat man at the motel's front desk Gunner had first met Tuesday afternoon. All the big man had volunteered today about Scales/a.k.a. Blue was that he was off on Fridays, thinking Gunner would compensate him to elaborate, but Gunner had managed to weasel a full name and home address out of him for free. All he'd had to do was say "or else."

"Or else? Or else *what?*" the big man had asked him, almost laughing.

"Or else I'll find him on my own. And tell him when I do that you sold his ass out for ten bucks. Or maybe five, whichever I think will piss him off more."

Five seconds later, Gunner was holding a sheet of Stage Door stationery with the name BYRON SCALES and the Stocker Avenue address scribbled on it.

By any name, Scales had just become the key to Gunner's search for Thomas Selmon. Gunner was kicking himself now for having needed to hear Clive Pritchard's inadvertent description of him—a muscular, dark-skinned young brother you didn't want to fuck with—to see that the janitor was worth a second look. It had been Scales, after all, who had connected Selmon to Johnny Frerotte. He'd portrayed himself as nothing more than a witness to the pair's meeting, when in fact he'd probably orchestrated it. Somebody somewhere had turned Frerotte and the Defenders onto Thomas. Why couldn't it have been Scales?

Scales lived on the first floor of the Stocker Avenue building, apartment number six, way in the back at the end of the courtyard. Gunner should have had to ring his unit on the phone out front to get past the security gate, but the return spring on the gate was shot so that it was ajar when Gunner tried it. The door and blinded window of Scales's apartment sat in the shade of a short, overgrown palm tree, shrouding them in darkness so complete, the marker on the door was damn near impossible to read. He stood beneath the umbrella of giant leaves and withdrew the Ruger from its holster with his right hand. He held the gun down and just behind his right thigh, then rang the tinny bell on the door, making no attempt to avoid the door's peephole. He wanted Scales to know who was calling.

"Who is it?" the voice of the man formerly known as Blue called out from the apartment's interior.

"Aaron Gunner. You remember me. We need to talk, Brother Blue."

He stepped up closer to the door, anxious now, and waited as Scales decided what to do. After a few seconds, the deadlock was thrown open and the door soon followed, Scales standing just behind it. He had tan trousers on, but no shirt and no shoes. His black chest looked like something cut from granite, and his abdominals were the most clearly defined Gunner had ever seen. He wasn't rubbing sleep from his eyes, but he resembled a man who'd just rolled out of bed, nonetheless.

"What the hell are you doing here?" he asked, showing Gunner the same foul attitude he'd displayed at the Stage Door three days ago.

Gunner didn't bother answering, just forced his way into the apartment, bringing the gun in his hand out from behind his back for Scales to see. Or that was the plan, until somebody standing to the side of the open door put a vise grip on his arm to wrench the weapon from his grasp. Gunner tried to turn, but a second man took him from the other side, his left, and wrapped an arm around his own, up high near the shoulder, so that between the pair, Gunner couldn't move an inch in either direction. Both men were wearing white hockey masks, and both were as strong as oxen.

As Gunner gamely struggled against them, they ushered him further into the room as Scales calmly closed his apartment door, grinning like someone who was about to become filthy rich. He came back around to where Gunner could see him and said, "When I heard you might drop by, something told me you might lead with the gun this time, so I invited a couple of my 'boys over. I hope you don't mind."

Gunner made one more effort to break free of his captors, realized it was a lost cause. He couldn't have been more at Scales's mercy if he'd been nailed to the floor with railroad spikes.

Scales finally laughed out loud, then threw a looping right uppercut into Gunner's stomach that the investigator feared would plow straight through him. He fell slack, wheezing desperately for air, held upright only by the two men at his sides. It was all he could do not to black out.

"That dumbfuck Barber Jack was supposed to whack you," Scales said. "That's why I put you on to him in the first place. But here you are, in my shit again." He shook his head and sighed. "It was up to me, I'd pop a cap in your ass right now and be done with it. But it's not up to me. Somebody wants to talk to you, hell if I know why."

Gunner wanted to hear more, but he still couldn't speak. Learning to breathe again took precedence over everything else.

"Stand him up," he heard Scales tell his accomplices, his voice filled with annoyance for Gunner's childlike helplessness.

The two masked black men lifted Gunner up as instructed, forcing him to his feet. Gunner found the strength to raise his head, only to do so just in time to catch the right hand Scales threw at his face without warning. The blow struck him flush on his left cheekbone, but didn't knock him out; Scales had taken something off it, not wanting him unconscious just yet.

"That was for your own protection," Scales said. "I don't want you thrashing around, making this any harder than it has to be."

Gunner's eyes rolled up, saw Scales inserting a hypodermic needle into the mouth of a small glass vial.

Oh, Christ, he thought, begging his limbs to move. But nothing would work. Every ounce of his strength was gone.

"I know what you're thinking," Scales said, seeing his distress. "A goddamn needle. Is it clean, or is it dirty? Did I just take it off a junkie with AIDS, or right off the drugstore shelf?" He laughed. "That's the beauty of using a needle, instead of chloroform or something like that. It messes with your head. I like that."

He laughed again, heartily, the point of the syringe in his right hand glistening like a gemstone, and stepped forward to give Gunner the injection.

He didn't know how long he'd been unconscious, but Gunner had the sense it had been several hours at least.

How he could know that, or anything else for that matter, was hard to say. Still feeling the effects of the drug he'd been doped with, he came to and found himself blindfolded and gagged, tied to a hardwood chair, arms behind him, like a deer to the hood of a hunter's pickup truck. He was blind, and mute, and half-frozen; his surroundings were as cold as a butcher's freezer and just as eerily silent. Multiple windings of the duct tape covering his mouth and eyes secured his entire torso to the back of the chair, so tightly he could barely inhale, while his wrists seemed to be fastened together with plastic cable ties. Even without the aid of sight, the futility of trying to free himself anywhere inside of forty-eight hours was obvious to him.

He sat motionless for several minutes, waiting for his drug-induced stupor to wear off completely as he listened for clues to his location, but no such clues were forthcoming. He was either in a soundproofed room, or one that was merely far removed from the usual cacophony of modern civilization. Gunner tried to imagine such a place, but couldn't, distracted by a growing awareness that his right biceps ached where Scales had put his beloved needle in.

When he finally lost patience with doing nothing, he tried to shift his weight to one side, to see if he could rock the wooden chair over and shatter it on the floor beneath him, but the chair didn't move an inch. Curious, he tried again, to the other side this time, and again the chair wouldn't budge.

"It's bolted to the floor," someone said.

The voice had been muffled and almost unintelligible, like that of a whispering highwayman wearing a bandanna over the lower half of his face. Gunner immediately thought of the hockey masks Scales's two friends had been wearing at Scales's apartment earlier.

Gunner tried to speak, forgot that he was gagged.

"Here. Let me get that for you," his host said. Muffled voice or no, he didn't much sound like Byron Scales.

Someone reached for the duct tape plastered over Gunner's mouth, ripped it from the investigator's face like they were trying to start an old outboard motor. Gunner screamed in anguish, his skin afire, knowing all too well as he did so he was providing the precise entertainment his kidnapper or kidnappers had been hoping for.

"Goddamnit!"

He expected to hear laughter, but none came. Instead, the silence he had awakened to returned, as complete and unnerving as ever.

"All right. What the fuck *is* this?" Gunner finally asked, containing his anger in deference to his utter inability to defend himself.

"Judgment day, my brother," the other man said, his voice circling Gunner buzzardlike from several feet away. If he and Gunner weren't alone in the room, he was the only one willing—or authorized—to speak.

"Scales? That you?"

"No. It isn't Scales. You and I have never had the pleasure, Gunner."

"Bullshit. You tried to kill me out at Jack Frerotte's house two nights ago."

"Is that right?"

"Damn straight."

"And why would I have wanted to do that?"

"Because you're a Defender of the Bloodline. You and Scales, and those boys who helped him jump me at his apartment."

There was a long pause before the other man said, "Yes."

"And Frerotte too, I imagine."

"No. Jack Frerotte was never a true believer. We understand that now."

Behind his back, Gunner was rubbing his wrists raw trying to stretch the cable ties binding them together, caring little that his chances for success were minimal at best. Sooner or later, his friend the Defender was going to tire of talking and move on to more demonstrative, perhaps even sadistic, ways of expressing himself, and Gunner had good reason to believe his life might depend on having his hands free when he did.

"So he was just a hired gun, then," the investigator said, just to keep the conversation going.

"A hired gun?"

"When he murdered Thomas Selmon for you. You *paid* Jack to do that, he didn't do it voluntarily."

After a moment, grudgingly: "Yes."

"You didn't expect to pay him?"

"I told you. We thought he was one of us. We would never have assigned him Selmon's execution otherwise."

The voice was on Gunner's right now, at approximately 2 o'clock.

"So maybe Selmon's not really dead. If Jack was only in it for the money—"

"We saw the body, Mr. Gunner. Jack took us to the grave site. That wasn't part of the original plan, of course, but our growing doubts about his sincerity made such guarantees necessary."

Then the photograph Gunner had found in Frerotte's basement had been for real. Not a fake the fat man had put together just to run a game on his friends.

"By 'we,' " Gunner said, "I take it you mean—"

"Our numbers are not important, Gunner. Except to say that there are far more of us than just the four brothers you already know about. That much I can assure you."

Now the voice was directly behind Gunner, precipitating at least a momentary halt to the investigator's struggles with the cable ties.

"Any of the others in here with us now, by any chance?" Gunner asked.

"Perhaps. Perhaps not. But you're not going anywhere either way, are you, brother?"

The truth in that, more than the sarcasm in it, stung like a cold razor at Gunner's throat. "Why don't you tell me what you want," he said.

"What we want? We want you to tell us whose side you're on, of course. With whom, exactly, do you stand, Gunner? The Judases— or God?"

Choosing his words carefully, knowing dangerous ground when he was about to tread on it, Gunner said, "That all depends. Which god are we talking about?"

"There is only one god, my brother. Allah, the Almighty. The father and protector of our people."

"The African-American people."

"The living seed of Mother Africa, yes. The very same seed being destroyed from within by the agents of the White Devil who live among us."

"You mean like Thomas Selmon."

"Yes."

"And that radio talk show host out in New Hampshire."

"Delbert Olney. Yes. You know about him?"

Gunner didn't answer.

" 'The Genius of the Ghetto' Brother Olney used to call himself. He hadn't lived in the ghetto since he was six years old and didn't give a damn about anyone who did. But he was an 'expert' on the problems of our people."

"So you killed him."

"Yes. He was only the first of many."

"You intend to kill all the Delbert Olneys in the world?"

"That is Allah's will, Mr. Gunner."

"And you know that because?"

"Because I've been *inspired to know it.*"

"Let me let you in on a little secret, brother. You're gonna run out of bullets long before you run out of victims. Or haven't you and Allah figured that out yet?"

The other man didn't answer for a long time. "We want you to step off, Mr. Gunner," he finally said, issuing a direct order. "Find something else to do with your time that has nothing to do with us and nothing to do with Thomas Selmon."

And there it was: the end of conversation Gunner had been dreading. Instantly rendering his struggles against the bands around his wrists pointless.

"What about my client?"

"Your client? Tell her what you wish. But you'd be smart to discourage her from pursuing the matter of her brother's disappearance, as well. That is, if you're at all fond of her."

"Meaning you'll kill her if she doesn't."

"That is precisely my meaning, yes." He came up unexpectedly on Gunner's left side, whispered right into his ear. "Just as we'll kill you. However reluctantly. If it was Allah's wish that we kill everyone who gets in our way, Mr. Gunner, you and Sister McCreary would already be dead. Surely you can see that. But that is not our way. We are Defenders of the Bloodline. We are assassins for the people, not common murderers."

He was telling what he thought was the truth. The distinction he was describing was as real for him as the earth beneath his feet.

"Give me Frerotte," Gunner said, playing the long odds that so presumptuous a demand wouldn't get him killed on the spot.

"What?"

"I need Frerotte. You let me nail him for Selmon's murder, and I'll do what you want. I'll walk away, and McCreary will, too. I give you my word."

"Your *word*?"

"You want me to forget you clowns tried to burn me alive Wednesday night, that's my price. I want Frerotte. The rest of you can go to hell."

Gunner's boldness struck his host silent again, filling the room with an eerie, almost palpable air of doom.

And then the Defender laughed.

Before Gunner knew what was happening, a hand took hold of his left arm, put it in a vise grip as a needle was punched into his flesh, feeding yet another injection into his veins.

"You're a lunatic, Gunner. And you're in no position to negotiate, as you have somehow failed to notice. *We* are in control here, not *you*."

"Wait! You don't . . ."

Already, Gunner could feel himself drifting into unconsciousness. Damning himself as a fool for overplaying his all but nonexistent hand.

"If someone tried to kill you at Jack's crib Wednesday night, it wasn't us. So the debt you seem to think you owe us is a false one." He paused. "The debt we owe Jack Frerotte, however, is not."

Gunner tried to speak, made only a small, pitiful murmur of discomfort.

"He deceived us. He presented himself as a fellow believer, when all he really was was a mercenary. Had we allowed him completely into our confidence, allowing you to deal with him now might pose some threat to us. But we were smart enough, at least, to keep him at a distance. He no more knows our names and identities than you do."

To Gunner, the Defender's voice was distant now, an ever-fading wisp of sound echoing in the dark.

"So it seems we have a choice to make, my brothers and I. Trust you to do as you say and let you live? Or kill you now and worry about Jack later?"

Again, silence descended upon the room. Gunner tried to wait it out, but couldn't.

Sleep had finally overtaken him.

13

There was no white light.
No hands reaching out to him from a shadowy void, no familiar voices calling his name, no friendly faces beckoning him toward heaven. But it was a near-death experience just the same. A murky, shades-of-gray spiral funneling down to perfect blackness. Silent, cold, terrifying.

And Gunner didn't know how it would end.

He was vaguely aware of a nagging regret. Had he brought this on himself? Was this the ignoble way he was going to die—pricked by a poison needle and put to sleep, like a tired old dog that hadn't the strength to bark anymore—because he hadn't had the brains to *lie* in exchange for his life? To just tell the man he'd fallen prey to what he wanted to hear, and nothing more? The words would have been so simple to say: *"Okay. You win. You want me gone, I'm gone."*

But he had tried to negotiate instead. To salvage some fragment of his self-esteem by insisting the Defenders give up Jack Frerotte. As if he had been in any position to bargain. Trying to dictate terms to someone who had nothing to lose by killing him had been the height of reckless machismo. Had it cost him all the days he'd had left to walk God's green earth?

The answer lay at the black, bottomless core of the gray spiral continuing to draw him down, closer and closer to what he knew was death. And in his ears, a slow, inexorable beat prevailed:

Thump . . . thump . . . thump . . .

The sound of a poor man's heart shutting down for good.

"I still say he ought'a see a doctor," Winnie Phifer said.

Gunner shook his head. "No."

"Winnie's right, Gunner. You don't know what them fools might'a given you," Mickey said.

"I'm fine. Get the hell out of here, both of you."

The trio was in Gunner's office, Gunner stretched out on his back on his couch, the others looming over him, watching him labor to keep their faces and the room around them all in focus. It was Saturday morning. Winnie had found the investigator unconscious in front of the barber shop's back door, rolled up in a ball on the ground like an oversize infant someone was trying to give away. She'd brought him inside all by herself, waited for Mickey to show up a few minutes later to decide what to do with him. Mickey shook him by the shoulders and slapped his cheeks a few times to bring him around, then asked him what had happened. Gunner didn't remember all of it, but he remembered enough to bring his two nurses to the brink of calling an ambulance for him.

Winnie snorted, her motherly concern gone unappreciated, and left. Mickey stayed behind, thicker skinned and harder headed than she. Dillett the Ridgeback was nowhere in sight.

"You gonna call the cops?" Mickey asked.

"No. Not yet, anyway." Gunner tried to sit up, changed his mind when his stomach started doing somersaults. "I don't suppose you've seen my car anywhere?"

"Didn't see it out front when I came in. Maybe it's around the corner, or somethin'. You want me to go look?"

Gunner nodded. He didn't have to tell his landlord why the car was a priority; a '65 Ford Cobra convertible in mint condition wasn't going to last five minutes left unattended anywhere, security system or no security system, and Mickey knew that as well as anybody.

"That cop Poole called you twice yesterday," Mickey said. "He said—"

"I know what he said. Forget about it," Gunner told him irritably, waving him out the door. He had meant to call Poole to ask for an extension on his forty-eight-hour deadline relative to the Everson case, but forgot. Now Poole would doubtless be on his ass all weekend.

When he was finally left to recuperate alone, Gunner did something that would have made his landlord proud. He said a silent prayer of thanks. He was alive. His head felt like an urn filled with sand, and his body ached everywhere, but he was alive. Some would have called him lucky, others blessed. Gunner was convinced he'd been a little of both.

After his fleeting moment of gratitude had passed, he made a second attempt to get to his feet, managed to pull the stunt off this time. He wobbled over to his desk and sat down before the thought occurred to him that he should check his pockets, make sure the Defenders hadn't added insult to injury by robbing him blind. They hadn't; his money and wallet were in their usual places, seemingly untouched. His keys, however, were gone, replaced by something else: a small hand-drawn map.

It was childishly rudimentary, just a series of labeled parallel and perpendicular lines directing him to a remote location in the Angeles National Forest, between forty and fifty miles north of Los Angeles proper. Beneath a small red cross near a crooked line identified as San Francisquito Canyon Road, someone had scrawled a brief message:

> We're gonna be watching you, brother.
> Thanks for the use of the ride.

A sure sign that Mickey wasn't going to find Gunner's car outside after all.

As expected, Gunner's cousin Del Curry bitched the whole drive out to the site depicted on the Defenders' map, pausing only to check his Hyundai's mirrors during lane changes.

Gunner had known the purpose of this expedition would shake the self-employed electrician up like this, but he was trying to suffer his cousin's whining in silence all the same, still feeling the last diminishing effects of his drugging the night before. It wasn't easy.

"I'm not a grave digger, man," Del kept saying. "Why the hell'd you have to call *me* for this?"

"I needed a ride, and you've got a car. Any more questions?"

"Mickey's got a car, doesn't he?"

"Mickey had to work today. You don't."

"But this kind of shit is police work, Aaron."

"I called the police. Poole was out in the field, and Emilio Martinez has the day off. Jesus, Del, you're acting just like an old woman!"

And so it went between them, Del crying like a baby, Gunner giving him hell for it, though in truth, Gunner was just as reluctant to do what they were about to do as his cousin. That the map was leading them to the location of Thomas Selmon's body, Gunner had little doubt, and after nine months in the ground, he knew the corpse was likely to be as appetizing a sight as an autopsy in progress. But he had demanded Jack Frerotte's head in exchange for his disinterest in the Defenders of the Bloodline, as misguided as that promise had been, and now it seemed he was going to get it, ready or not. Providing, of course, the Defenders hadn't ditched his car this far out in the middle of nowhere just to add an exclamation point to his kidnapping.

Gunner had suggested this last possibility to Del simply to try and quiet him, putting no credence whatsoever in it himself.

San Francisquito Canyon Road was a twisty, winding two-lane that climbed up into the Angeles National Forest eight miles above Interstate 5, between Castaic Lake to the south and Elizabeth Lake to the north. The terrain it sliced through was all rough and tumble, a rocky, heavily foliated landscape of steep angles and narrow ledges that seemed the very definition of desolate. It was a long way to go to dump a body, Gunner mused, but few places would have been better suited to the purpose, especially at night.

About nine miles into their upward trek toward Elizabeth Lake, Del pointed and said, "There it is."

The Cobra had been pulled off the northbound side of the road and left to rest on a slight strip of shoulder there, jammed into a small niche in the hillside. It was covered in dust, but otherwise appeared to be unharmed. Del turned his boxy little Hyundai in behind it, leaving the Korean car's tail protruding about a foot or two out into the road, and both men climbed out to inspect the red convertible more closely. They still hadn't seen more than two cars go by in either direction since they'd left Castaic Lake.

To Gunner's utter relief, the Cobra was indeed safe and sound. None of the indignities that could have easily befallen it under the circumstances—knife-shredded seats, soda-stained carpeting, a dented and key-scarred exterior—were in evidence. Apparently, whatever else the group was or wasn't, the Defenders of the Bloodline were not common vandals.

"I don't believe it," Del said.

"Yeah. Neither do I," Gunner agreed.

"Maybe something's missing. There's gotta be something missing, right?"

Gunner had already made a quick assessment. "The keys," he said.

Directing Del to watch for opposing traffic, nonexistent as it was, he opened the Cobra's driver's side door, felt around the floorboard beneath both seats. "Nothing," he said when he was finished, shaking his head.

"They had you come all the way out here to get the damn car, and didn't leave the *keys*?"

"No. I don't think so." He was looking past Del to the other side of the road, where the hillside fell off sharply to continue its descent to level ground.

"What?"

"Come on."

Gunner started across the silent highway, didn't bother to look back to see if his cousin was following him as instructed. He reached the edge of the drop and looked down, out over a wall of thick vegetation and jagged rock that would be difficult to traverse on foot, but not impossible.

Del came up behind him, said, "You think they threw 'em down there?"

"Not exactly. Do me a favor and go get those gloves I brought along, huh?"

"The gloves? You mean—"

"Just go get 'em, Del. Hurry the hell up."

Del reluctantly did as he was told, had to wait for a badly crumpled Toyota pickup truck easing its way downhill to pass before he could cross back to Gunner's side of the road. Gunner took the gloves out of his hand without a word, slipped them on, and then stepped over the guardrail, cautiously making his way down the treacherous incline, step by tenuous step.

"Are you sure you know what the hell you're doing?" his cousin called after him, staying put right where he was.

Gunner didn't even answer him, too busy watching his footing and looking for his missing keys simultaneously.

He was expecting a brief search, and that was exactly what he got. In less than ten minutes, he spotted his keys with relative ease, approximately twenty feet down the hillside from the road above, and out of its direct line of view. Someone had set them at the center of a small, level clearing, then arranged a circle of seven stones around them. Creating a marker only an idiot could miss.

"I think I found him!" Gunner shouted up to Del.

"Hey, you down there! Get up here now!" someone above him barked with authority. It was somebody other than his cousin.

Gunner stepped out to where he could see who the man was, though he already had a good idea. Squinting against the sun, he saw his cousin standing at the edge of the road where he had been earlier, joined now by a uniformed L.A. County Sheriff's deputy. The deputy had his sidearm out and trained at Del's waist as he tried to keep an eye on him and peer down the hill at Gunner at the same time.

Debunking the old myth, the investigator thought, that you could never find a cop when you needed one.

Six hours later, Yolanda McCreary was waiting for him when he got home.

She was sitting in her rental car out front, flipping through the pages of a magazine she had no genuine interest in. She looked like she'd been there a while. She got out of the car the minute he pulled the road-weary Cobra into his driveway and started toward him, giving him no chance to decide ahead of time how he would tell her the bad news. Not that a few more minutes would have made any difference; he'd been trying to solve that problem now since he'd left Castaic Lake and still he hadn't found the right words to say.

So he just came right out and said it: "We think we found your brother's body."

In the worst-case scenario he had pictured of the moment, McCreary would crumble, fall to her knees at the sound of this declaration and refuse to rise, spilling tears on the earth like a steady rain. But nothing as dramatic as all that happened. His client surprised him. All she did was turn her eyes away, bringing a hand to her mouth, and cry in silence. Gunner watched the tears run down her face unabated and said nothing, granting her the right to grieve as she saw fit.

After a while he broke down, said, "Come on inside, I'll get you a drink."

They entered the house and settled in the living room, side by side on Gunner's tattered couch. He offered her a beer, but she shook that off, asked if he had something stronger. He brought her some Crown Royal on ice and kept the beer for himself.

"What happened?" she finally asked.

He told her everything, omitting nothing but the agreement he'd made with the Defenders to win his release from their custody. He said they'd only snatched him to offer Frerotte on a silver platter, hoping the gesture would buy them some time, both with Gunner and the police. McCreary either believed that or never let on that she didn't. All she seemed to care about was the body Gunner had watched a Sheriff's Department anthropological forensics team unearth for the better part of the day.

"Are you sure it was Tommy?"

"We won't be absolutely sure until the coroner's office does a positive ID. But I'm pretty sure it was him, yeah. There was a wallet on the body full of your brother's ID, and the clothes seemed to match the ones I saw in that photograph I told you about, the one I found in Jack Frerotte's house Wednesday night."

McCreary nodded solemnly, bit her lip to keep from crying again. "How long will it take them to do an ID?"

"I don't know. A couple of days, at least. The body was pretty badly decomposed, dental records are all they're gonna have to work with, I'm afraid."

She turned, looked in his eyes directly. "So what now? I mean, what do you plan to do in the meantime?"

Gunner hesitated, disappointed that she'd found it necessary to raise the question now, so soon. Sitting this close to her, confronted yet again with the smoothness of her skin and the fine lines of her body, saying the words he was about to say was the last thing in the world he wanted to do, knowing as he did where it would lead.

"I don't have *any* plans for the meantime. My job is done," he said.

She gave a little laugh, thinking he must be joking. "What?"

"I've done what you paid me to do, Ms. McCreary. The rest is out of my hands."

She shook her head, said, "No."

"You hired me to find out what happened to your brother, and I've done that. You know he's dead, and you know who killed him. Beyond that—"

"That's not enough!"

"It's gonna have to be. I'm a private investigator, not a superhero. One crazy like Jack Frerotte I can handle, but a band of psychos like the Defenders is something else."

"They had my brother murdered, Mr. Gunner!"

"So let the police deal with them. They've reopened your brother's case, as soon as they get Frerotte in custody—"

"To hell with the police! *They* didn't find Tommy, *you* did!" She threw her glass across the room, shattered it against a distant wall, whisky and ice spraying everywhere.

"Now, wait a minute—" Gunner said.

"No, *you* wait a minute," McCreary said, leaping to her feet. "I want those bastards brought down! I don't care what it takes, or how much it costs. And if you don't have the guts to do it for me . . ."

Gunner stood up, took her by the wrist and said, "This isn't about *guts,* sister. It's about *brainpower.* How many fucking attempts on my life do you think your money *pays* for?"

McCreary tore her wrist free, glowered at him with open contempt. "You're a coward," she said.

Gunner was cut to the quick but refused to show it. "Call me what you will. But I'm not going to die for you, I'm sorry."

His client stood there a moment longer, saw in his face it was true, then took off running for the door.

Later that night, she returned.

Gunner had fallen asleep on the couch, depression having given way to exhaustion. He didn't know how many times the doorbell had rung when he finally heard it, opened his eyes onto the ceiling of his dark living room. She stood on the porch when he opened the door and said nothing for a long while. Then:

"May I come in?"

Gunner turned a light on in the living room and pointed her toward the couch, but this time he didn't join her there. He took a seat across from her instead. The clock on his VCR said it was a few minutes past eight, over two hours after she had fled the room earlier.

"I came to apologize," she said. Sounding reluctant, yes, but not altogether insincere.

"Forget it. I'm a big boy."

"No. I was wrong. Technically speaking, the work I hired you to do *is* finished. You don't owe me a thing."

Gunner didn't argue with her, just waited for her to go on.

"But I meant what I said. This isn't over for me. Until the people who put this man Frerotte up to murdering my brother are caught and brought to justice, it never will be."

"Listen," Gunner said. "There's something I haven't told you yet. Something I was hoping I'd never *have* to tell you."

"Yes?"

"It's not just *my* life on the line here. Yours is too. They made that very clear to me. They want us *both* to walk away. Find some comfort in the fact that the man who actually committed your brother's murder will eventually stand trial for it, and leave it at that."

"I can't do that," McCreary said.

"Sure you can. If I can do it, you can."

"Tommy wasn't your brother, Mr. Gunner."

"No. But I'm the one his killers have been stomping on for the last four days. Leaving in burning buildings to die, and poking with needles filled with God knows what. If anybody owes them, Ms. McCreary, it's me, not you."

"And yet you aren't going to do anything about it. You're just going to sit here and pretend none of it ever happened."

"I'm going to leave the apprehension of Frerotte's associates to the proper law enforcement agencies, and trust they're up to the task. That's what I'm going to do."

"I don't believe you."

"You don't *believe* me?"

"I don't believe you're that kind of man. That you're in the habit of letting other people fight your battles for you."

"You don't *know* me, Ms. McCreary," Gunner said.

"I know what I see. What I *feel.*" She stood up, came over to where he was sitting to hover over him. "I read you better than you think, Mr. Gunner."

Gunner looked up at her, tried not to let her proximity derail him. "Yeah?"

"You've wanted to be with me since the day we first met. Haven't you?"

Gunner didn't say anything.

"It hasn't been hard to detect. You're cool, but you're not complicated. I've been picking up your vibe from the start."

"Pardon my French, but that's bullshit."

"You saying it isn't true?"

"I'm saying the question's irrelevant."

"And if the feeling's mutual? Is it irrelevant then?"

Gunner looked up at her, searching her face for hidden motives. "You don't want to play this game with me," he said angrily.

"It's not a game. It's the truth," McCreary said. "Kiss me and you'll see."

Gunner stood up, gave her a long, hard look. "And if I did? You think it'd change anything?" He shook his head. "It'd only make things harder. For both of us."

But McCreary was undeterred. "Show me," she said.

And because she'd made it sound less like an order than a request, like something she needed as badly as he did, Gunner lost interest in arguing with her and did as he was told.

Praying every minute that he wasn't making the mistake of a lifetime.

Embracing the contours of a woman's body with his hands—the narrow corridor along the center of her back, the rounded underside of her breasts and buttocks, the tender hollow at the base of her throat—had always been a major part of Gunner's bedroom repertoire, but with Yolanda McCreary, these movements became more about his own pleasure than hers.

He had had more prolific sex before, sex that both energized and healed him simultaneously, but his experience with McCreary seemed to fill a spiritual void no one had ever touched in him before. He had been in love once, with a woman no longer alive, and the love they had made to each other before their inevitable parting had been warm, fulfilling, and remarkable in its own, unique way—but this went beyond that. This was more powerful and indelible. Almost life affirming.

And the feeling *did* seem to be mutual.

Of course, when their union was over, their world *had* changed, despite Gunner's promises to the contrary. Their relationship suddenly had strings attached, new and fragile though they were: invisible lines of emotion and sensitivity that had not encumbered them before. So while they still wanted the same things—McCreary Gunner's help in bringing her brother's murderers to justice, and Gunner the freedom to respectfully withold it from her—neither could refuse the other quite as easily as they had only hours ago. Life had just become more complicated than that.

One of them was going to have to lose. To surrender his or her position for the sake of keeping the peace between them.

It was either that or the seed they'd just planted was doomed to die before its ultimate potential could ever be known.

14

"We got a call from a guy
Friday night around eight o'clock, he says he witnessed a shooting,"
Poole said at exactly 9:17 Sunday morning. "A kid in a car at the in-
tersection of Exposition and Vermont, late Wednesday."

"I'm listening," Gunner said.

"This caller says he knows who the shooter was. Not his name,
actually, but what the guy looked like, and what kind of car he was
driving."

"What kind of car he was driving? I thought—"

"Hold on a minute and I'll explain," Poole said, making sounds
similar to that of a man moving a telephone handset over to his
other ear. "This caller tells us the shooter rear-ended him about fifteen minutes before Cribbs was shot, going southbound on Hoover
near Twenty-fifth Street. He tried to make a last-minute lane change
and didn't pull it off, slammed right into the caller's brand-new
Mazda.

"So the caller, he jumps out to check the damage, sees this black
giant in a blue sweatsuit step out of a silver Beemer, looking like he
wants to rip the caller's head off for gettin' in his way. He says the guy
had to be six-two, six-three, two-hundred and forty pounds, easy.
Medium to dark complexion, flat-topped haircut, shoulders wider
than a fuckin' movie screen."

This caller should have been a cop, Gunner thought to himself.
Only a camera could have captured Rafe Sweeney more accurately.

"Anyway, they argue for a while, the caller demandin' to see the
big guy's ID, the big guy orderin' the caller to get his fuckin' Mazda

out of the Beemer's way, 'til the big guy finally says *fuck it,* he grabs the caller by the throat and *forces* him to move his car."

"And then takes off."

"You got it."

"Naturally, the caller decides to follow . . ."

"And sees the guy put the hit on Cribbs. Yeah. All he wanted to do was keep the guy in sight until a black-and-white could turn up, and the poor bastard witnesses a carjacking instead."

Poole said the caller watched Sweeney cruise around a while, acting like he was lost, until he reached Jefferson Boulevard and the University Mall, where he suddenly seemed to get his bearings back. Gunner suspected this was merely where Sweeney had caught up to the car he'd been following before his accident—Sly Cribbs's Oldsmobile Cutlass Ciera—and started tailing it again. Unaware, apparently, that Cribbs had been in the mall at the One Hour Foto-Stop shop, dropping off the roll of film Sweeney was no doubt hoping to retrieve.

Had Gil Everson's bodyguard known the film was no longer in Sly's possession, none of what followed would have ever transpired. According to Poole's call-in witness, the big man in the freshly dented BMW had eventually parked his car fifty yards shy of Vermont on Exposition, slipped a ski mask over his head, then scurried on foot over to Sly's Oldsmobile as the kid calmly waited for the light to change. He ordered Sly out of the car, but the teenager wouldn't comply, so he shot him twice at close range before fleeing north along Vermont, still on foot, Sly's camera bag clutched tightly beneath one arm.

Not surprisingly, the man who had witnessed all of this from what he hoped was a safe distance fled the scene himself soon afterward.

"Is that a wild fuckin' story, or what?" Poole asked when he was through recounting it for Gunner.

"Yeah. Wild," Gunner said. "I assume you've run a check on the Beemer by now."

"Sure have. You wanna guess who it belongs to?"

"Rafe Sweeney. Inglewood City Councilman Gil Everson's personal bodyguard."

"Right again. You really *are* an investigator, aren't you, partner?"

"I know you won't believe this, Poole, but I really was going to hand him to you. I just needed a little more time to check him out, make sure he was the guy."

"Of course, of course. It's not like you've ever held out on me before, right?"

"Poole—"

"Save it, cowboy. I ain't been callin' you all weekend just to hear the usual string of lame excuses. All I want from you is the rest of the story. I wanna know what kind of pictures Cribbs was shooting for you, and I wanna know *now.*"

He thought he was demanding something of Gunner the investigator would be loath to surrender, but he couldn't have been more wrong. Gunner was happy to oblige him, now that he could do so feeling relatively certain that Rafe Sweeney deserved the LAPD's attention.

Poole listened quietly to his account of the Everson case, only expressed displeasure of any kind at its conclusion, when Gunner voiced some doubt that Sweeney's attack on Sly Cribbs had been committed at Gil Everson's behest.

"What the fuck do you mean, you don't know?" Poole said.

"I mean I *don't know.* Something about that doesn't quite jibe with me."

"No? Why not?"

"Because the pictures don't seem to be worth that kind of trouble, for one thing. All they show is him and what appears to be a cheap whore doing the nasty. Why the hell would he turn Sweeney loose on Sly over something as innocuous as that?"

"Hard as this may be for you to believe, Gunner, some people still find that kind of shit scandalous. And if some of 'em are registered voters in Everson's district . . ."

"So he'd lose the Bible thumpers' vote. So what? That's fifteen percent of his constituency, tops."

"So maybe his reasons weren't professional."

"Meaning they were personal instead."

"He's a married man, ain't he?"

"By definition he is, yeah. Though you'd never know it to watch him. Because the lady we're talking about isn't his only diversion. He's got a steady girlfriend, too, and he doesn't seem to care who knows it. In fact, if Mickey's any indication, the two of them have been a matter of public record for years."

"And that proves what, exactly?"

"That he doesn't act like a man who fears his wife. What she knows or doesn't know about his extramarital affairs doesn't matter to him."

Poole grew quiet, then took another tack. "Okay. Then maybe he was trying to protect the lady. The prostitute, not the girlfriend. You're sure that's all you can tell me about her? Her first name was Shelby?"

"That and the fact she struck me as somewhat familiar, yeah. I'm not sure why."

"You think Cribbs might know who she is?"

Gunner told him it was certainly possible. Getting Everson's girlfriend's name hadn't been part of his assignment, but Sly was just full of initiative. It wouldn't have been surprising if he'd compiled a mini-dossier on her and Everson both.

Poole snorted, said, "Yeah, well, if he did, he wasn't sharin' it with me. Every time I tried to ask him about the work you had him doing, he dummied up on me, started actin' like he was in too much pain to hear the question or somethin'."

Gunner had to chuckle at that, the idea that he had company in giving Poole a hard time. "Like I said. The kid's got initiative."

"Right. He's a real go-getter. So let's hear your second thing, wiseass."

"My second thing?"

"Your other reason for Everson not 'jibing' with you. You said 'for one thing' a minute ago, remember?"

"Oh. That one's easy. My 'second thing' is, you're not having this conversation with a *corpse.* Everson has Sweeney shoot Sly to retrieve the photographs, then leaves me around to tell you about it? Doesn't sound very likely, Lieutenant."

Poole thought about this a moment, said, "You know what? After careful consideration, I don't give a shit. If the councilman didn't put Sweeney up to hitting Cribbs, he ought'a be able to prove it. In the meantime, Sweeney's mine. Only reason he's not in custody now is, he and Everson are out of town. They're up in—"

"Sacramento," Gunner said. "I know, I talked to the councilman's secretary on Friday."

"Then you know they'll both be back tomorrow. When I'll be waitin' for 'em at the gate at LAX. You feel like ridin' shotgun, you're welcome to come along."

Gunner couldn't believe what he was hearing. Any other time, Poole would be promising him a year in the Gulag if he didn't take his act for a walk. But since Gunner had planned to do something of a more urgent nature with his time Monday . . .

"Or were you thinkin' about helping the boys out in Hollywood work the Covington homicide? Or is that the *Selmon* homicide now?"

Before Poole had explained his reasons for leaving Gunner five phone messages in two days—two at Mickey's, and three at Gunner's residence—he'd demanded to know what had kept the investigator from answering any one of them until now. So Gunner had told him: Friday, he'd been meeting the Defenders of the Bloodline up close and personal, and Saturday he'd been watching the L.A. County Sheriff's Department exhume Thomas Selmon's body.

"Actually, Poole, I—"

"Forget about it. They wouldn't appreciate the assistance, I can assure you."

"No, probably not, but—"

"You said you already gave 'em a statement, right? Yesterday, out at the grave site?"

"Yeah, but—"

"Then they already know what they need to know to work the case on their own, without any interference from you. Don't they?"

Knowing the question was one Gunner could only answer one way, Poole didn't bother to wait for a response, just asked the investigator one more time what it was going to be: Did he want to ride shotgun when Poole picked up Sweeney and Everson or not?

Gunner said he did.

Monday morning, Southwest Airlines Flight #313 arrived at Los Angeles International Airport from Sacramento, California, a little over five minutes early, just before 11:00 A.M., and Councilman Gil Everson was among the forty-seven passengers aboard. His bodyguard, Rafe Sweeney, however, was not.

"Mr. Sweeney is no longer in my employ," Everson said calmly when Poole and Gunner inquired about him. Poole looked like a boiler on the brink of exploding.

"What the hell does that mean?" the detective asked.

"It means I fired him. What do you think it means?" He was talking to Poole, but his eyes kept cutting over to Gunner, the actual focal point of his rising anger.

"Fired him for what? When?"

"In Sacramento. Saturday night. Look, what the hell is this all about?"

They were still standing at the gate he'd emerged from, the crowded terminal buzzing with activity around them, and Everson was clearly concerned that someone watching might recognize Poole for what he was: a policeman intent on questioning him.

"Where is Mr. Sweeney now, Councilman?" Poole asked, ignoring Everson's question.

"I have no idea. He checked out of our hotel immediately after I let him go. I assumed he flew back here."

"Shit!" Poole said.

"Are you going to tell me what this is all about, or do I have to guess?"

"We might want to talk about this somewhere a little more private," Gunner said, speaking to Everson for the first time.

"Like my office at City Hall, you mean? Not a chance, Mr. Gunner. Not until I hear what it is you gentlemen want with me."

Gunner looked at Poole, who glanced around quickly, said, "Looks pretty deserted over by terminal five. Come on."

The trio crossed over to the empty terminal, Poole leading the way, where the aircraft beyond the glass walls there stood to be the only possible witnesses to their discussion.

"Well?" Everson asked.

"He knows about the photographs, Councilman," Gunner said. "He knows everything I know, and maybe a little more."

Everson flinched once, but only once. "I don't understand."

"We've got a witness who says it was Sweeney who shot Mr. Gunner's assistant last Wednesday night," Poole said, "and we know it was you who put him up to it."

"What?"

"We talked about it at the Acey Deuce Thursday, remember?" Gunner said. "The carjacker who capped my young photographer friend? That was your boy Rafe."

"Rafe? I don't—"

"Like I said. We've got a witness," Poole said.

Everson closed his mouth, let whatever he was about to say die on the vine.

"You must have wanted those photos back pretty bad," Poole told him.

"That is an outrageous accusation! I had nothing to do with Rafe shooting that kid!"

"No?"

"No! I wanted those photos back, yes, but—" He cut himself off in mid-sentence, as if he'd been close to admitting something he'd only regret later.

Poole turned to Gunner, said, "Here it comes."

"I'm sorry, gentlemen, but I don't think I'll say anything further without an attorney present," Everson said.

Poole shrugged, so accustomed to hearing the words, they only barely disgusted him now. "Your call, Councilman," he said.

Gunner never actually read it, he only had its general content described to him by Poole, but the official transcript of Gil Everson's interrogation down at Parker Center that afternoon went something like this, shortly after Poole had introduced all of the parties involved:

POOLE: *Were you aware that Rafe Sweeney committed an aggravated assault against a young man named Sly Cribbs, late last Wednesday night?*

EVERSON: *No, I was not.*

POOLE: *Mr. Sweeney did not commit that assault on your behalf?*

EVERSON: *No, he did not.*

POOLE: *You didn't instruct him to retrieve the photographs Mr. Cribbs had taken of you and a female acquaintance earlier that evening by any means necessary?*

EVERSON: *Absolutely not. No.*

POOLE: *Who was that female acquaintance, Councilman?*

(a beat)

EVERSON: *No one. Just a friend.*

POOLE: *A friend?*

EVERSON: *Yes. A friend.*

POOLE: *You don't recall her name?*

EVERSON: *I . . . her name is Shelby. It* was *Shelby.*

POOLE: Was? I don't—

EVERSON: I only saw her that once, and all she gave me was her first name.

POOLE: She was a one-night stand?

EVERSON: Yes.

POOLE: Where did you two meet?

EVERSON: At the hotel. That afternoon, at lunch.

POOLE: The Marina Pacific Hotel?

EVERSON: Yes. How—

POOLE: We took a second statement from Mr. Cribbs about an hour ago, he told us that was where the photographs were taken. The Marina Pacific Hotel in Marina Del Rey.

(Everson does not respond.)

POOLE: Are you always in the habit of picking up strange women at the hotels you visit, Councilman?

DAVID GOLDBLUM *(Everson's attorney)*: I'm sorry, Detective, but that question is out of line.

POOLE: I was merely wondering if a pattern of such behavior exists for the man, Counselor.

GOLDBLUM: The relevance being?

POOLE: The relevance being that his wife seemed to know over two weeks ago that he might indulge himself in this manner. It's been that long since she hired Mr. Cribbs's employer, a local private investigator named Aaron Gunner, to provide her with photographic evidence to the effect that your client was doing the do with a prostitute of this Shelby woman's general description.

(Goldblum and Everson confer for a moment.)

EVERSON: My wife and I have been married now for almost thirteen years, Detective. She knows my likes and dislikes pretty well.

POOLE: In other words, it's a thing with you. Picking up prostitutes.

EVERSON: Yes.

POOLE: Prostitutes with a limp.

EVERSON: A limp?

POOLE: Your wife also suggested your friend would have a pronounced limp. Ms. Shelby doesn't?

(Everson does not respond.)

POOLE: Councilman?

EVERSON: I didn't notice if she limped or not. I'm sorry.

POOLE: What about drugs? Did you notice if she used any drugs while you were together? A little crack cocaine, or some heroin, perhaps?

EVERSON: No. Certainly not.

POOLE: And again, you never saw this lady before your meeting Wednesday.

EVERSON: No.

POOLE: Or after.

EVERSON: No. Never.

POOLE: Then you wouldn't know where we could find her today, I guess.

EVERSON: No, I would not.

POOLE: Were you aware that Mr. Cribbs had photographed the two of you together that evening, Councilman?

EVERSON: That evening? Do you mean—

POOLE: Did you know that same night that you and the lady had been photographed together?

EVERSON: No, I did not. I didn't know anything about the photographs until Gunner left one of them on my car the following day. Thursday.

POOLE: You didn't know Cribbs had taken them the night before?

EVERSON: No. I told you.

POOLE: Then Mr. Sweeney discovered this on his own that night. And took it upon himself to follow Mr. Cribbs from the hotel in order to get them back.

(Everson and Goldblum confer again.)

GOLDBLUM: *Mr. Everson can only assume that that is the case, based solely upon what you're telling him Mr. Sweeney has done.*

POOLE: *I see. Can Mr. Everson offer any explanation for Sweeney taking such drastic action so independent of his instruction, Counselor?*

GOLDBLUM: *Having no prior knowledge of Mr. Sweeney's intent, and being no more capable of reading the man's mind than you or I? No, he cannot, Detective, I'm sorry.*

POOLE: *(to Everson): But you can venture a guess, can't you?*

EVERSON: *Rafe always took his work very seriously. He probably thought he was doing me a favor.*

POOLE: *By shooting a seventeen-year-old kid.*

EVERSON: *By keeping him from using the photographs against me in some way.*

POOLE: *Like in a divorce action, for instance?*

EVERSON: *A divorce action? (shakes his head) No.*

POOLE: *You weren't afraid your wife might use the photographs against you in divorce court, Councilman?*

EVERSON: *First of all, as I've said several times now, I didn't know anything about the photographs. But if I had, I wouldn't have been concerned about Connie using them against me in divorce court, no.*

POOLE: *No? Why not?*

(a beat)

EVERSON: *Because we signed a prenuptial agreement before we were married. It would have done Connie no good to try and use those photographs against me.*

POOLE: *A prenuptial agreement?*

EVERSON: *Yes. Fifty thousand dollars is the most Connie could get if she ever filed divorce proceedings against me.*

POOLE: *Fifty thousand dollars?*

EVERSON: *Not a penny more, not a penny less.*

POOLE: *Even if you—*

EVERSON: *Committed adultery? Yes, Detective. Even then.*

(After a long beat)

POOLE: *Okay. Let's forget the prenuptial agreement and get back to Sweeney for a moment.*

EVERSON: *What about him?*

POOLE: *It's your contention that he retrieved the photographs from Mr. Cribbs on his own. Without your knowledge or consent.*

EVERSON: *Yes. Apparently.*

POOLE: *You're telling me he's that gung ho?*

EVERSON: *He can be, yes.*

POOLE: *Is that why you fired him? For being too gung ho?*

EVERSON: *I don't . . .*

POOLE: *Let me rephrase the question. Did you fire Mr. Sweeney in response to his assault on Mr. Cribbs?*

EVERSON: *No. I didn't know anything about any assault on Mr. Cribbs.*

POOLE: *You didn't?*

EVERSON: *No. I told you.*

POOLE: *Sweeney didn't simply overreact to your instructions to get the film in Cribbs's camera back for you?*

EVERSON: *No. I never told Rafe to go get anything back for me that night.*

POOLE: *Then why was he fired, Councilman?*

(Everson does not respond.)

POOLE: *What did he do in Sacramento so terrible that you couldn't wait two days to give him his pink slip here in Los Angeles?*

EVERSON: *I'd rather not answer that. That's a private matter between Rafe and myself.*

POOLE: *Excuse me?*

EVERSON: *I had reason to believe he couldn't be trusted anymore, so I let him go. It's that simple.*

POOLE: *He couldn't be trusted anymore? Trusted how, Mr. Everson?*

(Everson does not respond.)

POOLE: *Did you suddenly begin to doubt his abilities to protect you as a security man? Was that it?*

EVERSON: *No. It wasn't . . . it didn't have anything to do with that. His professional duties.*

POOLE: *Then what* did *it have to do with?*

(Everson does not respond.)

POOLE: *It wouldn't have had anything to do with a woman, would it?*

EVERSON: *I told you. I'd rather not say.*

POOLE: *Was he shtupping your wife, maybe? Could that've been it?*

GOLDBLUM: *All right, Detective. Enough, already. I believe the question you've been trying to get to here is whether or not Mr. Sweeney's firing had anything to do with the photographs you allege he assaulted Mr. Cribbs to retrieve, and the answer is no. Let's move on, please.*

POOLE: *After your client gives me a simple yes or no answer to one question, Counselor. (To Everson:) Were Mr. Sweeney and your wife having an affair?*

(a beat)

EVERSON: *Don't ask me. Ask* her.

POOLE: *I think we'll do that, Councilman. Thanks for the tip.*

The transcript came to an end shortly thereafter.

Poole learned almost immediately following his interrogation of Gil Everson that Rafe Sweeney had indeed returned to Los Angeles from Sacramento Sunday afternoon. He'd been booked on an American Airlines flight that had touched down at Burbank Airport in the San Fernando Valley just a few minutes after its scheduled arrival time of 2:45. Only Sweeney had not gone home. Poole and Gunner went looking for him at his Studio City apartment and found it unoccupied, his banged-up BMW missing from its parking space.

When they decided to ask Connie Everson if she and Sweeney had been lovers, as her husband had suggested Poole should, they discovered that she, too, was not home. But unlike Sweeney, her whereabouts were not exactly unknown.

For a few minutes past 12:30 that afternoon, toward the end of Poole's vigorous questioning of her husband downtown, Gil Everson's wife had been found dead at the foot of her bed by the family housekeeper, the victim of an apparent drug overdose. A later autopsy would reveal that she had consumed a deadly cocktail of phenobarbital and vodka over eleven hours earlier, a recipe for suicide she could have mistaken for nothing else.

No note explaining her motives was ever found.

15

The LAPD wasn't crazy about reacquiring the Thomas Selmon missing person–turned-homicide case, but they had taken it off the Sheriff's Department's hands in deference to proper protocol. The two Hollywood Division detectives assigned to the case were named Moreno and Loiacano. Gunner had spoken to them both out on San Francisquito Canyon Road late Saturday afternoon. He didn't know Moreno, but he and Loiacano had met once before, when Loiacano's partner had been a far less likable man than Moreno appeared to be. Perhaps this was why Loiacano took the time to call Gunner at Mickey's Monday afternoon to leave him a brief message.

"He said he just thought you'd like to know," Mickey said when Gunner used the phone on Matt Poole's desk to check in. "Barber Jack's on the loose. And so is somebody named Byron Scales."

"What?"

"He said they went out to the hospital for Jack yesterday morning and he wasn't there. He checked himself out Saturday night without anybody knowing, they don't know where he is."

"Jesus."

"Yeah. And when they went to get this guy Scales, whoever he is, they found his apartment cleaned out. He's missin', too."

Gunner ran a hand across the top of his scalp, said, "Great. Just great."

"Scales I don't know about, but Jack I know is trouble. I hope the fool's smart enough to know, he comes over here lookin' for *me,* I'm gonna take my bat and bust his fuckin' head open first, ask him if he'd like a little cream in his coffee later."

"If he shows up over there, Mickey, it won't be to see you," Gunner said. "But do me a favor: Bust his shit open anyway, will you? Just to give me one less thing to worry about for a while?"

"Wish I could tell you that's all the bad news I've got for you, man, but there's one more thing."

"Damn."

"You also had a couple of visitors this mornin'. One white and one black, both of 'em wearin' suits and ties. I'll let you guess what company they work for."

"Don't tell me they were Feds."

"They left their business cards. I'm lookin' at 'em now. 'Federal Bureau of Investigation,' agents Leffman and Smith. Smith was the black one, he did all the talkin'."

"What the hell do the Feds want with *me*?"

"They didn't say. They just said to have you give 'em a call as soon as I heard from you. You want the number?"

Gunner said no, he'd get it from him later. Whatever Leffman and Smith wanted, it would have to wait. Gunner's dance card was all full.

"The Feds, huh?" Poole asked when Gunner hung up the phone. "How nice." He grinned and threw himself back in his chair, more at ease being an asshole here at his Southwest Division digs than he was almost anywhere else.

"Connie Everson didn't kill herself, Poole," Gunner said, trying to restart the conversation he and the cop had been having before he'd paused to call Mickey.

"Are we back on that again?"

"She was an unhappily married woman. Not a manic depressive. She didn't fit the profile."

"Gimme a break. Women like Mrs. Everson commit suicide every day. You think *you'd* wanna live being married to a prince like the councilman?"

"So her husband was a philanderer who liked to play john every now and then. By all appearances, she'd known that for a long time. Why the urgency to end it all now?"

"Embarrassment. Humiliation. Guilt. She was, in a way, responsible for all those holes Sweeney put in Cribbs's chest Wednesday night, right?"

"Yeah, but—"

"And she'd just suffered one hell of a setback. If you and Cribbs had come through with those pictures for her, she might've been able to divorce the good councilman and keep her account open at Neiman-Marcus, too. That prenup she signed be damned."

"What do you mean, the prenup be damned? If it wasn't invalidated by adultery—"

"Who said anything about it being invalidated? I'm talkin' about it bein' torn up. Rolled into a little ball and run through Gil Everson's shredder by Everson himself, no less."

"You just lost me, Poole."

"The word is 'blackmail,' Gunner. It's usually committed for money, but not always. Sometimes the person holding all the dirty pictures is after something else. Like a fair and equitable divorce settlement, for instance."

Gunner thought that over for a minute, then shook his head. "No. I don't think so."

"Look. I'm not sayin' that's what happened, but the lady had to've had *some* reason for wantin' those photographs taken, right? Otherwise, it was all for nothin', which it ended up bein' anyway. So . . ." Poole pantomimed the act of pouring something down his throat.

"I hear what you're saying, Lieutenant, and I can't say it doesn't make a little sense," Gunner said. "But . . ."

"Something doesn't 'jibe' again."

"That's right. Something doesn't."

Poole watched him scribble aimlessly on a corner of the blotter on his desk, finally sighed and said, "Okay, 'Marlowe.' What is it, then?"

"I don't know," Gunner said.

"You don't *know*?"

"I can't figure it. Not yet. But I will. Give me time."

"Time, huh?" Poole sat up in his chair, lowered his voice curiously.

"Well, don't look now, pal, but I think you just ran outta all yours." He nodded his head once, urging Gunner to turn around.

Two men in blue suits were walking leisurely toward the detective's desk, one black, one white. They were physically dissimilar in every way, but their faces bore the same unmistakable stamp of humorlessness all civil servants succumbed to sooner or later.

There would be much rejoicing in the hallowed halls of the FBI this evening, Gunner thought. Agents Smith and Leffman had found their man.

Carroll Smith looked like a baby, fresh out of training; skin as smooth and brown as kid leather, eyes round and unblinking, a voice like that of a nine-year-old trying to play grown-up. If he was a day over twenty-seven, it didn't show. Irv Leffman, on the other hand, was growing old fast. Heavyset, pink skinned, and full of nervous twitches, he could have passed for someone forty-five to fifty without an ounce of effort. The hair was all but gone on his toaster-shaped head, and his face was a road map of worry. He was nobody's grandfather, but he would have made a fine stand-in for one in a pinch.

Poole had found an empty office at Southwest, somewhere for the two Federal agents and Gunner to retire to, showing more kindness to the Feds than Gunner had ever seen him express before. The space was better than an interrogation room, at least from Gunner's perspective, but one of the fluorescent lamps overhead kept blinking on and off intermittently, something Gunner found almost as annoying as having a strobe light trained on his face.

"Now that we all know each other, Mr. Gunner," Smith said, after all the IDs had been flashed and names exchanged, "we'll get right down to the reason we're here today."

"Please do."

"Tell us what you know about the Defenders of the Bloodline."

Gunner hadn't really needed him to make the formal request—it had dawned on him that this was what they wanted the minute he'd seen the pair marching through the station house toward Poole's desk.

"The Defenders of the Bloodline?"

"We have it on good authority you've recently had an encounter with some people who refer to themselves by that name. That isn't true?"

Gunner shrugged. "I guess it's true enough. But I didn't think they rated this kind of interest."

"They didn't present themselves as a nationwide band of political assassins?"

"Actually, they did."

"But you didn't believe them."

"I wasn't convinced all their talk was for real, no."

"I see. Well. Just for the record, Mr. Gunner, the Defenders of the Bloodline have murdered two people that we know of for certain so far, and a man named Thomas Selmon may yet make three. Is that 'real' enough for you?"

Gunner didn't say anything.

"We'd like to hear the details of your experience with them," Leffman said. Mickey had been right about Smith being the talker between these two, but Smith's partner liked to speak up every now and then, just to prove he wasn't mute.

"Tell me who your good authority is, first," Gunner said.

"Our what?" Smith asked.

"You said you had it on good authority I'd had an encounter with the Defenders."

"I did?"

"I'd like to know who it was."

"Is that important?"

"It is to me. I'm curious that way."

"You understand we're under no obligation to tell you?"

"Sure. Same way you understand I'm under no obligation not to get up and walk the hell out of here."

Smith conceded the point by way of actually smiling. "We've asked local authorities from coast to coast to keep an eye and an ear out for any cases that may relate to the Defenders. Since the group is considered by most of these authorities to be a joke and little else, few take our request seriously. No one claiming to be a Defender has ever been identified, after all. Still, there's a few law officers out there who listen when the FBI speaks. Some of them work here in Los Angeles. Out of any number of divisions. Southwest, Rampart—"

"Hollywood," Gunner offered.

"Exactly. Does that answer your question, Mr. Gunner?"

"I think so." Gunner tried to decide which of the two Hollywood Division detectives he'd talked to Saturday out at the Thomas Selmon grave site—Denny Loiacano, or Loiacano's affable partner, Sal Moreno—he could see most easily running home afterward to call the local FBI office with a hot tip, and settled on Moreno. Not because Loiacano wouldn't do such a thing, but because, now that Gunner stopped to think about it, Moreno might not have been "affable" at all—just eager to please. Some cops were like that.

"Good," Smith said. "Let's talk."

They kept him there for over an hour. He told them the story of his Friday kidnapping once, twice, then answered all the questions they could think of that back-to-back recountings of the event had somehow left for them. He held nothing back, all too aware that there would be no point—he was part of the manhunt for the Defenders now, whether he wanted to be or not.

"You cut a deal with them for your release?" Smith asked.

"In a way, yeah," Gunner said. "But I don't think that was the only reason they let me go."

"No? What other reason was there?"

"If the man I spoke to can be believed, they don't think of themselves as simple murderers. The people they reserve for killing fit a very specific profile, and they're reluctant to expand beyond it, apparently."

"But they would have killed you anyway if you hadn't promised to back off," Leffman said, his disapproval evident.

"Maybe. Maybe not. I guess I should have tested them to see, huh?"

"But you *were* bluffing," Smith said.

"Insofar as I had no intention of just looking the other way. I thought for once in my life, I'd just hand the cops the ball and let them run with it."

"And if we require you to do more than that now? Can we count on you to cooperate?"

"Cooperate how?"

"We need a worm on a hook," Leffman said straightforwardly. "You're the first person we've seen get this close to them and live to tell about it. They must like you for some reason."

"Hey, I'm a likable guy. What of it?"

"We think they'll approach you again," Smith said. "Either to court you for membership, or kill you for lying to them. We want to be there when they do."

"Lying to them? Who says I lied to them? If they've been paying attention, I haven't moved a muscle on the Selmon case. Every cop I've been with since Friday has come to *me,* not the other way around."

"True. But I think you'll admit that's a very fine distinction. It's possible they'll fail to recognize it, and if they do—"

"Hold it, hold it. They aren't gonna 'fail to recognize it' unless somebody *helps* them to. And who the hell would do a fucked-up thing like that?"

Smith fell silent, and so did Leffman.

"Yeah. That's what I thought," Gunner said.

"With or without our assistance, we believe they'll decide that you've broken the deal you made with them, and can no longer be thought of as a neutral party," Smith said. "If not today, then tomorrow. Or three weeks from now. Paranoia's going to set in eventually, and they're going to come after you when it does. Wouldn't you be better off letting us accelerate the process so that somebody's watching your back when they make their move?"

"If I could trust you to watch my back? Maybe. But I can't. I don't know you guys that well, I'm sorry."

"But you don't—"

"Look. What the hell do you need with me? I gave you all the leads you could possibly want. Scales and Pritchard, right? The brother over at Empowerment Printing? Why don't you go talk to him, see if *he* wants to be your goddamn 'worm on a hook'?"

"We've already determined that Mr. Pritchard can't help us. We questioned him this morning, his only link to the Defenders is apparently Scales, for whom he had a phone number and nothing else."

"So concentrate on Scales, then. He's bound to turn up eventually."

"Somebody's already told you he's gone missing?"

"Guess I've got friends in Hollywood, too."

The two Federal officers shared a glance, made a joint mental note to find out who the leak was in their otherwise airtight ship.

"We could wait for Scales to reappear, sure," Leffman said. "But that could take time. And these people are murderers, Gunner, no matter how you slice it. Being discriminating in their choice of targets doesn't change that."

"So what do you want from me? Just spell it out, boys, I won't laugh."

"We want you to work the case again," Smith said. "Rather than lie back like you've been doing, let them see you at least going through the motions of trying to hunt them down, Scales in particular."

"You'll be under surveillance twenty-four-seven," Leffman added. "You'll be in no danger whatsoever."

"Now there's a comforting thought."

"You'll be at some risk, of course," Smith said. "But we're convinced you would be, regardless. This way, at least, you won't have to worry about having eyes in the back of your head. We'll be those eyes for you."

"And if I don't feel like playing along? If I say you're free to watch me as long as you want, but I've got better things to do with my time than *pretend* to be working a case?"

Smith smiled again and shook his head. "Come on, Gunner. We're the dreaded 'Feds.' You don't really think you have that alternative, do you?"

Leffman first chuckled, then began to laugh outright, unable to contain himself. Smith joined in right after him. The FBI wasn't known for its sense of humor, but these two would have made a good start to a great party.

And Gunner had to give them credit for one other thing: They knew how to tell it like it was.

16

For the next day and a half, Gunner went along with the program.

He went back to Byron Scales's empty apartment in Windsor Hills and made a show of peering through its windows, as if he didn't know Scales had abandoned the premises long ago. He revisited the Stage Door Motel to hassle the fat man at the counter, demanding to know where Scales, a.k.a. Blue, was presently holed up. He even made a second run to Empowerment Printing, looking for Clive Pritchard, and acted like he was disappointed when someone he'd never seen before told him Pritchard didn't work there anymore. Gunner did everything possible to portray a man bound and determined to turn Scales up, driving his red Cobra from one end of the city to the next, and he did it all knowing he had more to fear than just Scales and the Defenders of the Bloodline.

For Jack Frerotte and Rafe Sweeney could have just as easily been watching him as the Defenders, and both had their own reasons to wish the investigator harm. Despite the unmarked FBI sedan that was diligently following his every move, its drivers so good at doing surveillance, he himself could hardly tell they were there, Gunner was uncomfortable enough playing clay pigeon to three separate, hostile parties that he found it necessary to make his own preparations for disaster; little tricks of the trade he had learned to fall back on in anticipation of worst case scenarios.

And it was all for nothing.

Because by 4 o'clock Tuesday afternoon, no one had made a move toward Gunner. Either because they were too smart to take the bait, or because their vow to watch him had been empty, Scales and the Defenders of the Bloodline never once showed themselves, and neither did Frerotte nor Sweeney. Smith and Leffman's "worm on the hook" had failed to get a bite, and Gunner wanted off the line. Had Smith not greeted him with good news when he checked in with the FBI man shortly before 5 o'clock, he would have said anything he had to to get the Feds out of his life again.

The pay phone connection wasn't the best, so Smith had to repeat himself before Gunner was sure he'd heard him correctly the first time.

"We've got 'im," Smith said again.

"Scales?"

"He turned up at an aunt's place in Plainview, Texas. Alone. He'll fly back tonight for questioning in the morning."

"And the others?"

"No word on any others yet. As you might imagine, Scales isn't saying much. We're hoping that'll change."

"And if it doesn't?"

"If you're asking whether or not we're prepared to continue our surveillance of you indefinitely, Gunner, the answer is no. We're not. The objective was to get our hands on a Defender. That objective has been met. On behalf of Agent Leffman and the entire bureau, I'd like to thank you for your cooperation and wish you a pleasant day."

Gunner didn't think it was funny, being used and discarded like a disposable diaper, but he had to make light of it or take serious offense, go see Smith in person to loosen a few of his teeth.

"You forgot something, didn't you?"

"What's that?"

"My hearty handshake."

The FBI man hung up.

Gunner left the pay phone he was using and went straight in to Mickey's, both to unwind and pick up his dog, the latter something his landlord and Winnie had been on him about since Saturday. Winnie had the crazy idea little Dillett could help protect him somehow in this time of imminent danger; Mickey just wanted the animal out of his shop. Somewhere around Imperial Highway and Avalon, less than five miles from his office at Mickey's, Gunner saw the ubiquitous unmarked sedan peel off behind him, never to be seen again. Those relentless watchdogs of the American taxpayer's money, Smith and Leffman, apparently worked fast.

Gunner put a call in to Yolanda McCreary as soon as he reached his desk, not having seen her now for over twenty-four hours. They'd been together nonstop from Saturday evening to Monday morning, when he'd left the house to meet Gil Everson's plane at LAX with Matt Poole, but once he'd started work trying to draw the Defenders' fire for the FBI, he'd deliberately steered clear of her. He sent her back to her hotel room and told her to stay put, hold onto the key to his home he'd given her sometime Sunday until he gave her the okay to use it. They had spoken over the phone two or three times since then, but that was all.

Now, he couldn't even reach her that way. No one answered his call when he rang her hotel room.

His heart sank. He slouched back in his chair, riding himself for calling at the exact moment she'd left her room to eat, or something—and then stopped, suddenly realizing what he was doing. He'd known McCreary for all of eight days—*and he'd given her a key to his home!* What the hell had he been thinking? Being alone had been wearing thin on him lately, it was true—his last long-term relationship with a woman had crashed and burned more than fourteen months ago—but that could hardly excuse a fall of this magnitude. McCreary had blindsided him, no less so than Byron Scales had down in Johnny Frerotte's basement—assuming that *had* been Scales—and now he was left to wonder whether her effect on him would prove permanent or merely temporary.

He considered the question quietly for a while, finally had to admit to himself that he was hoping for the former.

No messages had been waiting for him from either Poole or Denny Loiacano, so it seemed safe to assume that both Frerotte and Rafe Sweeney were still at large, but Gunner placed a call to Poole at Southwest just the same, just in case Sweeney had in fact been picked up and the cop was simply too busy to let Gunner know about it.

"Not a chance," Poole said, after he'd heard how Gunner's work for the Feds had ended.

"Everson's story still the same?"

"Yeah. Why shouldn't it be? He's in the clear as long as Sweeney's not around to point the finger at 'im. And his old lady's suicide still looks like a suicide."

"What about his girlfriend? The working girl?"

"We're still tryin' to find her. The people at the Marina Pacific remember seein' her, all right, but that's it. They say she wasn't a guest there, and they never saw her and Everson together. If she stayed overnight, they say it had to be in one of the two suites Sweeney registered in earlier that day."

"Sweeney?"

"Yeah. It was his name and credit card on the books, not Everson's. The councilman's got a reputation to protect, remember?"

Gunner fell silent.

"Bottom line is, we need Sweeney to put it all together for us," Poole said. "Without him—"

"So what are you doing talking to me? Get out there and find his ass, already," Gunner said.

"What, you worried he might hold a grudge or somethin'?"

"Let's just say I'd feel better walking the dog tonight if you had him under lock and key."

"Dog? You got a dog, Gunner?"

"It was just a figure of speech, Poole. But yeah, I've got a dog."

"What, an attack dog? Tell me you got an attack dog."

"Close. It's a Rhodesian Ridgeback."

"A Rhodesian Ridgeback? Does it know how to fire a Tec-Nine?" He laughed. " 'Cause if you were thinkin' of siccin' it on Sweeney *without* one . . ."

Gunner hung up the phone on the would-be stand-up comedian and went to find his dog.

Johnny Frerotte was sitting on the living room couch when Gunner walked in.

Dillett was the first to notice him. The little dog scurried into the house and immediately went to the couch, where Yolanda McCreary was sitting on the floor between the big man's legs, a large kitchen knife being held to her throat. Its blade was actually drawing blood.

"Get that . . . fucking dog . . . out of here," Frerotte said, referring to the animal now standing in McCreary's lap, excitedly yapping at his legs.

As he had out at Martin Luther King Memorial Hospital four days ago, Frerotte still sounded like an emphysema victim with a plastic bag over his head, and he was still wearing the shoulder harness and neck brace his doctors had fitted him with. Left arm bound uselessly to his chest, his field of vision seriously limited by the neck brace, the big man sported a two-day growth of stubble on his face, uncombed hair, disheveled clothing—and a stench not unlike that which might have emanated from a sun-ripened lump of roadkill.

"You don't look so good, Jack," Gunner said.

"I said put . . . put this . . . goddamn dog away!" Frerotte tried to bark. He brought the knife up higher on McCreary's throat, forced her to tilt her head back and eye the ceiling to avoid being cut.

"Aaron . . ." McCreary moaned, tears rolling down her face.

Gunner called the dog by name, followed the command with a whistle, silently ruing the absence of men who had only hours ago been standing guard outside, waiting to protect him from just such an ambush as this. If only Carroll Smith had been good enough to extend the FBI's surveillance on him for the remainder of the day . . .

Dillett turned at the sound of his name, started trotting back over to his master. Gunner was amazed. He held the door to the closet behind him open, shooed the little Ridgeback in with his foot, and closed the door again. Predictably, the dog began to bark incessantly in response to this indignity.

"Now," Frerotte said, "get your . . . piece out and . . . and toss it over here to . . . the girl. *Easy.*"

No surprise there. He was going to need a gun eventually, otherwise he was in no shape to kill Gunner and McCreary both.

Gunner slid the Ruger out of its holster with his right hand, slowly, so that Frerotte might see he had no intention of using it. It didn't take a genius to see that there was nothing he could do with the gun from here that could keep Frerotte from cutting McCreary's throat, even if only as a dying man's final reflex action.

He tossed the weapon underhand to McCreary, who caught it clumsily with both hands.

"Better tell her . . . what'll happen if . . . she tries to use that . . . thing on *me,*" Frerotte suggested.

And Gunner shook his head at her, having had the same thought as Frerotte. "Don't try anything," he said sternly. "He'd only need a split second. I'd never get to you in time."

"Damn straight," Frerotte said.

Dillett's barking was becoming harder and harder to ignore.

"Put the gun . . . down on the couch be . . . beside me," Frerotte told McCreary. "Over on my . . . right side."

McCreary did as she was told, reaching back behind her to lay the Ruger flat on the cushion next to the fat man's thigh.

"Now, get up real . . . slow, and don't . . . turn around. Just start walkin'. You turn around I'll . . . I'll put this fuckin' knife . . . in your *back!*"

Again, McCreary complied, rising carefully to her feet, barely breathing as the knife slid down and away from her throat, first between her shoulder blades, then on to the small of her back. All the while, Frerotte's eyes were pinned to Gunner, daring him to make a move. Wisely, Gunner never did.

"Go," Frerotte said.

McCreary eased forward now, toward Gunner, and Frerotte quickly exchanged the knife in his hand for Gunner's gun, using the woman's body as a shield for the maneuver, executing it flawlessly before the investigator could even think about stopping him. McCreary reached Gunner and turned around, found Frerotte grinning, training the Ruger at their faces with unabashed malice.

"Let her go, Jack," Gunner said. "You've got nothing to gain by killing her."

"Bullshit. Wouldn't none of us . . . be here . . . if it wasn't for her," Frerotte said.

"You cut her brother's throat and buried him in a hole out in the Angeles National Forest. She wasn't supposed to care about that?"

Frerotte frowned, unpleasantly surprised. "Who the hell—"

"The Defenders gave you up, Jack. They led me to the grave site in exchange for a little breathing room. I get Selmon's body, and they get a head start out of Dodge."

After a long pause: "You're lying."

Gunner shook his head. "You were a hired gun. Not a dues-paying member of the club. How much loyalty from those crazies did you expect?"

The big man ignored the question, asked one of his own, instead. "Where's the . . . body now?"

"With the county coroner. Where else would it be?"

Frerotte just stared at him, his already grim countenance darkening rapidly. "You stupid . . . motherfucker," he said.

"Don't blame me. Blame your boys."

"I blame *you*! You've fucked up . . . everything! And you're too damn . . . ignorant to know it!"

The little Ridgeback in the closet was mixing whimpers and howls in with all the yapping now, just for the sake of variety.

"Biggest payday I was . . . ever gonna have," Frerotte lamented. Sounding like somebody who had just watched a mugger run off with his winning lottery ticket.

"What are you talking about, Jack?" Gunner asked.

"I'm talking about . . . *a hundred and fifty . . . grand,* god-damnit!" He turned toward the closet, said, "Tell that . . . fucking dog to . . . shut the fuck up!"

"A hundred and fifty grand? How? For what?"

"Doesn't matter now. It's . . . over." He lifted the Ruger, pointed it directly at Gunner's head. "And so are *you.*"

He pulled the trigger as McCreary began to scream.

When nothing happened, the big man panicked, uncomprehending. His confusion lasted all of three seconds, but that was enough to ruin him. Perhaps if he'd had a clearer head, had the room been silent, and not filled with the continual, nerve-jarring cries of an eleven-week-old puppy, he would have recognized what was wrong immediately, and recovered in time to save himself. But he didn't.

He tried to fire the gun again, once more failing miserably, giving Gunner the chance to reach behind his back and withdraw the .45 caliber Para-Ordinance P10 that had been resting against his spine, in the waistband of his pants, for most of the last two days. Eschewing preamble of any kind, Gunner put three rounds in Frerotte's upper body as fast as he could get them off, then braced himself to fire three more, if needed.

Frerotte fell back, bleeding all over the couch, before sliding to the floor and collapsing on his face. He died with Gunner's 9-millimeter automatic still clutched in his right hand. Fully loaded and fully functional, but useless to him, all the same.

As it would have been to anyone, Gunner mused, who'd forgotten to take its safety off.

17

"Poole says this is a regular thing with you," Denny Loiacano said, hanging up Gunner's phone.

"That's a gross exaggeration."

"Somehow, I don't think so. This makes two bodies in four days, Gunner. Fatality rates don't come much higher than that."

Gunner kept waiting for the cop to smile, but Loiacano wasn't trying to be amusing. He and his laughing boy partner Moreno had wanted Jack Frerotte alive, and conversant, and here Gunner had gone and drilled three holes in him, pretty much ruining any chance they might have had of hearing what had happened to Thomas Selmon in Frerotte's own words. Their disappointment was such, in fact, that had Yolanda McCreary not been here to verify Gunner's version of Frerotte's shooting, the cops might have been inclined to slap a pair of cuffs on the investigator and run him out to Hollywood for a good, old-fashioned Q & A party.

"I didn't want the fat bastard dead any more than you did, Loiacano," Gunner said, watching the boys from the coroner's office carry Frerotte's body away.

"I can see that. That's why you only put three bullets in him, instead of four."

"He was armed. I'd've been a member of *your* union, that would have earned him a full clip, I believe."

Loiacano looked over at Moreno, who was still questioning McCreary in the kitchen, and said, "That a dig at the LAPD, Gunner? 'Cause if it was, this ain't the time."

"Sorry. My bad."

"Better tell me again how the deceased was too stupid to know you've gotta take an auto's safety off before you can shoot somebody with it. I think I missed something the first time around."

He meant the first *two* times around, but Gunner didn't correct him; he understood that Loiacano was entitled to his skepticism. For the kind of luck that had saved Gunner's and McCreary's lives did not come around every day. Because first and foremost, they'd been fortunate that Jack Frerotte was a knife man, someone who had probably held a gun in his hands about as often as he did a full house; and secondly, that Frerotte had picked today to come looking for Gunner, and not sometime sooner, before his work as bait in an FBI trap had moved the investigator to start carrying the Para-Ordinance around as a backup to the Ruger. Had either of these things not been true— had the fat man not taken three seconds to remember the Ruger's safety, or had Gunner not had ready access to the Para-Ordinance— *two* homicides would have almost certainly occurred in Gunner's home this afternoon, rather than just the one.

"I don't know, Gunner," Loiacano said after Gunner had described yet again the circumstances of Frerotte's death. "I'd say it sounds pretty fishy, except . . ."

"Except you know it happens."

The cop nodded. "Yeah. I've seen a lot of guys more gun-friendly than Frerotte pull the trigger on a nine without flipping the safety off first. None of 'em were geniuses, of course, but they did it."

"Then you believe me."

"I believe you, sure. Doesn't mean I'm happy with you. Armed or otherwise, we needed Frerotte alive. You could've shot the fucker once, just to put him down, then let him have the other two if necessary."

"If I'd been alone, I might have tried that. But I had the lady's safety to consider, as well as my own."

"Sure, sure. I'm just wondering how the hell we're gonna make sense of this mess now, that's all."

"Yeah."

"Take this hundred and fifty grand you say Frerotte mentioned. What the hell could that've been about? You said he'd already been paid for Selmon's murder, right?"

"He had. Five thousand dollars in two installments."

"So what the hell was this hundred and fifty grand? A bonus?"

"I don't know. I asked Jack that question myself, and he wouldn't answer me."

"You know if Selmon was heavily insured?"

"He had a modest life insurance policy through his job, from what I understand, but nothing that would have made killing him worthwhile. You were thinking maybe the wife and Frerotte knocked him off for the insurance money?"

"It was a thought."

Gunner shook his head. "Benefit was just fifty thousand. Even if you gave Frerotte all of that, it wouldn't add up to a hundred and fifty."

"No. It wouldn't."

"There could be another possibility, though. I've been thinking about it ever since Jack went down."

"Yeah? What's that?"

"It's gonna sound a little far out. But it fits in a weird kind of way."

"What?"

Gunner paused, doubting the wisdom of continuing, and said, "I've been told Selmon was thinking about writing a book. A memoir. He had a title for it, and everything, from what I understand."

Loiacano got tired of waiting for him to elaborate, said, "The Covington missing persons report mentioned he called an agent in New York before he disappeared, yeah. So he was writing a book. What's that got to do with Frerotte?"

"Probably nothing. Except that Selmon had the idea the book could be worth a few dollars, and chances are good, he was right. The *Press Examiner* scandal was pretty big news once, and a book about it, written by the scandal's central figure, might have caused a few heads to turn in New York."

Loiacano looked at him quizzically. "What? To the tune of a hundred and fifty Gs?"

"Or more, yeah. Happens every day."

"And you're suggesting Frerotte had this book, is that it?"

"I'm suggesting that's the only way I can see Thomas Selmon being worth a hundred and fifty thousand to Jack, dead *or* alive."

"So where is this book now, Gunner?"

The investigator shook his head, said, "I don't know. It could've been lost in Jack's house fire, or . . ."

"Or?"

"Or it may never have existed at all."

"Excuse me?"

"Near as I was ever able to determine, Detective, the book was all in Selmon's head. No one ever saw him writing it, and not a word of it has ever been found."

"But you just said—"

"I know what I just said. And it doesn't make a whole lot of sense to me, either. Unless—"

Loiacano watched Gunner grow pensive, tried to guess what was on his mind. "Unless Frerotte was thinking about writing the book himself."

"Yes. I know that sounds far-fetched, but Jack had a stack of research material on Selmon down in his basement before someone torched the place. And almost every book he owned was of the true crime/inside story variety, exactly the kind of sensational, kiss-and-tell book Selmon's would have been had he written it. I had a look at Jack's bookshelves just before the fire, that's all he ever read, apparently."

"And that proves what? Because he liked to read the stuff, he must've been able to write it?"

"No. Reading it and writing it are two different things, obviously. But think about it, Loiacano. Jack and the Defenders were the only ones who knew Selmon was dead. Everyone else believes he's still in hiding, just as he had been for the last five years. If Jack had approached a publisher or agent in New York claiming to represent Selmon, manuscript in hand . . ."

"They might've gone for it."

Gunner nodded.

"Sure. Why not? The dumbshits have done it before."

And they had. The Howard Hughes "autobiography" of 1972; the Hitler "diaries" in 1983 . . .

"Of course, Selmon turning up dead would have soured the whole deal," Gunner said. "Jack would've have had a tough enough time convincing somebody the manuscript was genuine as it was. If it came out Selmon had been murdered, the level of scrutiny he'd have had to deal with would've been too much to overcome."

"Right."

"When he told me I'd messed up the biggest payday he was ever gonna have, I wasn't sure I knew what he meant. But in this particular context . . ."

"It does kind'a fit, like you said. Assuming Frerrote could write as well as he could read, that is."

"Yeah. Assuming that."

The two men fell silent, until Loiacano said, "Too bad none of this has anything to do with Selmon's murder."

Gunner eyed him, said, "What's that?"

"I mean, it's all very interesting, but it's all after the fact, right? It's not relevant to our case."

"So *I'm* supposed to pursue it, is that it?"

"That's up to you. All I know is, *I'm* not gonna. Why the hell should I?"

Gunner couldn't think of an answer for that, because Loiacano was right: Technically speaking, Thomas Selmon's murder had been solved, his killer brought to justice. Anything Frerotte might or might not have done to try and profit from Selmon's murder afterward was immaterial now.

"But we don't know that the book wasn't Jack's primary motive for killing Selmon," Gunner said. "The money he got from the Defenders—"

"Was what? Just icing on the cake? Come on, Gunner. That's bullshit, and you know it."

"But—"

"Look. I've already got a motive for Selmon's murder, and one's all I need. Doesn't matter how many Frerotte had in all, what matters is that he's the perp I've been looking for, and he's no longer out on the street. The end.

"Now. You wanna call every agent and publisher in New York to see if somebody's holding a Thomas Selmon manuscript, be my guest. Just remember it ain't gonna change anything at this point. Selmon's still gonna be dead, and so will Frerotte." He looked over at his partner, said, "Hey, Sal! We about ready to wrap this up?"

Moreno grinned, overflowing as usual with good cheer. "Any time you say, yeah."

"Let me know what you find out, Gunner," Loiacano said, putting his little leather-bound notebook back in his jacket pocket. "I'd be interested to hear if you were right about this book thing, or not."

"Sure thing, Detective. Thanks for all your help," Gunner said.

Managing to keep the sarcasm in his voice down to an almost imperceptible level.

Gunner made eleven phone calls, then one more, just to make it an even dozen. It was this last he should have started with, the way things turned out.

A literary agent out of Manhattan named Karen Fielder said she'd talked to a man calling himself John Frerotte about a Thomas Selmon memoir back in mid-December, but was still waiting to receive a completed manuscript. Frerotte had sent her a six-page proposal of the book initially, and she'd jumped at the chance to represent it, providing the author's identity could be verified prior to the manuscript's submission to publishers. Learning now that both Frerotte and Selmon were dead, and that the book she'd been anxiously waiting to receive would not be forthcoming, nearly devastated her.

"I can't believe it," she told Gunner again and again.

She said Frerotte had asked what kind of money she thought the Selmon book might bring on the open market upon its completion, and she had told him an advance in the mid-six figures would not be unreasonable, providing the book delivered everything the proposal seemed to promise.

"The *mid* six figures?" Gunner asked. "Not the low?"

"The *low?*"

"Say between one and two hundred thousand."

"Well," Fielder said, "it may have gone for as little as that, I suppose. But that would have been something of a disappointment, to be quite frank with you."

"You didn't suggest to Mr. Frerotte that he could expect an advance of a hundred and fifty thousand?"

Fielder thought about it, said, "I imagine I could have. If I'd been concerned about overstating the market value of the manuscript. But I'm almost certain we could have gotten much more than one-fifty for it, and I've felt that way from the start. You're sure there hasn't been some kind of mistake? There really is no Selmon book?"

"The way things look right now, Ms. Fielder, no. There isn't. I'm sorry."

He asked her if there was any chance she could send him a copy of Frerotte's proposal, and naturally, she balked, smart lady that she was. He gave her Denny Loiacano's phone number out at Hollywood, requested that she reconsider if the cop would be good enough to vouch for him.

Fielder said she'd think about it.

"What does it mean?" Yolanda McCreary asked.

"It means Jack was smarter than I ever gave him credit for. He found a way to get paid twice for killing the same man."

It was just before nine at the Acey Deuce, and Gunner and McCreary were two of the mere six people in the house, including Lilly Tennell and Pharaoh Doubleday. The TV over the bar was tuned to a Clippers game, but Pharaoh and the two guys at the bar were ignoring it, Lilly was off in the back storeroom somewhere, and the set was nothing but a blur to Gunner from where he was sitting, at the same remote booth he'd shared last Thursday with Gil Everson and Rafe Sweeney. Not that actually seeing a Clipper game ever really mattered; it was always a safe bet the team was getting hammered, regardless of who they were playing or where. It was just one of those universal laws of sports-oriented physics.

"I don't understand," McCreary said. "You're saying Frerotte was writing the book Tommy had been talking about writing himself? About the scandal at the paper?"

"Yes. Either that, or he'd sent this agent in New York a six-page proposal for nothing."

"But where would he have gotten the idea to do that? From Tommy?"

"I think he probably got it on his own. Jack was a heavy reader of that sort of thing. Seeing a book in your brother's story would have probably come naturally to him."

"So where is the manuscript, then? If this agent doesn't have it—"

Gunner shook his head, said, "I don't know where it is. I went through Jack's house pretty thoroughly last Wednesday, but I never made it up to the second floor, and my search of the basement, as you may recall, was rudely interrupted. It could be over there somewhere, I guess. Assuming it survived the fire."

"How can we find out?"

"If it's there or not? Sift through the rubble, I imagine. Are you asking me to do that?"

"Am I asking you to do it? Sure. Why not?"

"Well . . . I just thought you might be ready to let this thing go and move on. But if you want me to stay on it—"

"Move on? How can I move on? If this book was the reason my brother was killed—"

"What? Finding it will bring him back? Or punish Jack Frerotte beyond the grave for having killed him?" He paused, allowing McCreary to consider the question before going on. "Loiacano was right, Yo. Your brother's dead, and so is the man who killed him. Finding this manuscript Jack may or may not have been writing might satisfy our curiosity about a few things, but that's about all."

"Yes, but—"

She stopped, deferring to Lilly Tennell, who had suddenly appeared at their table, smiling, acting like she knew how a real hostess of the public was supposed to behave. "How you folks doin' over here? Can I get you another round?"

The timing of the question irked Gunner, but he knew to show Lilly any attitude would be tantamount to flushing the rest of his and McCreary's evening here down the toilet. "Thanks, Lilly, no," he said.

"You sure? Sister's glass is empty."

Gunner looked, saw that she was right. "Would you like another?" he asked McCreary.

"Please," McCreary said.

"My name is Lilly, honey," Lilly said, holding her right hand out for McCreary to shake. "Since this fool you're sittin' with is too ignorant to introduce us properly."

McCreary shook the big bartender's hand and smiled warmly. "Yolanda. Pleased to meet you, Lilly."

"I like that name. Yolanda."

"Lilly . . ." Gunner said.

"Anybody ever tell you you look just like Simone Grant? That girl on *Love Conquers All*?"

"Oh, yes," McCreary admitted, blushing slightly. "Many times."

"You got that same smile, and you wear your hair the same way she does. For a minute there, I thought you was her."

"No, no, thank God. Simone is *terrible!*"

"Ain't she, though? Erica Kane and Dorian Lord, all wrapped into one!"

Both women fell out laughing.

"Somebody wanna clue me in on the joke?" Gunner asked.

McCreary stopped laughing, said, *"Love Conquers All* is a daytime drama on TV, and Simone Grant is its star bitch."

"A 'daytime drama'? You mean a *soap*?"

"Don't nobody call 'em soaps anymore, Gunner," Lilly said, obviously insulted.

Gunner shook his head. "Jesus."

Less than a year ago, being laid up at home with a serious concussion had left the investigator with little to do for nearly a week but spend his daylight hours watching soap operas—*All My Children, The Young and the Restless, General Hospital,* and yes, now that he thought about it, *Love Conquers All*—and the experience had damn near lobotomized him. In the all-too-addictive universe of 'daytime drama,' monogamy was a joke without a punchline, one child was born out of wedlock for every fifteen minutes of airtime, and wealth without beauty, or vice versa, was a physical impossibility.

They might not spell the ruin of modern civilization, Gunner conceded, but soaps sure as hell would never do anything to advance it.

"You think she's gonna marry Dr. Burton now?" Lilly asked McCreary. "Now that his wife has agreed to a divorce?"

"Simone? I don't think so," McCreary said with some confidence.

"I don't either. 'Cause Ramona said Friday, she's only givin' that man a divorce so she can clean his ass out, excuse my French. And Simone—"

"Won't wanna have anything to do with Dr. Burton after that."

"Exactly," Lilly agreed.

"You were supposed to be bringing the lady a fresh drink," Gunner reminded her.

The big woman glared at him, trying to decide whether or not his insensitivity to the subject of discussion deserved a slap upside the head. She turned to McCreary and said, "White Russian, right, honey?"

"Yes, please," McCreary said.

Before Lilly could look his way again, Gunner added, "Nothing for me, thanks."

Lilly grunted at him, then slowly lumbered off.

"That was a little rude, wasn't it?" McCreary asked.

"We were in the middle of a conversation. Maybe you remember it."

McCreary thought about defending Lilly further, but realized he was right. "You were telling me why it makes no sense for us to look for the book Frerotte may have been writing."

"That's right."

"Because finding it won't change anything."

"Because finding it won't tell us anything we don't already know. We know your brother's dead, and we know who killed him. The only thing we don't know at this point is *why*. Did he murder Tommy for the sake of the book, or the five grand he got from the Defenders?"

"And the book wouldn't answer that question."

"No. It wouldn't. At least, I can't see how it would. But it's your call, Yo, like I said. You want me to look for it anyway, I will. I'll start tomorrow, if that's what you want."

McCreary grew still, testing the weight of his argument against the insistence of her curiosity. Meanwhile, Lilly brought her her drink, smiled, then left them alone again without comment.

"All right," McCreary said finally. "I'll let it go."

Gunner gave her a long look, uncertain of her conviction. "Yeah?"

"Yeah. Why not? It'll leave some questions unanswered for me, but that's okay. What counts is that we know what happened to Tommy now, and that the man who murdered him is dead. I never really wanted any more than that." She smiled. "Besides—I can't afford you anymore, Aaron. It's time I went home and put all of this behind me."

"Home?"

"Back to Chicago. I live there, remember?"

"Sure, I remember. I just thought you might want to wait a while before heading back. Give us a chance to spend some quality time together."

"Is that what you want me to do?"

"I wouldn't have brought it up if I didn't. I thought we had an understanding. About what I'm looking for here."

"We did. I just . . . was a little unsure about it, I guess."

"Yeah? How so?"

She faced him directly, said, "I don't know you, Aaron. We've known each other for all of eight days."

"And?"

"And a woman needs more time than that to trust her *own* feelings about a man, let alone his for her."

"Okay. So how much time do you need?"

"I can't answer that. I don't *know* how much time I'll need. I only know that I want to take things slow with you, Aaron. Real slow. So that neither of us gets hurt mistaking this for something it isn't." She reached out, took his hand.

"And in the meantime, you won't be selling the family farm back in Illinois," Gunner said.

"No."

"Or handing your friend the fireman his walking papers."

McCreary hesitated, said, "No. Not yet." She smiled. "But I'm here until the end of the week. Maybe you can change my mind by then."

It sounded like a tease, but it wasn't. It was a spoken dream, a wish for something wonderful and God-given made aloud.

He could see it in her eyes.

18

Thursday was the day

it all came crashing together.

The quiet and uneventful Wednesday that preceded it had given no warning of what was to come. As of Thursday morning, Poole was still combing the streets for Rafe Sweeney and/or Gil Everson's prostitute girlfriend, Byron Scales had yet to utter a word that might assist the FBI in its effort to track down his fellow Defenders of the Bloodline, and Gil Everson's damage control strategy of one part professed ignorance mixed with two parts stubborn silence was in its third day of going strong. Time, in other words, had not exactly stood still since Tuesday evening, in the aftermath of Jack Frerotte's death in Gunner's living room, but it hadn't produced anything remotely useful to the investigator's various causes, either.

Perhaps if it had, Gunner would have found something more vital to do Thursday morning than attend Connie Everson's funeral. He detested funerals, and any excuse to avoid one would have been welcome. But lacking other business on his agenda, and as the late Mrs. Everson *had* been a client, Gunner felt obligated to pay his last respects, rather than sit at his desk back at Mickey's and pretend he wasn't feeling guilty about it.

The service took place at Inglewood Park Memorial Cemetery, literally across the street from the hospital room at Daniel Freeman in which Sly Cribbs—who had himself only narrowly missed becoming the Everson affair's first fatality—was slowly mending. Gray skies were fitting for funerals, and this one was as gray as they came: dark as charcoal, even black in places, blocking out the sun like an iron ceiling. It was only 10:00 A.M., but it could have easily passed for early nightfall.

Gunner hung back at the grave site like an interloper, watching them lay his former client into the ground with quiet dignity and grace. Councilman Everson, of course, was the chief mourner among the thirty or so people in attendance, darkly resplendent in a black, double-breasted suit, his grief composed but in clear view of all. If it was an act, Gunner thought, it was a good one. But then, guilt could often move a man to depths of emotion sorrow alone could not.

When Everson's face flashed briefly with surprise, his eyes affixed to something off in the distance no one but he had yet to notice, Gunner almost missed it. The councilman's recovery from the shock had been immediate, nearly instantaneous. But Gunner was lucky; his own gaze had been focused upon Everson at the time, and he'd caught the change in his expression right away. He turned to see what the councilman had found so disturbing . . .

. . . and saw a frail-looking black woman thirty yards away, *limping* down the paved road leading to the street.

Gunner stepped back, distancing himself further yet from the gathering at Connie Everson's grave, and took off at a dead run after her, not really giving a damn if Gil Everson saw him, or not.

"Connie was my sister," Shelby Charles said. But Gunner had already known that, of course.

He had known it the minute he'd caught up to her just short of an hour ago, outside Inglewood Park Memorial Cemetery. He saw her face again and suddenly knew two things: why she had come to see his former client buried, and why she had always struck him as vaguely familiar. They hadn't been identical twins, Connie Everson and Shelby Charles, but their resemblance to one another was there, however understated it might be.

It had taken him fifteen minutes to talk her into turning herself over to the police. He had feared that her brother-in-law's black lim-

ousine would exit the cemetery, then stop on the street to let Gil
Everson whisk her away before Gunner could even begin to question
her, but the lead car in the funeral procession just cruised right past
them instead, Everson probably deciding against giving the television
news crews hovering outside the cemetery a scene he would never
be able to explain away.

In the same room at Southwest in which Gunner had endured the
smarmy brow-beating of agents Smith and Leffman two days earlier,
Gunner and Poole sat down with Shelby Charles and coerced her
into revealing, little by little, how she had unwittingly been the cat-
alyst to both Sly Cribbs's shooting and her older sister's suicide.

According to Charles, she and Gil Everson had been engaged to
be married years before Everson had married Connie Charles instead, when all three had been students at Howard University in
the Charleses' native Washington, D.C. Connie had always had de-
signs on Everson, and he had always appreciated the attention.
When Shelby was nearly crippled in a tragic car accident in the
spring of 1982, one which left her with both a permanent hitch in
her gait and a dependence on prescription pain killers, Connie
moved in for the kill, and Everson jumped ship, finding it difficult to
envision himself achieving his political goals with a less than flawless
mate by his side. Unfortunately for Everson and his new bride-to-be,
however, he could not make himself care for Connie Charles the
way he cared for her sister. Even after a crushing depression drove
her to a life on the street, where her drug addiction quickly ex-
panded far beyond prescription medication, Shelby Charles remained the future Inglewood councilman's one true love, and Connie
Charles was both perceptive and realistic enough to know it. In fact,
it was her greatest fear that Everson would eventually respond to
this dilemma by either returning to Shelby outright, or keeping her
as his mistress.

So Connie Charles found a way to make these options anathema
to him.

"Christ. Is that one for the books, or what?" Poole said, after he and Gunner had stepped outside to leave Shelby Charles alone, having heard what they felt would forever remain the most relevant part of her testimony.

"I've heard of a lot of weird clauses to prenuptial agreements," Gunner said, "but yeah, that was a new one on me."

"It was smart, though. Damn smart. She turned the agreement around on his ass. He didn't want her hand in his cookie jar, he was gonna have to keep *his* off her little sister."

"Otherwise, the agreement was null and void."

"Right."

"Odd how Everson never mentioned that, isn't it? All he said was, adultery didn't invalidate the agreement."

"As opposed to adultery with a *specific lady.*"

Gunner nodded.

"I bet Everson damn near had a cardiac when she wanted that clause put in. But she probably wouldn't sign it any other way."

"And I'm sure he thought it wouldn't matter, in any case. At least in the beginning." Gunner grinned. "Because we all like to think that way, don't we, Poole? That no one woman's got our number? We wanna stay away, we can stay away, no problem?"

"Yeah, right," Poole said, laughing. "Still, you gotta give the fucker credit. He held out for longer than either of us could, I'll bet. Damn near thirteen years."

Shelby Charles had said it had been that long before Everson showed up at her home in D.C. eleven months ago, talked her out of tricking and into a detox center, in preparation for spending quality time with him again.

"So I guess if the good councilman didn't have a motive for sending Sweeney after Sly before," Gunner said, "he's got one now, huh?"

"Oh, yeah. I'd say so."

"So when do you bring him in again?"

Poole thought about it, shook his head. "I don't know, Gunner. This ought'a shake him up pretty good, but . . ."

"You still need Sweeney."

"Yeah. Sweeney was the triggerman. Havin' a solid motive for Everson's nice, but it ain't worth bubkes if we can't connect it to Cribbs's shooting. And right now, nobody can do that for us but Sweeney."

Gunner nodded, sat down at the empty desk behind him. Poole found a second chair nearby and did likewise.

"So where is he?" Gunner asked after a short silence.

"Beats the hell out of me. We should've found 'im by now."

"You think Everson sent him underground?"

"That's certainly possible. Except . . . somethin' about that doesn't jibe with *me.*"

"Yeah?"

"Yeah. Sounds odd, I know, but I really think the councilman was on the level about Sweeney being fired. Either that, or he's a helluva better actor than he is a politician."

"You think Sweeney and Connie Everson were really getting it on?"

"Yeah. I do. Everson seemed genuinely pissed when he talked about it. He never said they were gettin' it on in so many words, actually, but he sure as hell implied it."

"What did he say, exactly?"

"You expect me to remember that now? Shit, I don't know. He just basically said he couldn't trust Sweeney anymore. Not professionally, but personally."

"And you took that to mean Sweeney had been doing the nasty with his wife?"

"Yeah. I did. It was just somethin' about the way he was actin'. Like Sweeney had hit 'im where it hurts a guy most, at home, with his old lady." He spun in the chair he was sitting in, just like a kid, only made it turn one half a revolution. "Funny thing is, I never knew he gave a—"

"Wait a second," Gunner said, waving a hand at Poole's face to get his attention. "Run that by me again. Slow."

"Run what by you again?"

"That bit about Sweeney hitting Everson where it hurts a guy most. At home, with his old lady."

"What about it?"

"I just had a thought. You said Everson never said it was his wife Sweeney was fucking around with, right?"

"Right. He just implied it."

"You mean he implied that Sweeney was fucking around with his *old lady.*"

"Yeah. What—"

"What if it wasn't his *wife* he was talking about, Poole? What if it was somebody else? Somebody he might've felt just as possessive of, if not more so?"

"Like who? What the hell are you talkin' about, Gunner? Spit it out."

"I'm talking about a platinum blonde with a dynamite figure," the investigator said, scanning the squadroom for a free phone. "Looked to me to be somewhere in her early twenties. I don't know her name, but Mickey does. Don't ask me why." He got up, walked over to the telephone on the desk at his right and started punching in Mickey's number.

"Give me a second, Poole, and I'll get it for you," he said.

Rafe Sweeney was arrested without incident at the Westchester condominium of Chelsea Seymour a few minutes past three that afternoon. He was hiding in the blonde's bedroom when Poole, accompanied by a pair of backup uniforms, called on Seymour to see if Gunner's theory that she and Sweeney were backdooring Gil Everson was viable. One of the uniforms outside spotted the giant black man through a bedroom window, and Poole subsequently managed to talk him into surrendering without attempting to blast his way out of the condo first. Or maybe Seymour's impassioned pleas that Sweeney give himself up had moved him to do so, it was hard for Poole to tell which.

In any case, Sweeney was in lockup by eight that evening, and the circumstances surrounding his assault on Sly Cribbs were no longer a mystery. Which was not to say that Sweeney himself had confessed to anything, because he hadn't; in fact, he hadn't said three words to the police since his arrest. It was his girlfriend Seymour who had been doing all the talking, and there seemed to be no end to her co-operation with authorities. Knowing a tight spot when she was in one, Seymour had jumped at the chance to appease the LAPD and the DA's office by answering every question they put to her, and the result was a noose around Sweeney's neck he would never be able to shake off.

In short, Sweeney had attacked Sly Cribbs in order to keep his girl-friend living in the manner to which she (and he) had become ac-customed. Chelsea Seymour was a kept woman, and Councilman Gil Everson was the man who'd been keeping her for the last six years, and neither she nor Sweeney had any interest in seeing what life would be like for her if Everson's pockets were to suddenly go dry. Which, of course, would have been the likely outcome had Connie Everson been able to prove in divorce court that her husband had been seeing her sister Shelby again. Seymour knew about this loop-hole in the prenuptial agreement her sugar daddy shared with his wife because Everson had been fool enough to tell her about it once, and naturally, she in turn had mentioned it to Sweeney. It was no wonder, then, that both were gravely concerned when Everson began flying Shelby Charles into Los Angeles three or four times a month for two- and three-day romantic rendezvous.

Sweeney was so concerned, in fact, that after he'd spotted Sly Cribbs photo-documenting a tryst between the pair at the Marina Pa-cific Hotel eight days ago, he had required no instruction, from either Everson or Seymour (by Seymour's account, anyway), to first re-lieve Cribbs of his camera and film by whatever means were necessary, then issue a strongly worded Cease and Desist order to the kid's suspected employer, Connie Everson, the following day. An order, it now seemed clear, the councilman's wife had taken very much to heart.

If Gil Everson had only proven to be as gullible as Sweeney believed him to be, and accepted the bodyguard's claim that he had acted as he had for Everson's sake alone, Sweeney might never have been forced to make the incriminating move of running for the cover of Seymour's condominium. But Everson was no dummy. As the councilman himself thought it might be wise to explain only hours after Sweeney's arrest Thursday night, Everson had known his security man had not gone after Sly Cribbs and his wife with such calamitous zeal strictly to protect his employer. Despite what Everson had told Poole earlier, Sweeney was not that devoted to duty. He could only have taken the action he had, therefore, in the interests of one person—the *only* person Everson could think of who might have feared the financial consequences of Cribbs's photographs nearly as much as he: Chelsea Seymour.

Saturday night in Sacramento, when Everson had put this accusation to Sweeney directly, the bodyguard failed so miserably to plead innocent that Everson felt compelled to cut him adrift without a moment's hesitation, both to punish the bodyguard for betraying him, and to separate himself from the fallout he knew was most certainly to come.

In light of all this, this convoluted medley of cross-infidelity and greed, aggravated assault and duplicity, it was actually possible, Gunner realized, to see Gil Everson as a victim, the unwitting centerpiece to Sly Cribbs's shooting and Connie Everson's suicide, respectively. He had no claim to actual "innocence," to be sure, as the days of intense media scrutiny awaiting him would prove, but he wasn't the story's key villain, he was only one of several, so it could have been argued that he was nearly as deserving of his constituents' pity as he was their contempt.

Sadly, if Everson had been expecting such arguments to save his seat on the Inglewood City Council, he was setting himself up for yet another huge disappointment.

Less than three hours before the stroke of midnight could officially bring Thursday to a close, a weary Aaron Gunner finally got around to checking his day's mail. It was in this seemingly innocent manner that the second case he had been embroiled in now for the last eleven days—the Thomas Selmon missing persons case—took its own hard turn toward a conclusion.

Of course, Gunner had thought the case had already made that turn with the death of "Barber Jack" Frerotte two days ago, but that was before he'd slipped open the manila envelope he'd received Thursday morning from the Karen Fielder Literary Agency and read the book proposal inside. Or, perhaps more to the point, the tentative title its author had therein suggested for the book he intended to write:

> The Devil's Byline
> The Thomas Selmon Story

"So?" Yolanda McCreary asked when Gunner brought the title to her attention, the two of them sitting on Gunner's bed with a pile of partially opened mail and Dillett, who lay fast asleep in the crook of McCreary's lap. "Why is that important?"

"Because Jack Frerotte's not the one who came up with that title," Gunner said. "Your brother is."

"My brother?"

"His old pal Martin Keene told me that was the title Tommy had for the book when he was trying to recruit Keene to co-author it: 'The Devil's Byline.' "

"So . . ."

"So how the hell could Jack have known that? The *precise title* your brother had in mind for a book he hadn't even written yet?"

McCreary shook her head, unable to answer the question.

"It's possible Jack got it from your brother before he actually killed him, sure, but . . ." He shook his own head. "I can't see it. How would the subject have even come up between them?"

"Maybe this isn't Jack's proposal," McCreary suggested. "Maybe it's Tommy's. Maybe this is something Jack stole from my brother before he . . . before Tommy was killed."

"That would fit, except for a couple of things," Gunner said. "No one's ever found a shred of evidence to indicate Tommy wrote a word about this book before he died. Not a word. No notes, no outlines—not even an instrument he could have been using to write the book *with*. Like a typewriter, or a computer . . ."

"And?"

"And he never made a physical submission of any kind to anyone, either. His only attempt to sell the book that we know of was the one phone call he made to a New York agent from his motel room the night he disappeared. An agent, by the way, different from Ms. Fielder here. If Tommy had already written a proposal, why would he have bothered making phone calls, when he could have just started mailing proposals out instead?"

"I don't know," McCreary said.

"I tell you what. Let's you and I read this thing, see what it sounds like," Gunner said, before starting to read the proposal out loud, McCreary scanning the pages over his shoulder as he did so.

Eight minutes later, they were finished. And afterward, each was equally convinced that, whoever had written this outline for "The Devil's Byline," he had known "The Thomas Selmon Story" damn near as well as Selmon had himself.

19

Gunner had never learned anything by going through someone's trash, so this was a first.

Garbology, as the study of garbage was scientifically known, was supposed to be the mainstay of the private investigator's craft, a simple and cost-effective method of collecting information about people, but all Gunner had ever gleaned from the practice was how grossly some individuals liked to feed themselves, and to what level of debt they could allow themselves to plummet. It was a great way to ruin good clothing and attach foul smells to yourself for hours on end, but beyond that, as far as Gunner was concerned, trash digging was a fairly pointless exercise.

And yet, Friday morning at eight, Gunner dug a hand through some of Martin Keene's garbage anyway, as Friday was collection day in Silver Lake and the bins were all sitting right there on the street, openly inviting the investigator's scrutiny. Like his neighbors, Keene had been provided with three separate containers by the city of Los Angeles, all of them pretty much identical. Narrow, three-foot-tall plastic bins on wheels, the green one was for yard trimmings, the black for miscellaneous, and the blue was for recyclables, this last divided into two parts: paper goods to the left; plastic, glass, and aluminum to the right.

Gunner started with the paper side of the blue bin, never had to open any of the others.

About fifteen minutes later, he rang Keene's bell, and this time Martin Keene himself came to the door, looking very much like he'd been on his way out to play yet another round of golf.

"Mr. Gunner," Keene said, smiling. Covering it well if the sight of the black man unnerved him in any way.

"Hope you don't mind that I came by so early," Gunner said. "But I wanted to make sure I'd catch you at home. Is this a bad time?"

"For me? Not at all. I have a tennis game at ten, but that's over an hour away. Come in, please."

Gunner stepped into the cool air of the foyer, declined his host's offer of a drink. When Keene asked him where he would prefer to sit down, inside or out, Gunner chose the former, not wanting either of them to be distracted this morning by the beauty of the lake beyond Keene's veranda. They settled down instead in the house's dark living room, Keene sinking into the cushions of an off-white couch, Gunner doing likewise in a matching, equally comfortable chair. If Mrs. Keene was home, she was either still asleep, or maintaining the silence of a church mouse somewhere out of Gunner's view.

"Well?" Keene asked, still smiling. "How can I help you today?"

"You can tell me where Thomas Selmon is," Gunner said.

Keene almost laughed. "What?"

"I know we're all supposed to think he's dead, but he's not. He's alive, and I think you're hiding him somewhere."

"And why would I want to do that?"

"To get a piece of the book he's writing, I imagine. You remember the one: 'The Devil's Byline, the Thomas Selmon Story'? Either that, or you're actually helping him write it, like he asked you to earlier."

Keene's smile did a slow, painful fade. "I don't know what you're talking about, Mr. Gunner."

"Sure you do. But I'll run it down for you anyway, in case he's only told you half the story. Selmon came here last October looking for a co-author to lend the big money autobiography he wanted to write some credibility, but you turned him down. So he ended up cutting a deal with someone else, a man named Jack Frerotte."

"I don't know anybody named Jack Frerotte."

"No, you probably don't. But then, neither did Selmon. Frerotte had been hired by the Defenders of the Bloodline to assassinate Selmon after one of them recognized him out at his Hollywood motel, only Frerotte never did the job. He just faked it, instead. The coroner's office will be announcing any day now that the body Jack buried out in the Angeles National Forest last October, strictly for the benefit of the Defenders, is that of someone other than Thomas Selmon."

"You're not making any sense, Mr. Gunner," Keene said.

"Hold on. This is where the tale gets interesting. Either because he got the idea on his own, or because Selmon gave it to him in the course of begging for his life, Frerotte let Selmon live in exchange for a big slice of Selmon's book. He hid Selmon away in his basement to write and waited for him to produce something Jack could sell to New York. And by mid-December, Selmon had: a six-page proposal that Jack submitted to an agent named Karen Fielder, who's been watching her mailbox for the finished manuscript ever since."

"Look. What the hell has any of this got to do with *me*?" Keene demanded.

"Nothing. Not a thing," Gunner admitted.

"Then why the hell are you here?"

"Because I inadvertently spooked Selmon out of hiding two Wednesdays ago, and it's my guess he landed here. He would've had nowhere else to go, Mr. Keene."

"That's ridiculous."

"I was having a look around Jack's basement, and he blindsided me. Burned the house down to cover his tracks, and left me inside to go up with it. I thought it had been a Defender, but I was wrong. I realize that now."

"I haven't seen Tommy Selmon since last October. That was true when we spoke last week, and it's still true today!"

"Really? Then how do you explain this?" Gunner eased a folded sheet of white paper from his jacket pocket, opened it up, and began to read the printed text on its face: " 'The pressure Sandra was exerting against me daily had finally become too intense to ignore. Her demands for a feature story "with teeth" would not go away, so that it eventually became clear to me I was going to have to come through with something, anything, to appease her, and quickly. Martin had suggested months ago that I do a story about Chicago's inner-city drug culture, thinking because I was black, I could write such a story with real substance, since I, unlike my white contemporaries, could just go down there and interview every crackhead in sight without fear of repercussions. Naturally, I kept putting that idea off.' " Gunner stopped reading, looked up to face Keene again. "I don't have to tell you what this is, do I?"

Keene put his hand out, his face having suddenly grown ashen, and said, "Let me see that."

He looked the printed page over carefully, reading and rereading its contents in silence, and Gunner just let him, knowing he'd ask the obvious question sooner or later.

"Where did you get this?"

"Outside. In your trash," Gunner said.

Real or fabricated, Keene's incredulity looked genuine. "What?"

"Looked like just the first hundred or so pages of the manuscript, but there could've been more. I would've had to dump the whole bin out in the street to know for sure."

"You're lying. What you're saying is *impossible!*"

"No, Martin," Pat Keene said. "It isn't."

Her voice had been almost too hushed for either man to hear. She had entered the room from the back of the house without making a sound of warning, and now stood at its outer perimeter stock still, looking down upon them with sad, lifeless eyes.

"I should have thrown it away last week. Or burned it," she said. "But I didn't. I couldn't. I don't know why."

Keene sat frozen on the couch, waited a long time before speaking. "Pat. What are you saying?"

"I couldn't believe he had the nerve to come back. After everything he'd done to you. To us." A tear rolled slowly down her left cheek. "You weren't home. I tried to make him leave, but he wouldn't go. He pushed past me into the house and . . . and sat down. Right there where you're sitting now. He told me he wasn't going anywhere until he talked to you. So . . ."

Keene stood up, said, "Stop. Don't say another word. It isn't—"

She shook her head, determined to go on before she lost the nerve. "I went and got your gun out of the bedroom drawer. I pointed it at him, trying to scare him away, but he . . . he just laughed at me. He *laughed*!"

"Pat! Please!" Keene pleaded, going to her now.

But she put a hand out to keep him away, sobbing uncontrollably, and said, "He was an evil man! He had no *right . . .* to come here like that. To force his way back into our lives after all we'd done to put what happened in Chicago behind us!"

"Pat . . ."

"Where is he now, Mrs. Keene?" Gunner asked, before her husband could inevitably silence her.

"Don't answer that," Keene said firmly, taking his wife into his arms, stroking her brow with his right hand lovingly. "Don't say another word until we talk to Steven."

"But I *want* to answer it," Pat Keene said, the words coming out as a long, heavy sigh. "Please, Martin. I have to tell him." She turned her eyes up to him, showing him the weight she'd been carrying around for over a week without his knowledge. "I can't live with this another minute."

Poor Keene, Gunner thought. His position was completely untenable. She was asking him to step aside while she cut her own throat, to choose between protecting her and easing her pain. No-win propositions didn't come any worse than that.

When Keene finally nodded his head and looked away, freeing her to do as she wished, Gunner had to wonder if it wasn't the bravest thing he'd ever seen a man do for the sake of the woman he loved.

20

Pat Keene had dumped
Thomas Selmon's body into some heavy foliage on a hillside in
Elysian Park, between the hours of 10:00 and 11:00 P.M. two Thurs-
days ago. He'd been shot just once, right above the left eye, with a
.38 caliber Smith & Wesson revolver, nearly twelve hours previous.
Mrs. Keene had never killed anyone before, but she followed up her
first homicide—justifiable as her attorney would suggest in the
weeks to come it was—remarkably well. She cleaned up the blood
Selmon's shooting had left behind in her living room, wrapped
his corpse up in a sheet before dragging it out to the trunk of her
car, and waited for Martin Keene to fall asleep that evening before
driving out to Elysian Park to dispose of their old nemesis
from Chicago. Until Gunner's second visit to the Keene home in
two weeks, Pat Keene's devoted husband had never suspected a
thing.

No one in either the local or national press recommended Selmon's killer for sainthood, exactly, but they came close, treating her
story as that of someone who by no means deserved to be punished
to the full extent of the law.

As for Yolanda McCreary, the news that her brother had actually
been alive as recently as eight days ago hit her fairly hard. It didn't
seem fair to have come so close to saving him, only to have him killed
less than a twenty-minute ride on the freeways of Los Angeles beyond her reach. And yet, she was not inconsolable. Like many people, the last few days had reminded her all over again what a
manipulative, self-centered sociopath had lain at the heart of all

Thomas Selmon's various guises and/or identities, so that it was difficult, even for her, to much regret his passing.

Still, she accompanied her brother's body back to St. Louis and attended his funeral there before returning home to Chicago, doing what she could to console the family his greed had essentially denied a husband and father. The only promise she made to Gunner before leaving was that she'd stay in regular contact, talk to him on the phone at least once or twice a week, and maybe even exchange a letter or two. And if or when it became clear to her that their feelings for each other were of genuine substance, not something time and distance could easily erase, she'd put Ken the fireman down gently and come running back to Los Angeles as fast as modern aviation would allow.

It was the smartest approach possible to the care and feeding of their budding romance, Gunner knew, but he couldn't help feeling disappointed, all the same. His best case scenario had her staying here in Los Angeles and reversing the process, only going back to Chicago if their relationship proved a failure.

But he did the sensible thing and let her go, anyway.

Confident a man who'd been alone for most of his adult life could live that way for another few weeks, at least.

"This shit will kill you. I assume you know that," Carroll Smith said, biting into a Garbage Burrito at the El Rey taco stand on Normandie and Martin Luther King. The El Rey's signage said it was the "home" of the Garbage Burrito, and Smith, for one, believed it. Big as his hands were, he'd never had as much trouble keeping a tortilla closed in his life.

"Once every three months, how much can it hurt?" Gunner asked the FBI man, tearing into his own meat-and-cheese-packed house specialty.

"It's not that I'm into tofu, or anything, but you might have picked a more healthy establishment, that's all I'm saying."

"Relax. I'm sure your partner Leffman will eat more than enough broccoli at lunch today to compensate for both of us."

Smith glanced around uneasily, the open-air accommodations of the taco stand making him feel more conspicuous than he really was. "You're probably right," he said.

"So what can you tell me?"

"Very little, I'm afraid. Scales is playing the stand-up guy right to the very end."

"You haven't picked up *anybody*?"

"Not yet. We can't turn the son of a bitch."

Gunner just shook his head, afraid that if he said anything, he wouldn't know how to stop.

"But it doesn't matter. We're going to get the rest of them eventually, with or without his help. I promise you that."

"You wanna promise me something? Promise me the next time you need a civilian to draw fire for you, you'll take it down the street."

"Take it easy, partner. We found Scales in Texas, remember? If he bailed, the others may have, too. They've gone mobile before."

"From New Hampshire to California, you mean."

"Yeah. Chances are, you don't have a thing to worry about."

"But you're gonna keep an eye on me, anyway."

Smith nodded. "At least for a week or two. Maybe longer. We'd be stupid not to."

Gunner finished eating, piled all his trash onto his tray. "Thanks, Agent. It was a pleasure doing business with you."

He started to get up, but Smith said, "Wait a minute."

Gunner did.

"You were there, and I wasn't. So I have to ask. No one's in a better position to say than you."

"Say what?"

"How sincere they sounded. About killing you if you didn't back off."

"If you're asking was the man laughing when he said it, the answer is no. He wasn't."

"Then you're genuinely concerned they'll come after you. Sooner or later."

Gunner was silent for a moment, then said, "I don't know what they're going to do. And frankly, I don't much care. Running scared doesn't pay the bills, Agent Smith. The Defenders come looking, I won't be hard to find."

Smith nodded again, solemnly this time, and said, "In that case, I'd like to give you something. Call it a parting gift for playing the 'FBI Game.' "

He opened the attaché case sitting beside his chair, removed a leather, holstered automatic and slid it to the investigator's end of the table. Gunner immediately recognized it as the weapon Smith had loaned him earlier in the week, the one he had used to put Jack Frerotte down for the last time.

"Your Para-Ordinance," he said.

"We've already got transfer-of-ownership in the works," Smith said, "but that'll take about thirty days to go through. I'd appreciate it if you could find a way not to use it until then."

Gunner was nearly speechless; generosity from the Feds was something he'd never seen before. "It's a lovely gesture, Agent, but—"

"Forget it. The Bureau pays for 'em, there's plenty more where that came from."

Gunner still hadn't picked the gun up.

"Take it," Smith said. "It might not make *you* feel any better, but it will *me*. Go on."

Gunner did as he was told and nodded a wordless thanks.

That night when he went home, Gunner stepped through the front door with his Ruger drawn, didn't holster it again until he'd made a pass through the entire house, room by room. He'd been doing this now for three days, and was destined to go on doing it for several more. By the eighth day, however, his belief that the practice was worth his while had all but dissipated, leading him to abandon it.

Only once was he tempted to take it up again.

Exactly thirty-four days after his Monday afternoon lunch with Carroll Smith, he was sitting at his desk at Mickey's, opening a three-day accumulation of mail, when he came upon a letter in a plain white business envelope bearing no return address. Unsigned, the letter's simple, block-lettered content consisted of a single line:

ALLAH IS ON OUR SIDE

Gunner read the letter three times, then put it away in a desk drawer, where it would remain for two days, or until Carroll Smith could come out to take it away for forensics testing.